Tale of
of
Three Ships

Copyright © 2023 by Darcia G. Laucerica

All rights reserved.

No part of this publication may be reproduced, distributed, or transmitted in any form or by any means, including photocopying, recording, or other electronic or mechanical methods, without the prior written permission of the publisher, except as permitted by copyright law. For permission requests, contact: darciaglezl@gmail.com.

The story, all names, characters, and incidents portrayed in this production are fictitious. No identification with actual persons (living or deceased), places, buildings, and products is intended or should be inferred.

Book Cover and Cover Lettering by Logan Howard.

Content Warnings

-Swearing.
-Violence.
-Vomit.
-Descriptions of abuse (domestic and familial).
-Mentions of miscarriages.
-Kidnappings.
-Grief and loss.
-Claustrophobia.
-Drowning.
-Fire.
-Descriptions of corpses.

Contents

Book One: The Outsider	1
1. Taking in Strays	3
2. Sirens and Mages	23
3. Goliath Epistolary	49
Letter: New Friendships	69
4. The Dusk Market	71
Letter: Confidants	91
5. The Blind Escape	93
6. Murky Waters	107
7. Waterlions	121
Letter: Brewing Escape	137
Book Two: The Cursed Eel	139

8. Pirate Talk	141
Letter: The Plan	155
9. Pirate´s Haven	157
10. The Crown´s Persuasion	177
11. Mama Ruth's Home	195
12. Cold Plunge	211
13. An Invitation	225
14. Masquerade	243
15. A Desert Mission	259
Book Three: The Conviction	279
16. Edbris´ Waves	281
17. Storm Memories	293
18. Talking Corpses	305
19. The Drowning Kraken	321
20. Silent Docks	345
21. Fire at Sea	367
Acknowledgments	395
Fullpage Image	399
Map of Castiah	401

Book One

The Outsider

1

TAKING IN STRAYS

The port of Rera was dangerous to them early in the mornings but Glenlivet refused to set sail in the cover of night.

For all the sailor's superstitions and "rules" of piracy the captain mocked every day, not leaving the docks when it was dark was a personal boundary she swore by ever since acquiring *The Outsider* eight years ago.

Glenlivet stood on the deck of the ship, surveying the busy port with her sunken brown eyes. She barely blinked as she tracked every patrol guard who walked past. Celeste had paid off most of them, more than she could afford, so they'd leave them alone. But not all of them could be bought.

They had been on land for far longer than they were

comfortable with due to bad weather, and Glenlivet could sense the general feeling of restlessness starting to affect the crew. Her anxiety only grew with every sigil-embroidered cloak she spotted. The symbol of the Rera-Goliath alliance, the "vulture shield" as Augie called it, burned behind her eyelids.

"Captain!"

The young voice pulled Glenlivet out of her thoughts and she turned toward it, only to be met with a tall stack of books. Roma, the mage´s apprentice and assistant, shared the captain´s love for the written word but she was testing the limits of what their ship could handle in terms of weight. Glen inspected half of the stack of books while the young girl smiled apologetically.

As she had promised, most of them were medical journals and essays that their surgeon could use. Mel had been asking for new material, as she was afraid her knowledge was growing outdated from being at sea for months on end with no access to the latest developments of the capitals of Patriah. The other books in the pile were occult literature by Gaarian authors that Celeste and Roma would use for their craft and a pair of novels Glenlivet didn´t recognize. The captain offered a teasing look to Roma, as she eyed the romantic cover on one of the volumes, and chuckled when the girl flushed red and looked away.

Glenlivet sighed and shook her head while returning

the books to the apprentice´s arms. "Take them down before I change my mind."

Roma was quick with it, promptly disappearing again behind the books and waddling away with them. In her quick escape, she almost bumped into another woman who was carrying a wooden box full of produce onto the ship and blurted, "Sorry, Nona!"

As Nona cursed under her breath, the captain rushed to her aid, grabbing one side of the box that was about to slip. "Morning, sunshine," Glenlivet said. "What did I say about carrying heavy stuff all by yourself?"

The first mate of *The Outsider* was a tan-skinned shorter woman with brown hair bunched up in a low bun at the nape of her neck. The hair that she so meticulously set behind her ears every morning now fell in strands over her face. She blew air toward them to keep it from her eyes and chuckled. "I´m pretty sure you said I was perfectly capable and strong enough to carry a thousand boxes if I so wished, captain, cause to insinuate otherwise is ridiculous."

Glenlivet smiled, rolling her eyes, and pulled on the box to take it away from the other woman. Nona raised an eyebrow, with half a mind to trip her as she walked away, but instead followed toward the kitchen and got ahead to open the door for her, "You´re not the boss of me."

The galley was in a state from all the shopping done in

preparation for their departure. Blue, the cook, wasn't there, but their touch was apparent in all the notes they had left on the packages, detailing the contents of each one, as well as the place they were supposed to be stored. Glenlivet dropped the box on top of another one on the floor, and when she straightened back up, she reached for Nona's hair. Her fingers delicately placed the messy strands back in place and the first mate blinked in surprise.

"I quite literally am the boss of you, Nona," Glenlivet said, smiling.

The flustered shock that had slowed Nona for a few seconds quickly turned to entertained annoyance as she slapped the captain's hand away. Glenlivet was about to speak again when a young man ran into the room. Augie, winded from running, took off his wine-red hat to clean the sweat off his forehead. "Captain!"

There was an alarm to his voice that made both women frown.

"Yes, Augie?" Glenlivet said. "Any guards bothered you while coming back?"

The navigator had been sent off that morning to pay the owner of the shady inn they had been staying at while in port. Augie shook his head, visibly relaxing upon hearing Glen's voice. He continued, holding himself against the doorway, "Oh no, nothing like that.

No guards even saw us, we took the alleyways as you recommended. Celeste is doing a final inventory as we speak and then we are all set to go; unless you have anything else to do in town, of course, but to be honest—"

"Augie," Nona interrupted, cutting his rant short, "that hardly seems like an emergency. Why did you storm in like that?"

"Nona!" Augie´s head turned toward the sound of the first mate´s voice and his smile widened, two dimples showing up on his full cheeks. "I didn´t see you there! I hope I didn´t interrupt you two."

Both women rolled their eyes at that. Augie, navigator, and hurdy-gurdy player, was missing both his eyes and had the habit of making jokes about it whenever given the opportunity, then pretended to be offended if any of his friends laughed.

"Augie."

"Ah, sorry, yes! Two strangers are trying to board the ship," the boy said.

Glenlivet stared at him for a few seconds before rushing out of the galley, barely missing his shoulder on the way out.

Most of the crew had gathered by the gangway, blocking the passage of two individuals. The captain made her way through them to find Marcya, her weapons master, leading them all. Her sword was pointed toward the taller person, so close to the skin that the steel was cutting the beard hair that spread onto his neck. This alone was stopping them from taking another step.

"If you would allow me to explain—"

"Marcya. Back off, please," the captain said, putting a gentle hand on the woman's shoulder.

The sword lowered and the blonde woman turned to her captain, awaiting orders.

"Your crew is jumpy," the man on the gangway said, rubbing his neck.

"Can you blame them, old man?" She smiled at him, and Marcya frowned.

"You know this person, Captain?"

Glenlivet nodded at her, then turned to the crew. "Everyone, go back to work. It's under control."

While most did as ordered, a few curious ones hung back. Nona, who had run after Glenlivet, stood a few feet behind her, eyeing the two men.

"It's been a long time, Julian," Glenlivet said. "What brings you to Rera?"

The older man, about fifty and scruffy looking, took off his tricorn hat and smiled bright, revealing swollen gums and a few fake teeth. "I could ask you the same question, Glenlivet! But I think we both know my answer is always the same!"

"Chasing coin or chasing skirts this time?" Glenlivet

asked with a chuckle.

The gasp that came from behind Julian drew everyone´s attention. The captain had almost forgotten about the shorter person who had attempted to board her home. She did not recognize him. He also wore a hat, though a different style, a soft one that he had pulled down to his ears. A few ringlets of soft dirty blonde hair were visible from under it. The servant clothes he wore were too big on his frame, and he kept fidgeting with the handmade bag he carried.

Seeing Glenlivet´s attention drift to his companion, Julian smiled and slapped a hand on the boy´s back, who flinched at the contact.

"Let me introduce you to my friend here! This is..." The old pirate took a moment to look at him, moving his hand upward and grasping as if he could grab the name from thin air.

"Daniel. My name is Daniel Bardot," the boy filled the silence.

"Daniel! Yes, my friend Daniel," Julian said.

"He a part of your new crew?" Glenlivet asked, doubtful.

"I met the boy just yesterday, but maybe, if you will have us both," Julian said, shrugging, and when Glenlivet raised a confused eyebrow at him, he put a hand on her shoulder. "We are asking to join your crew. Or at the very least, passage out of this blasted country on your ship."

"You can join us as far as you want to go. As for him? I am not a nursery," she said, taking Julian's hand off her shoulder. "I don't know what the kid's deal is but he stinks of trouble. A newbie is not worth risking Goliath persecution."

"I'm a fast learner," Daniel said, taking a step forward.

Glenlivet stared at him, not expecting the meek little thing to advocate for himself. "This life is not for the faint of heart, kid. You have no—"

"It cannot be harder than what I am leaving behind," Daniel interrupted, raising his chin, and attempting to meet Glenlivet's height. "Julian said you took in misfits. That you offered a safe home to people who can't find freedom on land because of who they are. Was that a lie?"

The captain sighed, taking in the words, and shot a look toward Nona, who was watching the conversation unfold with a sly smile on her face. The kid was not wrong. While Glenlivet hadn't set out to do that when she had purchased *The Outsider*, things had developed that way naturally.

"You said it's not worth the risk," Daniel added, nervous about the silence. "I can make it worth your while."

Glenlivet watched, horrified, as the boy fumbled with the strap of his bag until he was able to open it and retrieve his money purse. The little leather pouch was heavy, the captain could tell just by the sound of it, but it became even more obvious as the kid opened it right there and then, to offer her coin.

"Oh my gods," she said, rolling her eyes and grabbing the purse out of Daniel´s hands. She closed it and threw it over her shoulder toward Nona. Her hands moved so fast that Daniel had no time to process it before the first mate caught the purse in the air and put it away in one of her belt hoops. He started to protest, but Glenlivet raised a hand to quiet him.

"As I said, this life is not easy. It´s especially difficult if you´re careless and stupid. Consider that your first lesson. Don´t show off all your money to a pirate unless you´re willing to fight them for it." And with that, Glenlivet turned and walked away, heading to her quarters.

On the way, Nona reached out to her, grabbing her forearm. The captain felt her fingertips press against the inside of her wrist, feeling for her pulse, "Are you sure about this?" she whispered.

Glenlivet nodded gravely. "He won´t survive long if we leave him here."

The first mate nodded, and let her go, watching as she walked away.

Julian chuckled to himself, finally stepping onto the ship and looking around at the working crew. "Said they'd welcome you in. Bit rough around the edges, but then again, which pirate isn't?"

"The captain is a woman," Daniel said as if this fact had just dawned on him. "You told me, but I didn´t fully believe it until now."

Julian turned to him, the smile on his face faltering as he considered the boy. "You superstitious or something?"

Daniel blinked a few times before correcting him. "No! Not at all, but I read that pirates were, I was just—"

"I recommend you forget all that you read about pirates when aboard this ship," Nona said, approaching them.

The first mate introduced herself, shaking Daniel's hand. The young man noticed the calluses on her palm as they did. Nona offered him a quick smile before turning toward the woman who had threatened Julian upon arrival. Marcya had returned to her duties but hadn't strayed far. When called by the first mate, she diligently approached and Daniel couldn't help but notice how her hand went to the pommel of her sword, as if by instinct. Julian, also noticing, raised his hands in mock surrender before walking away, in the same direction Glenlivet had taken.

"This is Marcya. She will show you where you'll be sleeping and lead you to the quartermaster," Nona explained, and the weapons master nodded. As Marcya grabbed Daniel's wrist and started pulling him toward the hold of the ship, the first mate called out to her,

"Make sure Celeste remembers to assign him his tasks!"

Marcya's grip wasn't harsh, but Daniel couldn't help but grimace at the touch anyway.

"You're going to be put to work. Don't think Celeste will go easy on you just 'cause you're new."

"Is she strict?"

"That mage didn't go soft on me when I first joined, I'll tell you that."

Daniel's eyes widened at that, his anxiety spiking. Marcya was about to open the door of the hold, a wooden hatchet on the floor of the deck when it sprung open and another crew member climbed out, rushing past them so fast Daniel struggled to see their face. He did notice, however, the pink coloration of their hair and the gills that flared just under their jaw as they ran past.

"That's Marina. Takes her a while to warm up to strangers, so give her space. You don't want to crowd her, or you'll regret it," Marcya recommended, holding the door open so Daniel could enter first.

For a moment, as Daniel walked down the stairs into the dark hold, he wondered if he was being swallowed by the ship, to never be seen again. Once in the hold, Daniel was relieved to see a normal space that held boxes with ammunition, and barrels, as well as fabrics. A wooden doll hung from the ceiling. He followed Marcya past a curtain into the crew's sleeping area.

A figure was hunched over on one of the bunks, focusing on several pieces of paper that sat on her lap. Her tattooed hands moved frantically over them, rearranging them to see a pattern Daniel could not even begin to comprehend.

Marcya had quite a laugh at Daniel's shocked expression when Celeste looked up and stood to meet them. She was a short woman with rosy cheeks and the warmest smile he had ever seen. The softness of her voice, though deep and rumbling like a fire in a cave, surprised him the most.

"Look at you, you poor thing!" Celeste cooed. "Marcya tried to scare you, didn't she?"

The snicker that came from the woman in question was enough of an answer, and Celeste shot her a disapproving look before turning to Daniel again.

"Well, don't you worry. I'll make sure nobody messes with you anymore. I'm Celeste. Resident mage and quartermaster."

Daniel offered his hand with a nervous smile. Celeste grabbed it with both of hers, rubbing the skin in comfort. Just then, the ship started moving, separating itself from the port.

He looked at the small high windows, realizing he was *actually* leaving. All this time, he had been waiting for someone to catch up to him, for someone to disturb his plans. But nobody had. Everything had gone his way for the first time in his life. However, the relief that took hold of him only lasted a few seconds. When he looked back at the woman holding his hand, she was staring at him with a deadpan expression and dark shadows under her eyes that hadn't been there before.

"Whoever you're running from isn't done with you. He'll come after you."

"She asked for her breakfast earlier than usual, Your Majesty. Indicates that, perhaps, this disappearance was premeditated and planned," Jona suggested. The soldier had dark brown eyes, with tattoos that started right under the waterline and ran down his cheeks. In his carefully pressed uniform and polished boots, he walked briskly down the corridor to keep up with the man he served.

King Micah Griffith of Rera opened the doors into the courtyard, only to be met by another royal guard, who bowed low upon realizing who had interrupted his entry.

"My King. I bring reports from downtown."

"Speak."

The soldier, a middle-aged man named Flick, who boasted a head of thick, dark short hair, relayed the information found on the market's side of the capital: "We found the queen's dress in an alley behind Old Evian's tavern. The bartender did not see Queen Danielle in the establishment, but he did recall a servant boy from the castle."

The king pushed Flick aside and started taking long strides toward the stables, "Where did the servant boy go?"

"Toward the docks, Your Majesty," Flick said, nodding curtly. "I've sent my best men to search the area already. They await us there."

Something in the old guard's eyes clued the king that something else remained to be said. His patience was growing thin with every second wasted as his servants saddled his best horse, a grey mare called Poison. He thumped the point of his scabbarded sword onto the ground, prompting the soldier to continue.

"Apologies. It is not good news. The servant boy was not alone. He left with an older man. Evian says this man wore a tricorn hat and a long brown coat. Shifty looking, he said."

Trinkets of all kinds littered the captain's headquarters. Every place Glenlivet had ever been to was represented in this room in the form of necklaces, crystals, books, tapestries... There seemed to be a particular fondness for stained-glass oil lamps. At least thirty of them hung from the ceiling, swaying with the ship's movement on the water.

Gale was fussing over Glenlivet's desk, the surface of it completely covered with maps and notes, as well as a compass, a watch, and pens aligned against a stack of books. In the midst of writing something down, the strategist barely registered the slow start of the ship as it separated from the port, but their careful note-taking was interrupted by the sound of the door as the captain walked into the room.

"Julian's here. He'll be joining us for a while," Glenlivet said. Gale blinked a few times, processing as she continued talking: "Word of warning: he´s not alone. Brought a young man with him."

Gale took one single step away from the captain who had gotten to the desk by then and reached toward a small red leatherbound notebook with jittery hands. Glenlivet followed the movement with her eyes, though she didn't need Gale to write down their thoughts to understand.

"I know it's out of the blue and we weren't planning on expanding the crew right now, but the kid is in danger. I don't know what, or who he's running from but it can't be anything trivial considering it's Rera we're dealing with. You of all people can understand that..."

Gale opened and closed their fist, their other hand

caressing the texture of the wooden desk. After almost a full minute, that Glenlivet used to look over the strategist's notes on the desk, Gale sighed and nodded. With quick movements, they opened the notebook and grabbed the small sharpened pencil by its side.

It will be nice to see Julian again they wrote down, quickly turning the notebook around so the captain could read it.

Glenlivet smiled. Shortly after, a knock on the room's door frame caught the pair´s attention. The captain allowed Julian entry with a gesture of her hand, and he walked in, admiring the room.

"You've become quite a collector, haven't you? Last I saw this place, it only had your little cot!" he commented, smiling wide, the fingertips of his left hand touching the bedpost. His eyes then went to Gale. "How have you been, wits?"

Gale bowed slightly as a greeting, a soft smile playing on their lips at the treasured nickname.

"Still not much of a talker, I assume? That's alright by me, gods know I speak enough for an entire crew." Julian sat on the opposite side of the captain's desk. He brought his feet up, his boots landing on the small free space on the table.

A blush covered the strategist's cheeks but the smile didn't falter as they shook their head and broke eye contact to focus on their maps once more. Meanwhile,

Glenlivet detached a bunch of old water-damaged letters from underneath her belt and opened the lowest drawer of the desk. She put the letters inside, then replaced them on her belt loop with an old rusted key before closing the drawer and locking it tight.

"Where are we headed, Captain? Hopefully somewhere with a sunny beach?" Julian asked with a smile.

Glenlivet smiled back but crushed those expectations immediately, "No such luck, old man. It's the Sodra Cluster for us this time." She tapped the map on the table, on the small conglomeration of islands they were headed toward.

Julian's boots fell off the edge of the desk and he threw his arms over the surface of it with a dramatic groan. "Not that old dump! Nobody likes it there and you know it. We all just pretend we like it so the tavern owners keep our tabs open." The last few words were muffled by the hat that slid down over his face.

"We have questions someone there might be willing to answer."

Gale's pencil scratched at their notebook paper with considerable speed, after which they ripped out the page and put it on the table for Julian to read. The older pirate pushed his hat back onto his head with a knuckle as he grabbed the note and read it out loud, stumbling over a few of the words.

"According to our informant in Rera, it´s been almost

a year since he last showed his face there, so our friend in Greene must have been misinformed. The trail has grown cold, so the Cluster is our best bet to find another lead." As he read, Julian's face grew paler and paler. His eyes traveled to Glenlivet, who considered him with a serious look on her face.

"You're still chasing after him?" He didn't bother to mask the incredulity in his voice. "After all these years... I thought you would have seen sense by now, child."

"We're not having this discussion again, Julian."

"You know how dangerous he is—"

"I do," Glenlivet interrupted, her tone sharp and final. "And I will have his head regardless."

They stared at one another for a long beat, a plea to reconsider on Julian's expression, and unmitigated stubbornness on Glenlivet's. Finally, the older man sighed and nodded, rubbing his face with his hands. The captain, dropping her gaze, locked her jaw and pressed her teeth together, eyes clouded.

"I heard about what he did to your last ship," she said. "I won't blame you if you decide to leave once we reach the Sodra Cluster, but you won't convince me to drop this."

Gale focused their eyes on the map, in the long but not very wide bay Goliath shared with the Iron Lands.

They had all heard about the affair. No pirate had been bold enough to steal so close to the capital of the world this side of Dread Water in years. Julian's last captain thought himself quick enough to go in and out unnoticed. A small cargo, taken from a Terafian ship that was docked there at the time. Small, but valuable enough to attract *The Conviction* too. The massive brigantine had trapped Julian's ship in the mouth of the bay as they attempted a quick escape and demanded the stolen goods.

The battle that ensued alerted Goliath's forces, effectively trapping Julian's crew between two enemies, and forcing them to surrender to one of the two for the slim chance of surviving. The captain thought that surrendering to Elric, the captain of *The Conviction*, would give them a better chance at escaping Goliath's imprisonment. And he would have been right if Elric hadn't been more interested in getting a head start. Blowing a hole in Julian's ship and setting it on fire once he had the cargo stopped Goliath from exiting their bay for a few hours, allowing *The Conviction* to leave without a tail.

Most of the crew, including the captain, perished in the incident, and most of the survivors ended up in Goliath's cells. Julian had escaped by pure instinct and luck, hiding out among dead tree roots in the Iron Swamp. It had taken him about three days to muster up the courage to get out.

"No." The old pirate's eyes were also trained on the map. "If you manage to kill him and get *The Conviction* back… I want to be there to witness it."

2

SIRENS AND MAGES

Life at sea was busier than Daniel could have ever imagined.

The first mate had taken full advantage of the good weather throughout the first three weeks at sea. Every morning Daniel and Roma were ordered to clean the floors as soon as they woke up. Then they'd assist the cook in making breakfast and have a bit of a rest while eating together.

It was during these meal times that Daniel got to meet most of the crew. It was overwhelming and chaotic and the first few occasions nearly brought Daniel to tears from cheer overload. The crew would pile on the galley door, banging their empty wooden plates on the frame, the floor, and their own hands, singing and clapping as they waited to be served their rations. They would sit where they could, all together, and share stories, ambitions, and their plans for the day.

Daniel kept quiet for the most part, anxiety brewing in the pit of his stomach. He was moved to see many would often cue him into the conversation, asking questions about his life in Rera and sharing their grievances with the country and its ruling. He kept his answers vague, nodded along, and watched their reactions in search of suspicion or doubt. The boy's eyes often focused on the captain during his inspections. He suspected she was the most likely to call out the flaws in his story. Glenlivet would eat with them every meal, generally quiet and observing them with smiling eyes, almost always arm-to-arm with the first mate, Nona.

One time, during the first week, Daniel leaned in toward Celeste and asked about their relationship. The mage, who had been busy trying to crack open a crab leg, smiled knowingly and shrugged, her eyes focused on the two women.

"Only the sea serpent knows," she whispered back.

Roma, on Celeste's far side, had rolled her eyes so hard that her pupils disappeared for a second. "Poor Daniel is too tired for your riddles, tata. Pass me one of those?"

The matter was settled and he hadn't asked again.

His exhaustion came mostly from the activities said

captain and first mate ordered after every breakfast. Glenlivet was a strict teacher and tested Daniel´s memory and patience with constant lectures and tests about sailing and navigation. The boy hadn´t lied about being a fast learner, however, and soon was helping the rest of the crew on more difficult jobs around the ship.

Nona, on the other hand, was partial to sword fighting lessons.

"I don't expect things to be quiet for long, so we must get you ready to fight sooner rather than later. When the time comes, we won't babysit you. You will have to look after yourself."

Daniel agreed, and the rest of *The Outsider* seemed to agree as well because they all rushed at the chance to watch Nona's lessons and to volunteer themselves as practice opponents. To everyone but Daniel's surprise, he had a decent stance and sharp reflexes that came in handy when sword fighting. Working against him, he was far too afraid of the blade to strike his opponents, and he kept pulling away too early and making himself vulnerable. Working past these issues was harder than learning how to sail and the frustration that overtook him when Nona managed to touch him made him throw his sword to the floor with a groan more than once. The first mate was incredibly patient, making him pick the weapon back up every time yet careful not to work him past what he could handle.

Marina was the only member of the crew Daniel hadn't been able to practice his sword skills against, or even talk to, for that matter. As Marcya had said, the siren was cautious around new people and so Daniel had given her space. His curiosity was reaching a boiling point.

"I've read a great deal about sirens," he said to Roma and the cook while peeling potatoes one day. "But I can hardly imagine Rera's books were faithful to the truth, no matter how much they swear on the gods."

"I'll say so," Blue said, chuckling and shaking their head. "Gara is constantly inventing new ways of justifying their trade of tails, and that king upon Rera's throne is a buffoon with jingly bells for brains for believing it all."

The young man laughed so hard tears sprung to his eyes, the potato that had been on his hand rolling now on the floor. The laughter continued until Roma and Blue joined in, so infectious it was, and until Daniel's ribs were aching. It was only after regaining his composure that he processed fully what had been said and scrunched his eyebrows searching for the best way to enquire further, "You said 'hunt us.' You mean…?"

The cook smiled wide. "Not quite. Only by half, so don't expect any long-distance swimming from me as you would from Marina."

It wasn't long after that conversation that Daniel

was able to interact with her. One cold morning as he mopped the deck, Augie rang the bell from the crow's nest. It startled the boy but it wasn't the emergency code he had been taught, so he stayed his heart and continued his chores. Glenlivet came running out of her quarters, dressed in loose trousers and a shirt that didn't belong to her. Daniel remembered having seen Nona wearing that shirt a week before, and smiled to himself as the captain approached one of the boxes on deck.

"A little help, please!" She had a smile on her face as she started to unfold and drag an enormous net out of the box.

The young man made his way over and helped her, with a curious look. "What are we doing, exactly?"

"Oh, right, you've never seen us do this before. We have to—" The captain interrupted herself, assessing him for a second before frowning. "Is it safe for you to lift a lot of weight with your bandages on?"

Daniel choked on his own surprise, dropping the net and raising his voice despite his best efforts not to. "What?"

Glenlivet looked over the side of *The Outsider*, toward the water. "We need to lift Marina back onto the ship but, and don't tell her I said this, the tail adds a lot of weight to her. Can you do that with your bindings?"

Daniel felt silly, hand raising to touch the chest so

carefully squished down and hidden behind plenty of medical gauze stolen from the castle infirmary. "My name is Danielle, not Daniel. I chose it because it was similar enough that I would still respond to it."

Glenlivet paused. "Well, is Danielle what you would prefer?"

The words started tumbling out of her mouth faster than she could think of them, her anxiety making her stutter. "I think so, yes. I didn't mean to lie but I needed to get out of there, and then time kept passing and it got weirder and weirder to confess the more time passed, I am terribly sorry, Captain, I truly—"

"Stop apologizing," Glenlivet interrupted the anxious rant, grabbing at Danielle's shoulders with warm, gentle hands. "If you wish, you can tell me all about it after we get poor Marina out of that cold water. It doesn't bother her now but she will be rather cross with me for making her wait."

Together, alongside Blue, who spotted them on their way out of the hold, they threw the net overboard and brought it back up once Marina had situated herself inside. With three people, they were able to get her up without a hitch, but Danielle felt just how true Glenlivet´s warning had been on the way her arms and chest started burning.

It was one thing to read about siren tails in the library of the castle in Rera, and another thing entirely was to see one in person. All thirteen feet of it, even squished inside a net, was a sight that made Danielle hold her breath for a moment as she watched Glenlivet allow Marina to get out.

For a terrible moment, she was listening to Micah describe how how he would cut tail from torso and send it off to the best taxidermist in the kingdom. A chill traveled up her spine. She rubbed at the back of her neck and coughed, taking in a deep breath and trying to shake away the memory.

"You ought to take your bindings off. It can´t be good to have them on for so long." Marina´s voice startled her. It sounded like a voice underwater even on top of the ship, a beautiful echo that drew you in. Danielle looked at the siren in a mix of shock and delight, but by the time she did, Marina was already looking at the captain. "And you! You have to figure out a better way to get me back up, this is ridiculous."

"And humiliating, I bet. But it's all we can do while the ship is moving," Glenlivet said, smiling and disposing of the net back into the box. "Get the spicy liquor, Blue, please."

As Blue ran to the kitchen, the sun hit the lower part of Marina's body, which was now separating, slowly and painfully, into legs. The cook approached her and sat next to her, giving her a bottle to help the process, and a blanket to cover herself.

"Anything to report?"

Marina nodded while taking a big gulp from the liquor. "It won´t be long before Marcya spots it from the crow´s nest. A Goliath ship, heading right toward us."

"Goliath?" Danielle´s shaky voice made them turn to look at her. "We´re avoiding it, right?"

"Oh, absolutely not. It´s been months since we had any decent fun." Glenlivet smiled wide, a twinkle in her eye that promised danger. "If they're returning to Goliath or Rera that means it's full of gold from all those taxes and debts they like collecting."

After that, controlled chaos erupted in *The Outsider*. The crew was woken up earlier than usual and they all ate breakfast while preparing the ship for battle. Danielle was surprised to find that excitement overrode the fear brewing in her stomach as she watched Augie exchange their pirate flag for a Sister Nations one, specifically the Agath variant. *The Outsider*, as a schooner, was very similar in looks to the ones Agath and Agara used for their trading, and the captain was not above trickery to seem innocuous or to go undetected.

Glenlivet watched the horizon as the Goliath ship appeared into view. "Easy, everyone! We're going to try to get out of this without bloodshed."

Marcya rolled her eyes and grabbed her daggers harder. "It's a Goliath. I bet you three gold pieces they start the fight."

King Micah was red in the face but silent, the shakiness in his hands only noticeable if you looked close. Nobody around him would dare to when he was in such a mood.

A dock worker had informed them that a servant castle boy had gone into a ship from Agath tagged as *The Outsider*. Jona had identified the supposed ´Agath´ ship as a relatively well-known pirate ship mentioned a few times in Goliath´s reports, with a captain famous for housing undesirables and fugitives. They were considered a minor threat in comparison to other infamous pirate crews, so no hunters had been sent out to find them specifically.

"This is perhaps the stupidest thing she's done by far," he muttered to himself, looking at his map.

He stared out the window, wondering how long it would take to reach Sodra. His ship moved as fast as it could go, having chosen a small vessel this time in order to catch up with them at sea. His crew was small but made of his strongest men, so overpowering cockroaches wouldn't be an issue. He still had some concerns, however, because if they made it to the pirate haven that was the Sodra Cluster before he could catch up to them, things could get complicated.

He had never been to the islands before. A place where degeneracy and thievery were allowed, and even encouraged, according to some. When he had been told *The Outsider* had sailed off in that direction, he had half a mind to leave Danielle to fend for herself among that crowd. Gods only knew what their kind would do to her. The thought amused him, and it would probably teach her the lesson she so clearly needed. But alas, she was the queen of Rera. Certain expectations about her were tied directly to him and his good name. He would not leave her in the hands of filthy pirates and destroy his reputation in the process. He would not have the empire's Council spreading gossip and diminishing his authority over it. She would learn her lesson by his hand alone, once they returned home.

"It's an attack!"

"Captain!"

"Pirates!"

Glenlivet felt a sick sense of pride at the fear in the men's voices. Her father had often spoken about that thrill. When cast away from *The Conviction*, she thought she would never be able to experience it for herself ever again.

By the time the crew of the Goliath ship was close enough to read the small plaque with ´*The Outsider*´ written on it, it was too late to escape in their clumsy, much wider vessel. The pirates opened the gunports and shoved the brass cannons forward, threatening dark mouths ready to fire.

Nona stood next to Glenlivet as the ships slowed side to side, wood plank resting against her shoulder. "May we have your hospitality, good sir?"

The captain she addressed was tall and had a short, well-kept red beard. He was dressed in Goliath´s uniform, and his chest was covered in patches and medals demonstrating his position as the commander of the ship. He looked around, eyes wide and lost. His mouth opened and closed without a sound. Glenlivet smiled openly, and using the gentle tone of someone who is not robbing a ship but knocking politely on someone's door, she said, "Don´t give any trouble and you will be able to return to your prosperous nation without any injuries. I promise it won´t take long."

Before the captain of the Goliath ship could answer, Nona was placing down the gangplank and Glenlivet was jumping on it. At the same time, Marcya was laying down another plank and walking across. Not long after, most of the crew was on the enemy's ship.

The ship was called *The Fiona*, stunning and ornate with polished wooden floors. Glenlivet whistled as she walked across the deck toward the captain. "Beautiful sails, Captain. You must count yourself lucky I am not in search of new ones, or else I´d be happy to take them off your hands."

The man was in such a state that he thanked her for the compliment before shaking his head and putting a hand over the grip of his sword.

"There is no need for that," Glenlivet said, smiling, while Nona pointed her pistol at the man. "I´ll just take your money box and send you on your way. I will allow you to keep other goods you may have, as well as your rations for the rest of your journey."

"My, you are in a kind mood," Nona teased, an eyebrow raised in mock surprise.

The second the captain of *The Fiona* took his hand off of the sword and nodded, Gale walked past him and into his quarters to retrieve the box.

Both crews were quiet, tension simmering. *The Outsider*´s first mate watched the people they were robbing with a careful eye. The captain was meek, and Nona recognized the features and attitude of a man raised by a rich Goliath family. The rich of the empire were negotiators with no real fight in them but with the capital to convince others to fight in their name. The rest of the men, as far as she could see, were from Rera, which wasn´t a surprise. They were experienced sailors, happy to be hired by Goliath. Her people were familiar with the fighting style of Rerans. It was the two men she recognized to be from Gara or Greene that could prove to be troublesome.

Upon closer inspection, the first mate noticed they were twins, probably identical but this was barely noticeable anymore; their faces were so scarred in different ways they were no longer that similar. One of them had had his nose broken in at some point and it no longer sat in the same position as his brother's. Both wore their hair in a low ponytail that hung over one of their shoulders. They were tall and dressed in brown old leather that stretched over muscled bodies.

They stood at the back of the crowd, looking sullen as they seemed to be analyzing them, just as Nona was. She followed the eyeline of the brother with the broken nose to Marina, and she watched him elbow his twin.

"Glenlivet!" Nona screamed.

Her captain hadn´t even turned toward the twins when one of them threw a dagger and slashed at her arm. As the fight broke out, Glen told herself to give Marcya three gold pieces as she grabbed the injury to stop the bleeding. Nona was next to her in a second, but the woman dismissed her with a shake of her head. "Don´t. He barely touched me. Go!"

Marcya rushed toward the man who had thrown the knife, slashing at him as he stepped back. His twin screamed at the crew to fight back against the pirate scum. The Rerans, though they were sailors and not trained swords, were armed. Now encouraged by the twins, they rushed forward and faced the pirates.

Glenlivet approached the captain of *The Fiona* in two long strides, sword to his chest. "Tell them to stand down. Now!"

"They won´t listen, I—"

She interrupted him with a groan and slashed at his chest. The startled scream that erupted from him distracted a few of his men, a chance the pirates took to subdue them. The captain did not care about this, however, as he patted his uninjured chest and cried with relief. The sword had avoided the skin but cut the patches and medals off of his uniform. The cries did not last long, as Glenlivet switched the sword to her other hand and hit him straight on the forehead with the pommel. The captain fell back on his ass, his back hitting the wall and the pirate turned to join the battle with the rest of her crew.

Julian had a young cabin boy moving back and forth, swords clashing against each other. Despite how young the kid was, he was a good swordsman, his footwork showing he had learned to fight in Rera, stiff and straight, probably taught by one of the royal guards.

"Your form is all well and good for land squabbles, boy! But..." Julian danced aside, giving way to Glenlivet as she walked past and kicked the boy behind the knees. The Reran kid fell onto the floor with a shocked yelp and Julian held his sword to his chin, "...you lose balance on a rocking ship."

The captain looked around the deck. Despite the mess of bodies moving and fighting, she spotted what she was looking for on the floor by the main mast. She threw the rope at Julian, who tied the boy's hands and legs and threw him down next to the unconscious captain of *The Fiona*.

Nona walked through the ship, avoiding swords left and right, looking for Marina. It was clear by the twin's stares that they were interested in her. The first mate shot a man who was about to attack Roma, and he fell over in pain. Roma took it as an opportunity to kick him and he grabbed at her leg, trying to bring her down. Celeste, who had stayed on *The Outsider*, ran across the gangplank cursing in three different languages, and reached into her satchel for a handful of yellow powder. She blew it onto the man's face and he fell back with a thud, unconscious.

"Thanks!" the girl yelled, taking her leg back, and Celeste prepared to get more powder from her purse.

As the mages kept running, putting any man from *The Fiona* to sleep, Nona's eyes landed on Glenlivet. The captain was in the middle of fighting one of the twins who had started the commotion. Her nose was bleeding, and he had managed to corner her but she was still putting up a struggle, her knee connecting with his groin twice. She was trying to create distance between them so she could use her sword properly but the man was an unmoving wall in front of her.

The sound of a pistol rang through the air, making Nona look for the shooter and whoever had been shot. Augie was standing on the poop deck of *The Outsider*. The X-shaped scars over where his eyes used to be glowed red. His free hand was outstretched in front of him next to the pistol. His hand, whose palm had a black hole the size of a Mangrath copper coin, closed in a celebratory fist as he cheered. The bullet had managed to hit the twin that was towering over Glenlivet, right in the ear. It fell to the gleaming wooden deck.

The man's scream made the pirate captain wince, and she tried pushing the twin away with her shoulder. As tall as he was and with the short space behind her, the man stood his ground, one of his hands pressed against his exposed ear canal. Blood rushed down his arm and sleeve, and all he could see was red because the splatter had reached his left eye, but he pushed against Glenlivet anyway.

Nona rushed through the distance between them, pushing and shoving everyone in her path. She watched as the twin grabbed her captain by the collar of her shirt. That was her shirt. She had left it in Glenlivet's room last night. A thought crossed her mind that Glenlivet wasn´t allowed to die wearing her shirt. Her legs burned as she ran faster.

Glen twisted her wrist and brought her sword down on the arm that was holding her up, legs kicking at his stomach. The blade went halfway through because of the odd angle and got stuck on the bone. More blood splattered onto them both, and his grip loosened.

Nona was four feet away from the man holding Glenlivet when she allowed herself to slip on the deck and slide the rest of the way to them, slashing her dagger at the back of the twin´s legs. The man let out another blood-curdling scream and his knees gave out underneath him, hitting the floor and completely letting go of Glenlivet.

"You bitch!"

The captain took a step back, grabbing the mangled arm and pulling. The forearm separated from the elbow and fell, rolling away with the swaying of *The Fiona*. The man´s cry died shortly after, the agony of all his injuries finally rendering him unconscious. Glenlivet now grabbed Nona´s arm, pulling her up to her feet.

"What would you do without me?" the first mate said, smiling, relief washing over her despite the battle continuing behind her.

"Probably die." The captain rolled her eyes, but couldn´t help smiling back at her. At the same time, she took the dagger from Nona´s hand and threw it over her first mate´s shoulder. It lodged into the arm of a Reran sailor who was running full speed toward them with a hatchet. Glen looked down at her blood-soaked garments and tsked, "I ruined your shirt, sunshine."

"Never mind that," Nona said, turning around and assessing the battle again. "We need to find this bastard´s brother. They wanted Marina."

She stepped over the unconscious sailor and ran, kicking and elbowing all in her way, with Nona close behind. Marcya was thrown onto the floor in front of them by someone. She caught her weight with her wrist and screamed when it twisted in an unnatural position. Glenlivet jumped over her and continued running.

"Nona! Take care of Marcya!"

Nona did as ordered, kneeling to grab Marcya and pull her out of the way of a sword. Using her last bullet, she turned and shot the man right in the ribs. He fell with a screech, dropping the sword as he grappled at the bullet hole.

"Marina!" Glenlivet called out, looking around.

Blue, who was in the middle of a group of three men when they heard Glenlivet scream, responded: "Quarterdeck, Captain!"

Glenlivet grabbed her other dagger from her belt and threw it at the cook, who caught it mid-air and started protecting themselves with it. "Thank you!"

The woman kept running, her head throbbing. "Marina!"

The youngest person aboard *The Fiona* was a ten-year-old boy called Tomás, and he was peeking his little head from the hold of the ship, watching with starstruck eyes as his father´s crew fought against the pirates. The screams and clashes of swords, as well as pistols firing, were so loud he was having trouble keeping his eyes open but he didn´t want to miss a single detail. He couldn´t see his father from his snooping spot but he imagined him triumphant over five pirates, his sword gleaming in the sunlight.

As the fight spread and moved like waves around him, his young, excited eyes spotted a pathway to the gangplanks the pirates had set up. It wasn´t difficult to cross. He was small for his age, and though his mother assured him he would soon have a growth spurt, his height helped him now, sneaking past the chaos of the fight and onto the pirate ship, unseen.

Danielle had been ordered to stay back. "To guard the ship," Glenlivet had said, but Danielle was more than aware this was to guard *her* rather than a genuine worry that *The Outsider* would be boarded. If it had been any other ship, she would have been allowed to participate in her first raid. But as this was a Goliath ship, they couldn´t risk her being spotted and recognized. Not when they were still so close to Rera.

She had taken off the binding around her chest and was in the middle of putting on a clean shirt when she heard the door of the hold open and close. It was done quietly, but whoever it was hadn´t been careful to move the latch out of the way, so the piece of rusted metal had complained out loud. Danielle suddenly became very aware that her sword was on the forecastle deck, where she had left it yesterday after practice with Nona. After looking around, she rushed toward the surgeon´s bunk, where she knew the woman kept a few small, sharp scalpels and a box of needles. In a scrape, those would have to do.

While rummaging through her things, Danielle´s ears were alert. The person approaching wasn´t any of her crewmates, that much she could tell by the sound and pattern of the footsteps; an ability she had been forced to learn to keep herself safe and out of her husband´s reach when he was in one of his moods. Listening attentively also told her that this person didn´t weigh as much as anyone in her crew because the floorboards weren´t creaking under them. Even Danielle, who had arrived at *The Outsider* emaciated, caused some of the old wood pieces to groan. This knowledge provided some relief as she finally found the scalpel and turned around to face whoever was just about to walk past the curtains and into the crew's sleeping quarters.

A child came into view. He couldn't have been taller than four feet, scrawny, dressed in shorts, a shirt, and a red vest that hung too low on his small torso. The inexperience and wonder were obvious in the way he walked into the room looking over his shoulder, not expecting any danger to come his way despite his surroundings. When he finally turned to look into the room, he squealed like a mouse upon seeing Danielle standing there, scalpel in hand. The reality of where he was suddenly dawned on him like a bucket of cold water as the pirate and boy stared at each other for several uncomfortably long seconds.

Tomás finally got out of his stupor and tried to unsheathe his short sword. It was a practice weapon, a dull thing that would have bruised Danielle at most if he had managed to hit her at all. She quickly got out of the way and dropped the scalpel, no longer inclined to use it against such a young opponent.

"Stop that right now!" she said, trying to sound stern as the boy swung toward her once more.

This time, the sword hit one of the wooden beams behind Danielle, who squatted to avoid it. Standing back up, she grabbed the sword by the blade and pulled it, sending the boy sprawling onto the floor. In a moment of panic, the former queen of the nation of Rera grabbed one of the heavy blankets from the cot to her right and threw it over the boy.

Marina stood in between the bowsprit and one of the brothers from Gara, who held a small throwing axe in his left hand. As convenient as it would have been, the siren knew he wouldn't risk losing his only weapon. She considered jumping over the railing and into the water but spending the early morning swimming to make sure the path ahead was clear for *The Outsider* had drained her energy too much to risk it. She was fast, however, and had thus far managed to dodge every blow from the man, whose build slowed him down.

The twin's eyes were bloodshot and his nose was as red as his shirt under his long coat.

"You filth," he groaned when she managed to avoid another swing by ducking to his left and stabbing him on the outside of his thigh.

"Marina!" Glenlivet's voice called from the stairs to the deck.

The siren felt warm relief wash over her. She wouldn´t have been able to hold him off on her own forever. It was in a very similar situation to this that Marina and Glen had met years ago, though the roles had been reversed then. The thought amused her, and she smiled, watching as her opponent looked in the direction of her captain's voice. The perfect opportunity to twist the sunken dagger and open the wound on the leg even further. This would ensure the tissue was destroyed so badly the skin would never heal completely. A reminder of what happened to men who hunted her kind, and maybe the key to getting out of his reach.

When the man's legs trembled from the pain, she dashed to the right, to meet her captain. The twin's hand shot out and grabbed her hair. His other hand, which had dropped the axe when he was stabbed traveled to the back of her neck and closed so harshly that Marina saw spots of light.

"Now where do you think you're going?"

The man curled his hand further, the tips of his fingers digging into the closed gills and scratching at the exposed wet skin inside. Marina's eyes rolled back and her mouth opened as she desperately tried to get away and lost air.

"Marina, no!" Glenlivet screamed, running full speed toward them, her sword drawn.

It was too late.

The siren's mouth opened even wider, the edges of her lips breaking like seams being pulled apart to let out a hiss from deep within her throat; so loud it sent Glenlivet flying backward. The man couldn't help letting go of her, stumbling away and throwing his hands onto the sides of his head, trying his best to stop the echoing sound. It was cracking his head open, he was sure of it.

Glenlivet tried her best to get back up but her arms failed her. "Marina!" She couldn't hear her own voice over the siren's distressed scream that kept repeating inside her skull. Her surroundings were spinning as she let herself lay on the deck and closed her eyes, trying to breathe. Her trembling hand moved toward the letters tucked away under her wide belt.

Marina's eyes were glazed white and her cheeks bruised blue around the wounds caused by opening her mouth so wide to scream. She turned slowly toward the man.

His ears were bleeding, as was his nose. The twin hoped the tears running down his face were just that. He blinked them away and discovered his body locked in pain as he watched the siren kneel in front of him. The woman's mouth was closed but the sound was still loud in his head.

Gara had published many works about sirens and the best way to hunt them, for they were dangerous and cruel. Many spoke of their beauty and bewitching spells that lured good-hearted people to crash against rocks. Everyone told tales of their songs, which calmed sailors into not realizing they were drowning and being fed upon. The truth about their voices, the man from Gara now realized, nobody had lived to write down.

He watched the siren open her mouth again. The pain

was too debilitating to move, to back away from her teeth. He prayed to the gods for the first time since he was twelve.

3

Goliath Epistolary

The fighting below stopped, and all heads turned toward the quarterdeck. The siren's cry had frozen them all and woken up the captain of *The Fiona*, who stared with wide horrified eyes as the echo of it transitioned seamlessly into the cries of pain of one of his men.

The sound didn't last long.

The bleak feeling that had overtaken both crews shattered as a man in a blue coat screamed and swung toward Julian. The fighting started anew, more brutal than before.

Glenlivet opened her eyes at the sound of battle. Her head ached, and the nausea was still threatening to make her spill out her breakfast but she sat up anyway and wiped the sweat off her forehead. "Leave him be..."

Her voice was weak and hoarse as if she had been the one screaming, but loud enough for the siren to hear, even over her wet chewing noises. With the threat taken care of and at her captain's order, Marina's eyes started shifting back to normal, her dark pupils appearing from under the white veil. Her hands released the man's head as if it had burned her. The sound of it hitting the wood made her look away, shaking.

"No."

"Yes," Glenlivet said, trying to stand by grabbing onto the railing. "Come on. You'll have time to feel guilty afterward. Let's get out of here and fix your arm first."

Marina looked down, confused. She felt no pain, but it became clear that the man had been able to get ahold of the axe on the floor and attempted to defend himself in his last moments. Her right bicep was slashed at three points and bleeding profusely.

The siren got up and backed away from the body, stumbling into Glenlivet, who winced as her surroundings started spinning again. The captain held on to Marina, careful not to touch her injuries, and turned to watch over the main deck. She was relieved to find every single one of her people was still alive and fighting, though some seemed to have sustained injuries of their own.

She brought her hand up to her mouth and whistled

as loud as she could, then bellowed, "Retreat!"

Her crew responded almost immediately, moving back toward the gangplanks while still defending themselves from attacks. The captain of *The Fiona*, who had managed to stand after a moment, was fueled by the sight of his men fighting and screamed above the chaos. "Don´t let them get away!"

Glenlivet groaned as they walked down the stairs as far as they could onto the main deck, "That pathetic excuse of a man grew a spine all of a sudden?"

"Gale!" Marina called out, seeing the strategist fighting nearby, the moneybox tucked under their left arm.

Their eyes followed Marina´s voice, widening at the sight of her state. Gale kicked the man they had been fighting on the knee, sending him to the floor, and rushed to meet the two women.

"Get Marina, I will cover for you both," Glenlivet said.

"Nonsense," Marina said, then turned to Gale. "The captain was close to me when I screamed. She´s hurt. You should cover us, I am fine to walk."

Gale nodded firmly and turned to do just that, creating a pathway through the battle.

Mel, *The Outsider*'s surgeon, was a woman in her late thirties with round cheeks, kind grey eyes, and dark mid-length hair that stayed out of her face with the help of a red scarf. She always stayed on the ship during raids —to protect it, yes, but to also protect her own hands that were in charge of patching up injured people.

On this particular raid, she had been in the kitchen. She was boiling water and preparing bandages for her crewmates´ return when Marina's scream pierced the air. The woman, just like everyone else on *The Fiona*, had frozen in shock, her muscles locked in place from the dread. When she was able to move again, she rushed toward the pantry and kneeled, moving boxes around to find the medicine she stored in the coldest area in the tiny storage room.

"Great Bear Yrena, protect my family," she muttered, hoping, praying, that none of her people were close enough to be hurt by the scream.

She cursed under her breath upon finding the vials. Two of them had gone bad, but the third would do. Mel was heading out of the kitchen and running to assess who needed her first when the hatch on the floor opened with a *bang*.

"Gods! What—"

A strange kid coming out of the hold interrupted her question. Before she could even open her mouth again, Danielle popped out behind him. She looked panicked and was holding the boy by the shoulder with one hand while her other one held his sword.

"He snuck in," she simply said when she saw Mel's questioning look. "What in Mydos' purse was that sound?"

"That was Marina," Mel said in a rush. "Someone must have hurt her real bad to force her into that state. Do me a favor, and don't judge her too harshly. I need to go." Mel turned to keep moving but just at that moment, Gale was helping Marina onto the plank to cross.

"Sweet girl, come here!" The surgeon said, helping her down and began to examine the arm that continued to bleed a deep crimson.

"You should see the other guy. Got what he deserved," Glenlivet said, jumping aboard her ship, Gale following close behind. She turned to *The Fiona* and cupped her mouth with her hands, "Everyone back! Now!"

The first to make it back was Roma, then Celeste and Julian. The process was slow, as the crew struggled to pull away from the attacking enemies. Danielle pulled Glenlivet's sleeve, grimacing at how blood-soaked it was, and shoved the kid toward her. The captain looked startled for a second, and Danielle explained: "He's one of them. Tried sneaking into the hold. I didn't know what to do with him."

Glenlivet struggled to find words, her brain still foggy from the siren's cry, but noticed the captain of *The Fiona* pushing his men toward the cannons.

The man was screaming at the top of his lungs: "The pirate scum will meet justice in front of The Empire's Council, or sink!"

"I'm afraid we won't be doing either of those things, sir!" Glenlivet replied. "We have something of yours I'm sure you would like returned."

"You can sink with the money box, we have—" The man's eyes traveled to meet the pirates, then his son and his bravery died in his throat. He scrambled to his men, stopping them from preparing the canons. "Stop! Stop right now! They have my boy!"

Glenlivet looked down at the kid, putting a hand on his shoulder. "What is your name, young man?"

"Tomás," he stammered after swallowing hard.

"That was very brave, sneaking into my ship, Tomás. You'll grow up a fine sailor, I think. Were you curious?" The boy nodded, and she smiled. "Did you get to see much of it?"

"Only the hold," he answered, slightly more at ease.

"Oh, that is not nearly interesting enough. My friend will show you the rest of it while I talk to your father, how about that?"

He nodded eagerly again and smiled back without reservations as if he had forgotten the battle happening behind Glenlivet. Gale offered their arm to the kid.

"Put down your weapons!" The commander of *The*

Fiona turned to his crew, who obeyed orders, if not a bit hesitantly.

"Very kind." Julian smirked at him and started helping the rest of the crew cross back to *The Outsider*.

The surviving twin from Gara had gotten up and was limping toward the planks, holding the space where his arm used to be. "What are you doing?" he screamed at his captain, "We can win! We outnumber them!"

"Stand down! They have my son!"

"Damn your son! They have a siren!" he yelled, in such a rage he didn't notice the looks his crew was giving him. "You could buy three boys his age with the money we'll get for its tail!"

Glenlivet grabbed the pistol from Augie´s belt. She shot the screaming man in the shoulder of the arm she had cut earlier, sparing him harm to the healthy one. He screamed, stumbling back.

"Speak about my crew like they're animals again. I dare you."

The man didn't respond, the pain too heightened for him to voice any more complaints. Glen wondered if he had realized his brother was dead. She wondered if he cared at all.

"Now give me back my boy!" the captain demanded.

Glenlivet frowned. "Surely, you can see why I can´t do that." She gestured toward the cannons that awaited on the deck of *The Fiona*. "How do I know you won´t try to sink my ship once you have your son?"

The man´s rosy coloration was no longer there as he stuttered and tried to come up with a response, but Nona spoke up before he could: "We have no use for your kid, sir. If you didn´t have your cannons, we would feel safe returning him and going our separate ways."

Glenlivet smiled wickedly, eyeing her first mate. "So smart, sunshine."

"Goliath ship coming toward us, Your Majesty."

Micah looked up from his few notes on the pirate ship he was following, with a raised eyebrow. Jona waited in the open doorway.

"And? What do you suggest?"

"Should we stop them to enquire if they have any reports on *The Outsider*?"

The king smiled, nodded, and waved his hand to dismiss him. "You know what to do."

Jona Ishim bowed slightly and left, his steps sure and rhythmic. Micah considered the map on his wall. If the reports of their direction were true, the Goliath vessel had probably seen *The Outsider* pass around midday. This would be a good confirmation of their path. He doubted there was any interaction between the two ships; as far as reports were concerned, the pirates often avoided open sea scuffles, preferring to hide like cowards and attack by surprise.

And yet something in his gut told him this was an important stop to make. Jona seemed to also think so. Normally he wouldn't pay any mind to his soldier's opinions about his decisions but Jona, like him, was a hunter. After many years of tracking, sniffing the air, and studying prey, one developed an instinct about these matters.

Mel needed all the helping hands she could get. None of them, thank Yrena, were fatally wounded but there were several bruises and cuts that needed to be taken care of, lest infection set in.

She had started with Marina, as the fighting concluded and the ships separated. With her, she needed to take precautions, of course. The siren had taken wine and a green powder that Mel had mixed together.

She then bit down on a piece of wood and covered her mouth with a piece of cloth tied at the back of her head. Even with all of that, Marina insisted on being strapped down, so there was no chance her defense mechanism would trigger and harm anyone else in response to the pain.

Mel cleaned the cuts on her arm and stitched the

wounds back up, relieved that there didn´t seem to be any major damage to the muscles or the bone. The man hadn´t had enough control of his body to cause any lasting harm.

Gale ran around with Augie, getting every injured crew member alcohol to calm the nerves and cope with the pain. Celeste and Danielle were sent with instructions to take care of bruises and sprains. Marcya cursed out loud when the mage tried to move her wrist in order to see how bad the situation was.

"Oh, shut up, you big baby," she said, smiling, and Marcya laughed as Celeste wrapped her wrist to keep it tight and unmoving. "Mel said is not broken, but that you shouldn´t move it for a couple of days. Keep it elevated too."

Marcya was about to complain, but Celeste gave her a look so fierce she closed her mouth immediately.

One of the men from *The Fiona* had managed to punch Julian on the cheek and had been wearing several rings. The cuts were not deep but required cleaning, especially with them being so close to his eye, and he was also refusing Mel´s orders to let her check the bruises on his ribs where he had been kicked.

"I´m fine, woman! You worry too much!"

"I worry the right amount, you old man," she said, pushing him down on a stool, "Lift your shirt and let me see. You might have broken ribs!"

"Impossible! My ribs are as solid as the Iron Forest trees!" He drank from the bottle in his hand as Danielle cleaned the cuts on his face. "Now go help the people who actually need it, Mel, my sweet."

The surgeon blushed and rolled her eyes. "Everyone is behaving and getting the help they need. Now stop being an ass and move your shirt."

The ribs were bruised and red all over, especially on the left side of his torso, but they did not feel broken. She breathed a sigh of relief.

"Mel, really... I'm fine."

"You are," she said, putting the shirt back in place and making sure it wasn't wrinkled. "But we needed to make sure anyway. Now go lie down. You might not have broken ribs, but you are bruised to all hell. You need rest."

"Rest is for the wicked, darling." he winked up at the surgeon.

"Exactly. So go rest," she answered, placing her hands on her hips and smiling down at him.

Glenlivet was sitting in her room, eyes focused on the ceiling where one of her stained-glass lamps swayed slowly, her feet propped atop her desk. Her neck and nose were starting to ache, the adrenaline from the fight already gone. She had cleaned the blood coming out of her ears but they were still sore, and a loud continuous ring still played in her head. She pressed the letters against her abdomen, finding comfort in the weathered texture of the parchment. A bit of blood had gotten onto them from the soaked shirt, but they were still readable. A part of her knew it didn't matter if they weren't. She knew their contents by heart.

"Captain?"

Nona's voice made her open her eyes and look toward the door. She smiled at her first mate and put the letters away in the drawer, locking it. The woman followed the movement with her eyes as she closed the door behind her. She knew the captain struggled after battles. Glenlivet wasn't a monster, as much as some people would like to see her that way. She was human. And more fragile than she allowed others to know. She preferred to rob ships without bloodshed. It weighed heavy on her chest for days afterward when fights broke out.

"How is your nose?" Nona asked as she approached.

Glen smiled and immediately winced at the movement that caused her nose to wrinkle. "Hurts like hell, but I've had worse, you know that. Come here..." She extended a hand toward her first mate.

Nona took her hand, not missing how cold she felt. The captain took her legs off the desk and brought Nona onto her lap, holding her close. Her arms circled her waist, face resting on her chest. She listened to her heartbeat and breathed out. She was alive. She was right there. She wasn't lost.

"Mel told me to give you this." Nona got a small vial out of the small bag on her hip and handed it to her. "She said it's not enough to treat you properly, so we have to make a stop at The Dusk Market."

Glenlivet groaned, but uncapped the vial and drank. "That stop will only give Elric more time to move and hide."

"This is not up for discussion, I'm afraid," Nona said sternly. "There is no point in catching *The Conviction* if you lose your mind to the echo."

The captain nodded, but her eyes remained hardened, avoiding Nona's. The first mate grabbed her jaw, turned her face toward her, and added, "And Marina would never forgive herself if you did."

At this, Glenlivet's eyes softened and she nodded again, this time with a sigh of resolution. Nona brought her close and rested her chin on top of her head, the scarf she wore soft to the touch on her cheek. She reached around her and freed Glen's hair from its tie. It fell to her shoulders and Nona softly ran her fingers through it.

"Don't think about that right now. Just rest."

She stood, pulling away from Glenlivet, who whined a bit before Nona made her stand along with her. Still holding her hand, the first mate led the captain to her small bed in the corner of the room. She made her lay down and watched as she closed her eyes and sighed again.

"Will you let Augie know we need to make that stop in Agara?"

"I will," Nona said, smiling. Sitting down on the side of the bed, she leaned toward Glenlivet, who opened her eyes to watch her. "Will you kiss me?"

"I will."

Glen reached up, cupping Nona's face in her hands, and pulled her down toward her lips. The kiss was soft but laced with tension from the battle. Nona pulled away, needing to get back to the deck. Glen still held her face, still in the trance of the kiss.

"I love you," Nona whispered.

Glenlivet stared up at her, hands leaving her face and falling to her sides. The soft smile that had been there a second ago faltered slightly. "You should go tell Augie about the stop."

"Glen," Nona said, almost pleading. Her chest and cheeks felt warm. Embarrassment made her hands shake as she stood up.

"Go," the captain said, that mockery of a smile still on her face. "Please. I'm tired."

Micah boarded *The Fiona* knowing his assumption had

been wrong. Even from his own ship, he could see that the Goliath´s vessel had dealt with pirates not too long ago. Its crew was busy on deck, cleaning blood from the fancy wood deck with soapy mops and rags. In a corner, they had placed two bodies under a pair of sheets.

"Your Majesty, it is an honor to have you aboard my ship. Captain Seth Kinrade, at your service."

The king of Rera assessed the captain of *The Fiona* with squinted eyes. Soft hands, gentle face. Somewhere in his semblance, Micah could see the ghost of the little boy he used to be and the insecurity of a person who was teased growing up.

"You should throw the bodies overboard," the king said. "They´ll spread disease among the rest of your crew."

The captain´s eyes widened, and he spared a glance at the sheets in the corner. "They were a pair of brothers. They have a mother waiting for them back home. We were hoping to offer them a proper burial."

Micah walked toward the sheets and lifted one of them. The sight that greeted him made him turn away with a grimace. "Their mother won´t want to see them like this. It would be best to keep a token and dispose of their remains now."

"A token?"

"From their uniforms. To give to their mother," Jona offered with a nod, from behind Micah. "I´ll aid your crew in doing this, sir, while you discuss things with the king."

Captain Kinrade nodded, a bit frazzled, and gestured toward his quarters for Micah to follow.

"I am hunting the pirates who attacked you, Captain," the king said as he entered the room. "Whatever you can tell me about them I would appreciate."

He was surprised to see a boy, around ten years old, laying on the floor reading a book. The captain, stepping into the room behind him, walked to the kid. "Of course, Your Majesty. Apologies, this is Tomás, my son."

The child stood from the floor and bowed politely while still embracing the book. Micah looked at it. An atlas of Castiah, the continent on the other side of Dread Water, was an odd choice for a kid.

"Sit over there and be quiet, boy. We have important matters to discuss." Once Tomás did as told, the captain sat on his desk and invited the king to sit across from him.

"Thank you, I´ll stand," Micah said, shaking his head.

Kinrade looked put off for a second before clearing his throat and standing too. "*The Outsider* was an average schooner, as far as I could see. Small crew but efficient. They worked well as a team and protected each other in battle. More than I can say for other pirates I´ve encountered," he started saying, nervously arranging papers on top of his desk but maintaining eye contact. "The captain was a woman, in her mid-twenties, I think. Brown skin and dark long hair in a ponytail. She was wearing a grey scarf with a pattern. Stars, I think."

"I must commend you. This is far more detailed than I expected," Micah commented, raising an eyebrow. "You sure got a good look at her during battle. I take it you fought her personally, then?"

The captain blushed, avoiding the king's eyes. "I can't say I did, Your Majesty. When they first boarded, they intended to take the moneybox peacefully, and we talked for a moment before Gareth and Jenne saw their siren and started the fight."

Micah's eyes widened as he stepped closer to the desk. "A siren? A pirate crew that small captured a siren?"

"No, Your Majesty. She was part of the crew. They named her and everything. Protected her."

The king knew *The Outsider* took in the bottom of the barrel of society, but hadn't considered the possibility of a sea monster being among them. A smile crept up his face despite his best efforts to contain it, and he looked around for a moment before asking, "Did they take anything else aside from the money?"

"They made us get rid of our cannons, so we wouldn't be able to sink them as they escaped. But they didn't steal anything else. Not that we have much else." The captain proceeded to look inside one of his drawers. "Aside from tax collection, we were tasked to deliver several documents to The Council, but the pirates didn´t seem to know or be interested in these."

Seth Kinrade set the documents on the desk, and Micah leaned forward, dragging them toward him across the surface. A few trial transcripts from judges and clergy in The Sister Nations that required signatures, a harvest inventory and a ledger from Agath specifically, and, most importantly, pirate hunting reports. Micah looked through these in search of any mention of *The Outsider* but found nothing. One particular page from the small Denea colony caught his eye, and he separated it from the others.

"I need a copy of this document and I shall get out of your hair, Captain."

Kinrade nodded. "I´ll have my calligrapher make you a copy. It won´t be an official document without the seal…"

"I know that," Micah interrupted, frowning before getting a hold of himself and forcing a smile. "I don´t need it to be, don´t worry. Feel free to inform The Council of our encounter, and tell them, if you´d be so kind, that I will make inquiries about this report on my travels."

"If I may ask," the captain said, a nervous hint in his voice that caused Micah to genuinely smile, "where are you headed next, Your Majesty?"

"*The Outsider* is going to The Sodra Cluster, so I will follow them into pirate country."

"They're not going to the islands, sir." The kid's voice coming from the chair in the corner startled both the captain and king. He had stopped reading a while ago, and his eyes were wide and shining with excitement.

"Tomás, what did I say about staying quiet?" the captain scolded, his heart beating hard as he watched the expression on the king's face. "And you must address the king properly."

"No," Micah said, lifting a hand to silence Kinrade, now walking toward the child. "Why do you say they're not headed to The Cluster? Speak."

Tomás swallowed, feeling nervous, but eager to help. "I heard them talking among themselves while I was on their ship. Their doctor, a woman dressed in red, was annoyed they were out of a tonic. She told another lady that they needed to buy more. The one with the kraken necklace said The Dusk Market would be their best option. The Dusk Market is in Agara, right? Not The Sodra Cluster."

The wolfish grin on the king's face only made Tomás more nervous, but the kid stayed put, not breaking eye contact with the man. The tension stretched on, as Micah thought about his next move, and finally nodded and exited the room in long strides.

"Did I do good?" Tomás asked his father, finally breaking the silence.

G.

I thank you for your letter, I really do, but I swear it almost sent me into a fit. I am not allowed correspondance, you see. It was quite a stroke of luck that I found the envelope before father did.
Don't misunderstand, please. You were perferctly polite and proper, but you have seen how he gets. You mustn't write to my house ever again.
Father doesn't like you much. Will you ever tell me why? He refuses to say, and gets cross if I insist on asking but I am so curious.
I know you said you are faithless, but I would like to see you again at temple. We could discuss a spot to hide all letters we exchange in the future...

L.

4

THE DUSK MARKET

"You all know how this works but you, Danielle," Glenlivet said as they entered the main street of the market through a stone archway. "If you see something you want in one of the side streets, always take someone with you. Don´t wander off alone. We´re pressed for time as it is."

The crew followed a buddy system every time they went ashore for supplies. It was a standard safety measure, but it was especially important when visiting The Dusk Market. They tended to avoid the place unless they had an emergency or odd purchases to make. None of them thought the place´s inventory was worth getting lost in the twisted and intricate maze of side streets. People told tales of folks disappearing to buy something and showing up days later, with the notion of only having been gone for a few minutes.

The place also had a habit of providing people with things they needed, regardless of whether the person was aware of that need or not. For example, this effect of The Dusk Market seemed set upon giving Glenlivet those stained-glass lamps that were hung all around her quarters. She always found a new one in her room every time she visited, which infuriated her to no end.

The market came alive as the sun fell. The stalls were manned by shopkeepers calling out to attract people toward their products. The main street workers, all sporting black masks that covered their noses and mouths, walked down the road lighting lanterns and greeting newcomers. The fire brightened the market stalls as far as the eye could see. It had rained earlier in the day, and the puddles on the cobblestones reflected the flames´ light.

A group of Agara children, with brown skin and hair that resembled Glenlivet´s and loose linen clothing and broken-in shoes, pushed through the group of pirates, accompanied by a dog almost the size of a small horse. At the sound of the animal, Augie jumped onto Blue, who tried their best to avoid laughing out loud and instead snorted. The sound joined the clamor of the market. Distant music poured out of side streets.

The smell was almost overwhelming. Danielle had to

take a second to close her eyes and take it all in. She recognized salted pork, fresh bread, and spices of all kinds. If she concentrated hard enough, she was convinced that, somewhere close by, they sold oranges too. But many of the scents were unfamiliar to her. When she opened her eyes, the group had walked ahead down the street and Roma, who was hanging onto her arm, had led her to a stall to the left.

A small man sat on a stool behind a mountain of tiny bottles. Some of them were labeled as fragrancies, most of them names of flowers she had never seen in person, much less smelled before. She was busy reading them as the man exchanged a few wheezy words with Roma. When she looked back to her companion, the mage apprentice was squinting as she handed the man some coins.

"They are pure, right?"

The man´s eyes grew wide at the notion of his product being doubted. "The purest, child! Mama Ruth herself verified them."

"Who?" Danielle asked, unable to quiet her curiosity.

"She´s a very famous mage around these parts, Roma answered quickly as she grabbed a bottle labeled ´anemone´.

"You´re new," the vendor said, his beady eyes focusing on Danielle. "Anything for you, fancy one?"

Danielle stammered, confused. She was dressed in

the servant's clothes she had stolen, though they had been washed a few days ago, and she looked down, searching for anything that might have made the man use that nickname. Before she could find it, or answer in any way, a hand on her shoulder made her jump.

"She's looking for clothing today, Val," Nona said from behind her, smiling. "Care to point us to your nephew's shop?"

"Ynos's mane, if it isn't Cromwell's kid! My, I thought you'd be dead by now," the man said, struggling to stand on the stool to get a good look at Nona over the hundreds of little bottles in front of him. Danielle couldn't tell if the man was happy or disappointed by the first mate's status from behind the bushy grey eyebrows and mustache, but kept silent when she saw that Nona's smile didn't falter. In the end, the man pointed down the main street, his thumb sticking out to the left. "He should be two corners down from here. That way."

As Danielle and Roma walked away after thanking him, they saw Val jump down from the stool and get out of his shop to hug Nona, who affectionately patted the man's back.

"They seemed close," she said, pulling Roma close.

"Val has known Nona since she was a little kid. He had a shop in Old Mehri before he relocated and settled here."

Danielle thought about the ruins of Old Mehri. One

day the glorious Ynos-worshipping capital of Mene, the next day a graveyard of sand, ash, and bones.

Roma redirected her attention back to her by opening her bag and letting out a delighted giggle. "Look!"

She did as told and spared a glance inside the bag. She was surprised to find two bottles in there instead of just the anemone one. "I wonder what I´ll need coriander petals for?"

Before Danielle could answer, Augie was intertwining his arm with hers. "Captain said you're off to see Val's nephew. I have orders to keep you safe."

The young man's infectious smile took over Danielle's face despite her confusion. "Keep me safe?" she asked.

Roma nodded. "Oh yes. We should stay close to Augie. He has a way of knowing how to move in this place."

Beaming, Augie said, "Just wait until you meet Uvol. He's the funniest guy!"

Uvol was not the funniest guy. His voice was so monotone Roma felt half in the grave every time he started a rant. But Augie found him hilarious solely because the man kept shoving his boot into his mouth when he was present.

"So good to see you again, Augie."

"If you would look over here—"

"As you can see, these patterns..."

"You won't be able to see any fraying of the fabric if

you press it every—"

Every time, Uvol looked in pain and distraught, only to make yet another insensitive comment a moment later, which caused the blind pirate to cackle, his whole body shaking, hands hugging his own belly.

Uvol had garments of all kinds to protect from the weather at sea. At the end of the session with him, Danielle had a shirt, coat, and trousers that fit her and would be perfect for sailing and working aboard.

"I have a contact by the bridge that could help with shoes and a belt," Uvol said, contemplating the clothes Danielle was stuffing into her bag. "Search for the stall by the Unity Bridge with the jar full of buttons at the top. If you tell her I sent you she will give you a discount... probably."

"Thank you!" Roma and Danielle said in unison.

"*See* you again sometime, Uvol!" Augie laughed, waving over his shoulder.

Nona had moved on to a jewelry stall while a bored-looking old woman with red hair waited and watched her.

"How was seeing Val again?" said a tentative voice behind her. She didn't turn around. "It's been a while. Must have brought back memories from home."

Nona felt Glenlivet's hand settle on the small of her back. A shiver ran up her spine. Despite herself, the tiniest smile reached her lips.

"Mehri isn't my home," she muttered.

"*The Outsider* is" was silent but loud at the end of her sentence and Glenlivet smiled, encouraged.

"Which necklace do you like? I'll buy it for you," the captain said, looking down at the stock of the shop, then at Nona's neck. The old kraken token attached to a frayed thread stared back at her. It was clear it had been around her neck for many years. Glen reached to touch the piece, her knuckles slightly touching the woman's collarbone. "That way you can throw away this old thing."

The smile on Nona's face dropped and she turned to walk away, breaking their contact. The captain walked close behind her.

"Sorry about the other day," Glenlivet murmured.

"You always are," Nona sighed, her voice quiet and cold. "I'm glad to see you've at least stopped avoiding me."

Glenlivet flinched. The five days it had taken them to get to Agara since the attack on *The Fiona* were a blur, the sound of Marina's cry still playing in her head. Louder, however, was what Nona had said after the battle.

"I wasn't trying to avoid you," she lied. "I haven't been

feeling well, you know that. Don´t be that way."

"What way?" Nona asked, shrugging and stopping by another stall. She didn´t look at it for long, moving again when Glenlivet caught up, to the middle of the busy main street.

The captain sprinted after her and stopped her, holding her wrist. "Nona, stop this, please..." She brought her hand to her lips and kissed the back of it.

The first mate pulled her hand away and looked around. "You stop it."

The captain smiled, unbothered by the crowd around her. "Are you that afraid of showing our affection in public?"

It was meant to be in jest, the light teasing they were so accustomed to. But Nona stepped up to Glenlivet and stared at her with stern eyes, her mouth a thin tight line, "And you´re afraid of it in private."

Her voice let the captain know the conversation was over, and Glenlivet looked away.

They walked together in silence, not even looking at the shops anymore. Nona was holding her old necklace in a tight fist when she heard the voice.

"*The Outsider*. Have you seen the crew around?"

The shopkeeper shook her head. The soldier he was talking to had his back turned to them, but she could see the sigil on his shoulder. Far worse news, a shorter man with long black hair stood next to him, arms crossed behind his back. His clothes were better quality and Glenlivet recognized the signet ring on his thumb. Nona grabbed Glenlivet's arm with one hand and pulled her scarf further down her face to hide her. They walked fast, almost running.

"Men from Rera. They're here for us."

"We have to get Danielle. Now."

The Unity Bridge that connected the colonies of Agara and Agath was impossible to miss. Red and orange stones from Mene's desert made up the structure and Iron Forest wood decorated the railings on each side of the bridge. Under the arches, what seemed like thousands of jellyfish had gathered and now swayed with the waves.

Danielle ran toward the bridge, eyes shining at the sight. She had learned of the construction as part of her education growing up. She watched as people walked casually across it, their clothes flapping back and forth with the wind.

"It's beautiful, isn't it?" Roma said, catching up, though her eyes were focused on the water below.

"More than beautiful!" Danielle said, breathless. "I dreamt of seeing it ever since I was a child. I can't believe I'm here. Back home, we are taught to keep the place in mind when praying to the gods for peace. It's a symbol of diplomacy and understanding. The Goliath structure that brought on dialogue between the two warring colonies."

Augie scoffed, his hands closing into fists. "So that's what they teach in those fancy schools in Rera..."

"I'm sorry?"

"Augie, be kind. She doesn't know," Roma interjected.

"Kind has led us nowhere with Rerans," Augie spat.

Danielle's eyes widened. She had never seen the young man angry in the whole month they had spent together at sea. Roma put a hand on Danielle's shoulder and turned her, so she'd look at the bridge again.

"Look closely, on the surface of the stone below, near the water," she instructed. "It's been destroyed for the most part, but you can still see it if you squint."

Danielle struggled to see anything for a while on the dimly lit surface. But with effort, she spotted what Roma referenced. In certain areas the waves splashed, you could see the remains of carvings, low-relief sculptures of people at war.

"My history books didn't mention the bridge having art on it," Danielle murmured.

"Once, the sculptures were the most beautiful part of the bridge," Roma said, then looked at the former queen. "You were right that Agara and Agath hated each other. They couldn't go a few months without a conflict breaking out. However, this was centuries ago, before Goliath inserted their government on the islands."

Danielle frowned, confused, and she focused once more on the ghost of the sculptures as Roma continued talking. There, in the shadow, Danielle saw the image of two men in different uniforms facing a giant together.

"When Goliath ships arrived, the two nations built the bridge together, with the aid of Mene, back when the nation still stood against the Empire. You're right that the bridge is a symbol. That's why Goliath sent Reran soldiers with mallets and knives to destroy the art that depicted them as invaders."

Danielle turned to look at Augie but the boy had walked away toward the stall with the jar of buttons on top. "I didn't know…"

"They did the same to his home. He's not angry at you, not really."

"He should be," Danielle said, bile rising in her throat. "I was queen, Roma. I should have at least—"

"You said it yourself, you didn't know," Roma interrupted, and placed an arm around Danielle's shoulders. They started to walk to join Augie at the stand. "Plus, from what you told us this past week, you didn't have the freedom to do much of anything. Your husband sounds like a proper dick."

The feeling of nausea didn't disappear entirely,

paired now with hot anger gnawing at her throat and threatening to make her scream, but Danielle smiled at Roma all the same.

By the time they neared the shop they had been looking for, the three were happy to see Blue, Marcya, and Celeste walking toward them. Roma rushed to Celeste, showing her the purchases she'd made, and started chatting about possible uses for the powders while Blue and Marcya approached Danielle and Augie.

As they did, Danielle saw the cook pause to inspect a poster on a wall, and rip it off. The poster contained a detailed description of the missing prince of Mangrath, and the reward set by his father for anyone who found him and brought the heir home. Dead or alive. Danielle was familiar with the posters, though they had been distributed with less fervor with every year that passed without the prince being found. She was about to ask Blue about it when she saw them crumble the poster into a ball and throw it into a trashcan.

"We got the medicine Mel requested," Marcya said, lifting the bag that contained the vials and smiling wide. Mel had given her the mission of buying the tonic for the captain and had stayed on the ship to look after Marina.

"So, we're ready to leave when you are," Blue added as they caught up.

"We still have to get a belt and some practical shoes

for Danielle," Augie said, and to the young woman's surprise, he seemed to be back to his usual self, returning Blue's smile. "Gale and Julian went to get the thing?"

The group started laughing, sharing a knowing look.

"What thing?" Danielle asked, glancing at each of them with a raised eyebrow.

"The captain thinks The Dusk Market gives her a stained-glass lamp every time she visits," Augie said, smirking at her.

"She mentioned that."

"Right. It´s not unheard of. *The Market* does tend to give out gifts," Marcya said, shrugging, but smiling in a devilish way that Danielle now recognized as the joy she experienced when fooling someone.

"Gale is the one who buys a lamp every time we visit," Celeste revealed now that she and Roma joined the group.

"Don't tell the captain. Swear upon your Reran subjects, Queen Danielle," Augie said, putting a hand on his chest and bowing.

Roma slapped Augie over the head. "Don't be so loud about that, you're going to get us killed."

Augie laughed, winking at Danielle, who sighed in relief that their new friendship wasn't absolutely ruined by her ignorance. The boy then turned to Roma, shrugging, "Nobody is around. Only Lavina, and she can't hear us right now. RIGHT, LAVINA?"

Lavina, the woman behind the button jar stall, was sleeping in a sitting position, her chin drooping onto her chest. Her loud snoring was interrupted every few seconds by a loud hiccup, but she didn't stir, even when Augie screamed in her direction. Marcya got close and jumped up, grabbing the jar from the roof of the stall, and shaking it aggressively. The sound of the buttons moving and clicking against the glass startled the old woman awake.

Upon looking up, Danielle noticed one of her eyes was a deep brown while the other was grey. She had a scar that expanded from her chin all the way up to her left ear, which was missing its earlobe.

"Put that jar back, you pirate scum!" the woman said, her voice rough and gurgling. "What do you want now? You were here just yesterday!"

"It's been almost two years, Lavina," Marcya said, smiling, but putting the jar back and taking a step back. "And I'm not here for me."

Danielle stepped forward, slightly intimidated. "I need a corset, shoes, and a belt... Uvol sent us?" The last part was tentative, as Lavina didn't seem to be listening to her at all, her eyes drooping as if she was going to fall asleep again.

At the mention of Uvol, however, she let out a piercing screech and laughed out loud. "That damn runt! How's he doing?"

"He's well," Augie said, smiling. "As funny as ever."

"Huh... Must be a different Uvol, then."

The woman turned, smiling a wide grin, and searched the boxes behind her, which were stacked on top of each other in dangerously tall piles. She muttered to herself, almost like a chant, as the group watched. She then turned like a doll, arms swinging almost as if they weren't attached to the body, and she sat back on her stool, immediately falling asleep again.

Blue sighed and took the jar. "It's my turn with it."

They shook the button jar next to Lavina's good ear, who stood up abruptly and continued with her task of looking through boxes. She screamed after a few seconds of doing this. "Belt, corset, shoes! What do you think I am? A *saleswoman*?"

"That is in fact what you are, Lavina," Marcya said, still smiling wide. For the first time, Danielle noticed the slight dimples on her cheeks.

"All right, all right!" The woman had found a belt and a pair of shoes that were Danielle's size despite Lavina never taking her measurements. "Corset should be over there in that box, girl," she said, pointing to a box on the floor by their side of the stall. "Five gold pieces for the lot!"

"Whoa! No discount? We're regulars," Blue complained.

"I've never seen any of you before in my life," Lavina

deadpanned, in a tone that Danielle couldn't decipher. If she was being genuine, she couldn't tell. Either way, none of the crew seemed to take it to heart. "If you want a good quality corset for cheaper, you'll have to cross the bridge. Most clothing in Agara is imported... except those peanuts. Those damn peanuts!" She shook her first toward the sky.

Danielle took a step toward Marcya. "Maybe we could check out Agath for the corset?" she suggested, thinking about how much money she had left.

Marcya considered for a second, looking briefly at the bridge before shaking her head and taking out her purse. "No. We don't cross the bridge. I'll pay for it."

"What? Why?"

"Captain's rule. We don't set foot in Agath," she said, shrugging, and before Danielle could protest, she had paid Lavina for the corset.

Blue placed the jar of buttons back, and almost immediately after they all heard the old woman's snores again.

"Marcya!"

At the shout, they all turned, the quality of their captain's voice agitated and hurried enough that they all straightened their backs in attention. "Cover her. *Now.*"

Danielle felt fabric cover her head, shoulders, and then her nose and mouth. Glenlivet looked at the group and counted them, making note of everyone missing.

"Celeste, signal Gale and Julian."

"What color?" the witch asked, already fumbling through her bag.

"Red."

"Red?" Danielle cried out, breathless from the surprise as the captain put one of her arms around her shoulders. Nona stood on her other side, flanking her, and they all started moving back toward the exit. "Red means Emergency Retreat, right? What's happening?"

Celeste had taken out what seemed to be a small red tube and a match.

"Your husband is here," the captain said, bracing herself.

"*Micah?*"

Just as she spoke that blasted name, the top of the cylinder in Celeste's hand exploded. Red flame and smoke came out of it, flying upwards above the stalls. Danielle could barely hear what everyone was saying from the sound of the explosion. The crew had explained the system of communication they had but she never thought it would be so loud. Glenlivet was sure all of The Dusk Market had heard it. Gale and Julian would know what to do.

"If we cross the bridge, it will be easier to evade them," Blue said, looking back.

The captain ignored that comment and turned to her navigator. "Augie."

"Yes, Captain."

"You have your music with you, yes?"

"Always." The boy took out a small and very old hurdy-gurdy from his bag.

"I need you and Celeste to intercept the king and his men. Distract them. Be smart."

The witch and the navigator nodded and ran ahead to do their part. Glenlivet watched them go, then said, "The rest of you, follow me."

The king of Rera was familiar with The Dusk Market. At least, as familiar as one could be with an annoying mosquito or a bothersome fly. He walked through it with no intention of buying anything and no intention of keeping any items the market might gift him. The less time he spent on these islands the better.

His eyes focused on the people walking by. He could spot a pirate a mile away. They were a very particular type of people and he was good at recognizing the elements that made them stand out, no matter how sneaky the rats were.

One of his guards appeared next to him. "This stall hasn't seen anyone suspicious either."

"Useless. All of them."

"Does royalty care for palm readings?"

He hadn't noticed the woman approach so her sudden voice, on his left, startled him slightly. She stared up at him with a smile, hand ready to receive his.

"Run along, witch. Your kind is no fit to talk to a king," the guard said, drawing his sword and taking a step in front of Micah to protect him.

Her smile did not falter, hand still out and welcoming, eye contact unbreaking. "I am a mage, Your Majesty. And I would do the first reading for free, of course."

"At ease, soldier," he said, so the guard took a step behind him and lowered his eyes. Micah scoffed. "What do you think you're doing? Keep asking around for the crew."

The man walked away, sheathing his sword. Micah turned to look at the girl once more. She had an agreeable face, but he could tell she was trouble on a good day. It was clear by her hands and demeanor that she was used to working. Tattoos traveled up her arms and disappeared under her clothes. Some sort of red powder made crescent moons under her fingernails.

"I don't approve of witchcraft, but..."

"Even the smartest of kings get curious sometimes. Nothing to be ashamed of," she said, fixing the shall that lay across her shoulders. "My name is Celeste, Your Majesty. What brings you to Agara?"

"I thought you would learn all that by reading my palm," he said, taking off his glove. "Go on then, Celeste.

What do you see?"

She grabbed his hand, a little forcibly to the king's surprise, but he allowed it. The mage stared at his palm, eyes raking over the lines. Reading palms wasn't Celeste's specialty, though technically she knew how to do it. What she did well was *seeing*. Most of the time, she did it by chance, when strong feelings resurfaced. And the king of Rera was troubled. A whirlwind of emotions knocked her back a little when she touched his skin. They weren't pleasant emotions, and it wasn't a pleasant sensation to feel them.

She couldn't help but grimace, something that Micah caught.

"Speak, witch. What do you see?"

"You're a hunter."

"Yes," he said, slightly amused. "My whole family was. That is no secret. We're famous for hunting monsters. But you knew that when you approached me, of course." He tried to pull his hand away, now convinced Celeste was a con artist. She held on harder, stopping him from moving away. Her nails sunk into his skin, and he winced even as he snapped, "Let go."

"No. No. No," Celeste said, not in full control of where her mouth was taking her. Her heart pounded hard. "You're hunting a human."

G.

I haven't gotten a lick of sleep since you told me about your upbringing. To think you have travelled all over Patriah... I haven't even crossed the bridge to Agara yet! How different lives we have led so far, only to end up in the same dump of a town.
"Agath has all we need," father says. Such a BORE! I am so grateful you showed up. Would you ever sail me away, sweetness?

I know it's silly but I hope you don't mind my daydreaming. Perhaps sailing is too ambitious of a start for a girl like me. Something smaller is first in order, wouldn't you say?
Something smaller like sneaking to The Dusk Market on Friday night?
Father won't find out if I slip out through the kitchen window.
Your woolgathering friend,

L.

5

THE BLIND ESCAPE

Celeste was looking through Micah´s eyes.

The hallway they stood in was large, painted white and green. He was in front of a mural of a roaring brown bear, her cubs behind her. The king was carefully observing the animals as the doctor to his right talked. His voice was muffled by the absolute rage Celeste felt inside Micah´s chest, growing and bubbling like acid, ready to spill.

"It´s simply too risky for her to go through another miscarriage, Your Majesty. I´m sorry."

Micah stared down at his hands, opening and closing them into fists until the ache disappeared. Celeste felt trapped, like she was drowning inside his body. She felt his desire to hit something. Someone.

"The queen is distraught, of course. I'll make sure to give her all the remedies to help the cramping, but the process is in Yrena's hands now." The doctor gestured to the protective bear on the mural.

"I understand, Doctor," he said, and Celeste couldn't believe how sad and kind he sounded in counterpoint to the tension in his jaw, his teeth grinding.

It was her. It was all Danielle's fault. She did not understand her place. She refused to learn. One way or another, she would fall in line and give him an heir. He would not offer up his kingdom to a Goliath envoy, not even over his dead body.

Celeste screamed inside the memory, overwhelmed by the images that followed. She managed to escape back into herself as Micah pulled his hand forcefully from hers.

Glenlivet had just turned fourteen the morning she was thrown to the rocks of Agath's shores. She still had a scar on her shoulder from the fall.

Elric Omar, the newly appointed captain of *The Conviction*, had grabbed her by the elbow and unceremoniously thrown her overboard while the crew cheered. She had never been friends with any of her father's crew. Their cheers meant nothing to her. But his silence— His silence as he betrayed her mattered a great deal. The new captain had been a teenager himself when she had been born, but was already the first mate. He had taught her everything she knew. She had considered him family.

"Elric!" she roared, tears breaking her voice. She saw him turn his back on her as he put that damn hat back on. Her father's hat.

The image of *The Conviction* faded away in her memory as she walked as fast as possible down the main street of The Dusk Market. They had managed to pass by four royal guards who were distracted by Augie.

The boy had promised them information on the crew they were looking for if they listened to a song and gave him some silver. Since the king was busy with the mage, they had agreed. Augie's left hand moved fast over the keys, while his right cranked the handle. He sang along to the music, twirling in place and around the guards, forcing them move to keep their eyes on him.

Danielle had trouble keeping up with Glenlivet's strides. While she wasn't running to avoid suspicion, she walked quite fast and was taller than her.

Hidden behind the fabric covering her face, Danielle saw the king out of the corner of her eye, looking agitated as Celeste held his hand. She knew that expression on Micah. She had seen it when she had started bleeding, just before losing her first pregnancy. He was scared. And when Micah got scared, he turned violent. Her hands trembled, fearing for the mage, and the full bag in her arms hit the floor, and she tripped over it. She couldn't help but yelp as she fell, hands splayed in front of her to avoid landing on her face. The scarf Marcya had placed around her head fell off as she did.

Glenlivet pushed Blue and Marcya to keep walking, to avoid the guards' attention on them, and Marcya pulled Roma after her. Their hands were clammy as they kept moving, their nerves making their hearts beat faster. Nona knelt by her side and did her best to cover her once more but it was too late. Danielle felt his eyes on her as soon as she tried standing. A month away wasn't enough to forget how his gaze felt on her skin. Shame rippled through her at the fear paralyzing her as she heard Micah call out to his soldiers.

Luckily, neither Nona nor Glenlivet were stuck in the same way, and she felt the first mate's hands pulling her up and pushing her forward. In her daze, as she ran, she realized the captain had grabbed her bag from the floor. She couldn't feel her own legs.

Augie reacted as soon as he heard the king's voice calling for his soldiers. The heavy instrument in his hands hit two of the men closest to him in the back of their heads, and they doubled over in pain and surprise. The hurdy-gurdy let out a strangled half scream.

"Augie!" Celeste cried out, shoving Micah away from

her and to the ground. He let out a stream of insults and threats in her direction but she ignored him. "Pistol! Now!"

The other two soldiers had drawn their swords while Augie pulled his gun from his belt. He fired twice, calculating where the two men were by sound, and prayed nobody would be near if the bullet went astray. One of the shots lodged into one of the guard´s arms while the other hit the armor hidden under his shirt, hurting like hell but not injuring him.

Celeste reached Augie just as this guard removed his helmet. He had brown skin and dark eyes, with tattoos under them. The mage grabbed Augie by the elbow and led him down the main street, in the same direction Glenlivet had taken. After a few blocks, the mage looked over her shoulder and felt a chill down her spine when she saw how fast the guards were catching up.

"We need to buy the captain time!" Augie guided Celeste down a side street on their left. The space was full of spice vendors who yelled at them for running and only screamed louder when they saw the four soldiers in their wake.

The king had continued down the main street, rushing toward the docks. Danielle was trying to escape on that ship again and he was not going to allow it. His men could take care of chasing and killing the pirates. Jona would make sure of it.

Augie took control of where they ran, turning on corners in what he hoped was a random enough pattern to lose the soldiers. The guards were close behind every time Celeste checked, but their build didn't help in the tight little streets Augie chose; they kept knocking over things and pushing people in order to pass. The navigator dragged Celeste into a tight empty alley between two buildings that connected to another side street of The Dusk Market. They paused there for a moment, breathless and sweating buckets.

"Maybe we can slip into one of the buildings?" Celeste said.

"We won't need to."

Celeste saw what he meant a moment later as two market workers blocked the way with boxes full of products. She walked toward them and knelt, peeking above them just enough to spot three guards rounding the corner only to reel to a halt, confused.

"We've lost them," she said, smiling, then cocked her head. "There were four of them. Augie, there are only three now. The one with the tattoos is gone."

"My name is Jona Ishim. I grew up in the side streets of The Dusk Market and I'm as old as the stone beneath your feet. Did you really think you would lose me in my own home?"

The soldier approached from the far end of the alley. Celeste shoved herself in front of Augie, arms open to protect him. She closed her eyes as the sword swung down toward her face.

The run to the docks took almost half an hour, and at the end of it Glenlivet was so winded she could taste blood in her mouth. Her jaw was clenched so tight she was developing a headache. The lights flashing in front of her eyes was also not a great sign.

"I'm not used to running on stone," she said, adjusting Danielle's bag over her shoulder. "I hate this place."

"It's not from being on land, you tit," Nona grunted, placing a hand on her forehead to feel her temperature. "You're near a fever from running face first into a screaming siren."

"Oh right." The captain smiled, and Danielle saw in horror that her gums were bleeding profusely.

"Come on, we're almost there," Nona said, turning a corner to the port.

Marcya grabbed Nona by the back of her shirt and pulled her back. "Soldiers," she warned and crouched behind a cluster of stacked barrels.

She was right. Two of the king's guards stood in front of the gangway to *The Outsider*. They looked bored, with their eyes closed and a relaxed stance. Glenlivet wasn't fooled though; their hands rested near their weapons.

"We can take those two," Blue said, sizing them up.

"Blue, no!" This time Nona stopped them, grabbing their arm. "Sometimes, I swear you have a death wish."

"We outnumber them," Roma said, frowning. "Why don't we fight them?"

"We don't know if there are other guards hidden nearby ready to back them up," Glenlivet said, her vision too blurry to allow her to look for more soldiers.

"I know those two," Danielle muttered, and everyone looked at her. When she noticed their eyes on her, she blushed. "The younger one is new to the job. Took the cloak when his father retired a few months ago. He used to supervise my walks around the gardens. He was always kind to me."

"Would you say he's a sucker for a pretty girl?" Nona asked.

At that strange question, Danielle only blushed harder and blinked several times before responding: "How would I know such a thing?"

Nona chuckled. "What about the other one?"

The distaste on Danielle's face was immediate as she focused on the two men again. "He's an ass. He thinks all women should be so lucky to be saved by him."

"I can use that." The first mate smirked, then cleared her throat and tilted her head upward, placing her hands around her mouth to project a sound Danielle wasn't sure any human could do before. The group followed Nona's sightline to the ship's crow's nest. The top of Marina's head was barely visible up there, but at the sound of a dowitcher coming from Nona, it moved and disappeared.

Glenlivet looked at Nona with a fondness in her eyes that made the first mate falter when she looked back at her.

"Smart girl," Glenlivet said.

"Shut up."

"Gross," Marcya said, though smiling wide. "Now what?"

"Mel will take care of them," the captain said.

"Mel?" a voice asked from behind them.

"Oh, gods!" Roma yelped, turning around to the new voice, a hand to her chest. "How did you get here so fast?"

"We took a side street and came out by one of the other exits to the forest," Julian explained, taking off his hat and crouching beside Gale.

Glenlivet turned to them, frowning. "That stupid move could have cost you a week in there. I hope you know we would have left without you."

"Liar," Gale whispered, eyes shining as they shook their head.

Julian snickered upon hearing the strategist's voice, but Nona shushed him before he could make a remark about it.

In silence, they watched Mel stumble out of the hold with two bottles of wine in her hands. The two soldiers turned to her when they heard her approach, their voices hard to hear from so far away. The two men were on guard, but the pirates watched as they grew relaxed talking to her. Mel was unarmed, seemingly drunk, and inviting them inside for a glass and some company. After a loud giggle from the surgeon, which made Julian roll his eyes, the older of the two soldiers walked up the gangway and into *The Outsider*.

"What an idiot," Marcya commented.

The younger man looked around him, unsure.

"Come on, come on… Be an idiot too," Glenlivet begged.

The guard followed after a moment.

Micah was going to murder them all. Every single one.

He had run as fast as possible behind Danielle and the women helping her, but that witch had given them quite a head-start. The pirates had gone through the market's gate at full speed. By the time he reached it, a merchant cart blocked his path. The enormous thing, full of olive barrels, had gotten stuck and the workers kept trying to shove it in at a weird angle. He had watched his prey disappear down the path to the docks.

He hadn't been too worried. He had posted two of his men by *The Outsider*. One of them was his second strongest, and the new boy was eager to prove himself. The two of them would stop them and give him time to arrive.

The wind was picking up as he reached the docks. He turned the corner out of the path and watched, frozen in place. The docks were empty, his men nowhere to be seen.

"Shit," he muttered, pushing his hair out of his sweaty face.

He started walking toward the ship, which seemed empty and was deadly silent, and started unsheathing his sword. He'd get the job done himself.

"Captain!"

He stopped dead in his tracks and turned to the voice.

The blind hurdy-gurdy player was running full speed, coming from another street that connected to the docks. Slumped over his back was the mage, her face bleeding onto the young man's shirt. Through the blood, her right eye was swollen and shut. Her other eye, shining white like it had been when reading his palm, focused on him.

"Get the ship moving now!" Augie screamed, and Micah watched as the crew appeared on deck and started moving.

The king started running again, now to the musician and mage, to cut off their path. Celeste raised a hand toward him as he got closer and her eye widened in a silent warning. It wasn't this that stopped him but the bullet hitting the ground right in front of his feet. He turned his head toward the ship, searching for the source. Danielle stood there, holding a pistol, a look of disbelief on her face. Next to her stood a taller woman with a star-patterned head scarf, helping her aim with a gentle hand on her arm. She was smiling.

"Displeasure to meet you!" she said, as she directed her crew to move the gangway.

The ship started pulling away from port, as Celeste and Augie reached the edge of the dock. The boy allowed the mage to get down from his back, and while she stumbled slightly, she jumped almost immediately. She fell on the deck of the ship, a hand pressing against the massive gash on her face. Augie hesitated, feeling the edge of the dock with the tip of his shoes. Micah saw his chance. He started running again, his free hand outstretched to grab the back of the blind man's collar.

"Jump! Now!" Glenlivet ordered, her voice steady and sure.

Augie's jump was clumsy, not calculated, and reckless enough that Marcya barely managed to catch him. She pulled him and fell backward onto the deck.

"My hero!" Augie gasped, holding onto her.

While Marcya rolled her eyes and pushed him off of her, Micah stared daggers into Danielle. He heard the sound of footsteps behind him, his soldiers arriving just in time to witness their objective escape.

"Your Majesty!" The captain called out. The superiority in her eyes made him sick to his stomach. "You're missing two of your idiots!"

Roma and Marina appeared on deck, carrying an unconscious and bound man between the two of them. They dumped him over the banister, and his body fell into the water with a splash that got Micah's shoes wet. A second soldier was dumped overboard, and the king heard his men rush to get their comrades out of the water before they drowned. He didn't even look down.

His eyes were focused on Marina.

6

MURKY WATERS

The days following the chase at The Dusk Market were quiet and heavy. They all knew, Danielle especially, that this wasn't the last time the King of Rera would attack them. The whole crew was aware that he probably followed close behind.

Celeste had been sleeping in the captain's room, being cared for by Mel and Augie. The navigator told Glenlivet how the mage had protected him from Jona's sword, giving him enough time to pull out his pistol and shoot the man in the thigh. The soldier had slumped against the wall, and Augie saw his chance to flee with Celeste. The young man asked to help Mel, and the surgeon allowed it. She only needed a few hours to sigh and announce that the mage had no hope of preserving vision in the injured eye, and instead focused all her energy on warding off infection after she stitched up the injury to the best of her abilities.

Glenlivet had been taking the medicine they had bought at the market under Mel's orders. She no longer had frequent headaches or heard the echo of that blasted scream, so while Celeste rested in her quarters, the captain slept on the mage's hammock. She had refused to take Marcya's bunk when she offered it.

"It's no issue," she had said. "I slept on a hammock all the time while at *The Conviction*."

It was under this hammock that Glenlivet found the new stained-glass oil lamp from The Dusk Market, giving the crew their first laugh in days. Danielle watched, amused, as the captain added the item to the collection with a whine. When Danielle looked at Gale, she had to hold back a cackle at the strategist's comically confused expression as Glenlivet spoke of the lamp.

While still worried about Celeste, that moment dissipated the grey cloud of tension over the crew. To Danielle's infinite relief, they went back to talking while having their meals on the main deck.

"Do you reckon we'll find a lead in Sodra this time?" Roma asked Glenlivet one evening. "We weren't very lucky there last year..."

"It's our best shot," she said, chewing on a piece of meat. "So unless Marina gives us a reason to change our course in the morning, we´ll go directly to the main island."

Marina raised her fork in silent agreement but otherwise continued eating. She had been in a sullen mood since *The Fiona* but had slowly returned to their routine, and with Celeste injured, had taken up more responsibility. Glenlivet swallowed her food and spared a glance toward Julian, but he wasn´t paying attention as he spoke with Mel about Celeste´s health. She then sighed, put her plate down, and looked at Danielle. Unlike the older man, the former queen had been alert, and she met the captain´s eyes.

"Danielle..."

"Yes?" She feared the worst from the conversation and had been working extra hard the past few days to avoid it.

"You´re going to have to make an important decision soon," the captain said. "Julian already said he would tag along but you have made no commitment."

The crew grew quiet, the remaining chatter low and far between. They were all listening in now, though pretending not to be.

"Once in Sodra you will have to choose if you continue with *The Outsider*, or if you find another way out of the Cluster."

Danielle broke eye contact to stare down at her bowl of food. She held it tighter, trying to stop her hands from shaking. Finally, she found the courage to say what had been weighing on her shoulders for the past few days. "I understand, Captain. Once we're in Sodra, I'll find someone else to take me on. I can pay for passage out of there in a merchant ship or something."

Glenlivet frowned but nodded and didn't respond, refocusing on her dinner. Roma, however, gasped and looked between Danielle and the captain. "What? No! She's part of the crew now, cap! Why—"

"Roma, stop," Danielle said, smiling softly at her and placing a hand on her knee. "I appreciate it, I do, but there's no helping it. If I leave, Micah will stop hunting you down and you will all be safe again. It's the smartest thing to do."

When she looked back toward Glenlivet and the rest of the crew for confirmation, she was confused to see them frowning at her with sad expressions.

"She didn't get it." Nona elbowed Glenlivet, prompting her to explain herself.

"Kid, you misunderstand. It's not that we want you to leave for our safety," the captain said as if the notion was ridiculous. "Roma's right. You are part of *The Outsider* now and protecting you is just part of the job. Our pasts coming back to haunt us isn't new to any of us."

Danielle bit the inside of her cheek in deep thought. "Then, why—"

"While we are willing to protect you from the king if

you stay," Glenlivet interrupted to finish her thought, "I didn´t want to assume you´d wish to continue traveling with us."

"We are hunting someone ourselves," Nona said, looking at her with a serious look in her eye. "Someone dangerous. Micah is nothing in comparison. All of us are willing to die on that mission."

"Well, I don´t know about all of that," Mel said, a cheeky grin on her face as she winked at Julian.

"Oh, shut it," Glenlivet said, sticking her tongue out at the surgeon but looking back to Danielle with a soft smile. "I don´t want you to feel like you have to be part of that fight. You have a choice here."

"Oh dear, don´t cry!" Roma rushed her, wrapping her up in her arms. Danielle hadn´t realized she had started to cry until the mage´s apprentice said it. "Look what you´ve done, you two!" Roma said, looking over her shoulder at the captain and first mate.

Danielle and the rest of the crew laughed at that, bodies shaking and feet banging against the wooden floor. When they had all calmed down and Roma was back in her seat, the former queen of Rera nodded, a decision made up in her mind.

"You said it yourself… I am part of *The Outsider* now." Danielle smiled at Glenlivet, who smiled back at her. "It´s my job to protect all of you now, too. I´ll face whoever you´re hunting alongside you."

Glenlivet raised a glass to her, and they all drank, cheered, and drank some more. The night closed around them before the subject was brought up again, this time by Danielle.

"Why are we hunting *The Conviction*?"

The crew got quiet again, looking at Glenlivet and anxiously awaiting her answer.

"I've heard the name being thrown around, but not much else," Danielle added.

"The captain of *The Conviction* is Elric Omar Enitan. He murdered my father."

Glenlivet stood, striding starboard to watch the waves. Nona looked at her go, and turned to Danielle. "Normally, and we are not the exception to that rule, pirates choose their captain. *The Conviction* is a very old ship, and they work differently. The captain always passes down the role to his first kid."

"Like a monarch with an heir," Danielle said. "What if the captain never had a child?"

"In those cases, the first mate would take over the ship," Nona explained. "Elric was the first mate when Glenlivet was born. By this point, that stupid superstition about women being bad luck at sea was spreading like wildfire, so Glen was raised as a boy to protect her from the rest of the crew."

Danielle widened her eyes and looked at Glenlivet, her back to them as the wind tossed her hair about her head. Only now did Danielle realize just how silly her disguise must have looked to Glenlivet when she arrived.

The captain spoke up: "He spent fourteen years pretending to be my friend, teaching me everything he knew. Training me so I could become captain one day. And then he threw my father overboard and abandoned me in Agath like I was nothing." Her voice had started low and calculated but cracked toward the end.

Danielle glanced at Marcya, who stared down into her drink as the captain spoke. At the mention of Agath, the woman met Danielle's eyes. The younger woman remembered what the weapons master had said by the Unity Bridge.

Captain's rule. We don't set foot in Agath.

The next morning Augie sat next to the helm, repairing his hurdy-gurdy. A small piece of wood had broken off when he hit the soldiers in Agara, and he was busy mending it as best as he could with old glue and a sharp knife. The small stick chart he used to help him navigate rested on his lap as he worked.

Gale stood next to him, one hand on the helm, the other holding a book. It was a fantasy novel, the corners of the pages folded over and over by the whole crew over time. It was a well-loved tome, with watermarks and even some burns here and there, but still legible. It was Gale's fifth time reading it.

"Roma bought new books in the market," Augie commented. "You should check them out."

Gale nodded. They intended to, right after re-reading *Stories of Hiladas*. They weren't hopeful about finding a story quite like this one in the pile, but they would give it a try. The protagonist was in the middle of planning his escape with his best friend, who also happened to be his accomplice in a crime against the crown and his lover. A prince with a duty he did not want to conform to. A soldier who had fallen in love with the very person he was supposed to protect. A couple meant to fail under the pressure of the world. A couple who succeeded against those odds. Gale knew there was a happy ending in a few pages, and that comforted them.

Most of the copies of *Stories of Hiladas* had been burned by Goliath emissaries on a pyre, along with the author. Gale had saved this copy from the flames when they were fourteen, long before they joined the crew. They had hidden it from their family upon returning to their home in Mangrath, had read it in secrecy wishing for such an adventure, and took it with them when escaping to sea. Since then, the whole crew had read it, sharing their feelings under candlelight on quiet rainy nights in the hold of *The Outsider.*

Marina made her way up the stairs to the quarterdeck, her hair still wet from the night swim. "Murky waters ahead. Captain says we are to dock in Melende, not Sodra."

Gale adjusted their course, while Augie tilted his head toward Marina's voice. "What do you think it is?"

Marina, who had been ready to leave again, turned and said, "Probably waterlions, considering the area... But they were acting really weird so I'm not sure."

"How so?"

"Well." Marina sat next to the navigator, looking unsure. "It was a big underwater storm. Waterlions usually create multiple smaller ones to confuse and catch their prey."

"Must be a big pack, then," Augie commented.

The siren bit her lip, looking toward the sea. "Maybe. Gave me a bad feeling though."

"No worries. Gale will go around them," the boy said, comforting her with a hand on her shoulder.

The strategist watched as she smiled softly before returning to the main deck to join the rest of the crew. Gale had seen Micah's eyes as the ship pulled away from Agara and recognized the spark of greed in his eyes when he spotted Marina. They knew it meant more trouble for them.

The image of a young Micah running through the halls of his family's dungeons struck Gale, a memory that hadn't bothered them for decades. The young prince of Rera had promised to show them his family's collection, with a wicked smile. Gale hadn't been able to stand staying in that place for long.

The dungeons served as a museum for the family's hunting tradition, the heads of multiple creatures hanging from the walls, rugs made from their pelts covering the floor. While the creatures had been preserved and treated to prevent rot, the smell was still overwhelming in the dark underground room.

Gale had run out and had made their mother promise to never bring them back to Rera. Weirdly enough, their mother had listened. Something in the horror behind her child's eyes must have moved her to listen. Every time their family traveled to Rera for any reason, Gale had been allowed to stay home.

"You all right?" Augie said out of the blue. "I know seeing Micah again affected you."

Damn him. How he managed to catch wind of everyone's thoughts, Gale didn't know. They sighed and looked down at the book in their hand, brushing their thumb over the pages. "I'm all right," they said, voice rough and groggy. "He didn't see me, so it's all good."

Augie smiled upon hearing their voice, and continued to fix his instrument. "Let's hope it stays that way. You belong here. With us."

Gale nodded, refocusing on the *Stories of Hiladas*

once again.

King Micah's hunger had increased tenfold. The soldiers all felt it in the air as they worked around the ship. Flick was used to the volatile nature of his job: If it wasn't a fight with rebellious mobs, it was a fight to stay in one piece around the man he was charged with protecting.

In a way, he thought, the king before Micah had been worse. Flick was approaching fifty and had been at the service of the crown of Rera since he was sixteen. In all those years, he had learned to navigate the royals' emotional outbursts and operate around them. Micah's father had rejoiced in openly hurting his enemies —and his own people. His son was partial to quiet humiliations.

Having been raised around the talk that his father's sadism spurred, the current king was self-aware enough to keep his cruelties private, which meant his temper was calculated and controlled. Out at sea, he feared there was nothing to keep that temper at bay. Micah hadn't spoken a word since they had returned to the ship. Flick had been too busy taking care of his men's wounds to watch out for his king's mental state. A part of him was sincerely relieved about that.

The man who had been shot first lay in his hammock,

blind drunk to relieve the pain. Luckily, the bullet hadn't lodged too far into his arm, so the extraction wasn't too difficult. The two men hit by that blind boy with the musical instrument were resting as well but awake, in fear of a concussion.

More seriously, Jona had been shot in the thigh while pursuing the pirates, but the man refused to allow Flick to inspect the wound, insisting he would sort it out himself. Flick had argued, but eventually, Jona had given him a look that made him drop the issue and leave the room as fast as possible.

The other two injured soldiers worried him the most. They had been dumped unconscious but alive into the water. The pirates had given them some sort of medication to make them sleep, and while he had managed to keep them alive the past three days, they were still not fully responsive. And even if they woke up, they had failed to do what they were ordered. They had blatantly disobeyed. He didn't know what their fate would be.

Flick left the hold for the king's room. He knocked on the door and waited, holding his breath. There was no response from the king, but he twisted the doorknob anyway. A dagger struck the casing of the doorway right next to his head. He let out a sigh.

"Your Majesty." He pried the dagger from the wood. "I've been informed *The Outsider* has changed their course northwest."

Sitting at his desk, the king's back was turned to the door. But at that, his head whipped around to look at him over his shoulder, eyes bloodshot and wide. "Why?"

Flick closed the door behind him and stood firm in front of it. "We are not sure, Your Majesty, but they're still heading to The Sodra Cluster. They may have decided to dock in one of the smaller ports."

The king took in the information with his mouth closed tight, mind racing, "We'll keep going straight ahead. It will be faster to reach Sodra than any of the surrounding islands. We'll receive the pirates there. Give them a welcome party."

"Very wise, sir," Flick responded, though he was not quite sure it was. The pirates were experienced in traveling to those islands. He figured there had to be a reason for their change in course, something only they were able to see or predict. But he wasn't going to be the one to defy the king. Not when he was in one of his moods.

He had turned to leave when the king spoke again.

"Flick."

"Yes, my king?"

"Where are those two who were foolish enough to get drugged by the pirates?"

Flick swallowed, grabbing the doorknob so hard his knuckles went numb. "Still unconscious, Your Majesty."

"When they wake... let me know immediately. I want

to personally slit their throats."

"Your Majesty… One of them only just turned twenty," he pleaded.

He knew he needed to shut up and mind his business. He hadn't made it to forty-nine by questioning his king's orders. Micah stood to peer out the window for a second before turning to face him. His expression had softened, though he wore a decisive smile that didn't reach his eyes. He was using the same body language he faced his court with back at the castle.

"Of course. Only twenty. He has barely lived."

For a second, Flick wondered if he had made it onto the list of people the king regarded with enough respect to behave in a humane way around. And then the smile reached his eyes. Flick took a step back. The dagger in his hand hit the floor with a *thud*.

"You're old enough though, right?"

7

WATERLIONS

Markl woke up startled, followed by immediate nausea and the sensation that his nose had been stuffed with sand. The swaying of the ship did not help. He looked around in the dark hold to find himself alone. Weird. With such thick darkness, Markl would have assumed most of the crew would already be asleep.

As he stood from his hammock, what happened in Agara returned to him and he had to sit back down for a moment. The last he could remember was following that woman into the pirate ship and being served a drink.

He knew orders had been ignored, and that would earn him some sort of punishment. It was his first journey with the king, but the other guards with far more experience had warned him several times about Micah's temper. Even so, Markl wasn't sure he believed all the stories.

He sighed, rubbing his hands over his face. His bangs were slightly wet for some reason, sticking to his forehead, and his clothes had been changed. Flick had probably taken care of him. He always did. Markl made a mental note to buy the old man a drink the next time they reached land. He stood again, trying to stop his stomach from expelling its contents, and staggered up the stairs from the hold onto the deck.

To his surprise, it was still early afternoon. The clouds were so dark he had believed it was nighttime. The sky threatened to pour at any second and the air smelled like chaos: a mix of salt, rain, and iron. He looked across the deck, where the crew was gathered around a pile of rags. One of his mates, Charles, looked over his shoulder toward him.

Markl walked toward them with a sinking feeling in his stomach. Charles met him halfway, almost tripping over his own feet. He grabbed Markl's shoulders to stop him. He was shaking. He saw Charles's mouth move, but the words didn't sink in. His eyes followed the rest of the crew. They were in the middle of moving the bundle of clothes into the burn bucket, a rusted old thing where they burnt any refuse they generated through the journey.

"Why are they burning those rags?" Markl finally managed to ask.

Charles grabbed his face with both hands, cradling it like one would a child's, and moved him so the scene was out of sight. "Those are not rags, Markl."

"The young one's awake!" a voice roared from the deck above them. "Let the boy see!"

With obvious reluctance, Charles released his face, to look down at his feet, grinding his teeth. Markl moved toward the bucket, surrounded by his silent peers.

"Let him see what happens when people defy orders."

King Micah's voice made Markl's steps falter, but he pressed on. He was now certain this was his punishment for leaving his post, but he didn't want to confirm it. He looked around at his fellow soldiers, who didn't dare meet his eyes. There was no sign of Hasan, the other soldier he had been assigned to guard *The Outsider* with.

And no sign of old Flick. His head snapped down to the burn bucket.

He heard the king's boots hitting the steps as he stared, unblinking, at the pieces of what used to be two people, quartered to fit into the bucket alongside their blood-drenched clothes. Two people he knew, who had mentored him and drank alongside him.

The nausea that he had managed to hold off came

bubbling up his throat and crashed against his teeth and tongue. He stumbled backward and threw up on his boots to avoid the bucket.

"The rest of you, get back to work!" the king ordered, and the soldiers did as told while the young man trembled and wretched bile and acid. "Markl, right?"

Micah approached to place a hand on his shoulder and pull hard, making him stand. The king shoved Markl toward the bucket again.

"You'll be the one to do the honors and set fire to your friends in there," the king said and held out his hand. Markl took what he offered without thinking, and the weight of them startled him, making him yelp, his elbows bending. He didn't dare look down; he knew the texture.

"I hate the smell of burning hair," Micah said conversationally, "so you will throw the heads to the sea. Think of them as an offering to Edbris, if it helps."

Markl managed to look at the king. He was smiling, almost in a comforting way, as if he was doing him a favor by making him do this 'ritual.' Almost numb, Markl tore his eyes away and approached the portside banister. The water was so dark it seemed a void. No sacrifice should be made to those waters, he thought. But with the king's eyes on the back of his neck, he did so anyway.

The two heads sank so easily into the ocean, a part

of Markl felt underwhelmed. And then something in his mind cracked like wood breaking as he realized he would now have to light a fire to burn the remaining pieces of his friends. "Please…" he murmured to nobody in particular. He wasn't even sure what he begged for.

The ship rocked violently to the side, making them stumble and fall on their backs.

'The giant eel is responding to our offering.' Almost immediately after the thought occurred to him, another violent push moved the ship in the opposite direction, and the king, who had been trying to stand back up, fell to his hands and knees.

"What is that?" he grunted, using Markl to steady himself up.

Markl stayed on the deck, and crawled over to the bucket, in case another push from whatever lurked in the water made it fall on its side and spill its contents. He found its lid close by and rushed to cover it with a sob. The crew moved frantically to their positions, screaming at each other to hold on, to avoid falling overboard when the next push came.

Jona screamed orders. They needed to pull the latches to open the underwater windows designed for Reran warships. Whatever was under the ship was alive and he could cut into. "Trigger the blades! Now!" At the same time, he secured a rope from the mast around his middle and prepared his stance to avoid falling.

"Waterlions!" shouted a man from the crow's next, "Hundreds of them, Captain!"

As soon as he managed to get those words out, the mass of waterlions hit the ship's hull once more. The soldier let out a scream, his voice cracking as he lost footing and fell from above. Markl, still hugging the burn bucket, cheek red from rubbing against the rusted metal, watched as the man fell. He cracked his spine on the banister, slumped onto the deck, and stopped moving.

Seconds later, a creature flung itself onto the ship, flapping its tail around to move toward the body. The waterlion's mane, wet and heavy, stuck to his face, and finger-length teeth were impossible to miss with his protruding snout. His nostrils flared, smelling the air in search of its meal. His two paws, almost the same size as his head, moved to drag his massive body across the deck toward the fallen soldier. Markl flinched at the sound of claws on the wood.

"The blades!" the king yelled.

In the hold, Charles ran toward the latch that would activate them. The waterlions pushed on the hull again, making him fall to the floor. "Damn lions," he grunted, trying to push forward as the ship settled. "Next push they'll keel us over!"

At last, he reached the latch and pulled on it with

all his strength, the wood creaking as the specialized gunports opened and sharp blades violently sprung out of them. From the hold, Charles heard the screeches of the waterlions that were surrounding the ship. When he sprinted up the stairs back onto the deck, he noticed it had started raining. The sea was no longer black, but dark red, tainted with the blood of all the creatures that were in the way of the blades when he had triggered them.

He saw Markl, who was still hugging the bucket, with no lifeline. He ran toward him, grabbing two ropes from the main mast system. As he approached his friend, he secured the rope around his middle and fell to his knees next to him, securing his own lifeline as the man sobbed.

"It ate him. It ate him," Markl was repeating over and over.

Only then did Charles realize what Markl was looking at. A waterlion was fully immersed in the rib cavity of one of their men. He couldn't even tell which one of their crew was the body being ripped apart.

He forced himself to look away, his hands shaking as he pried his friend's fingers off of the bucket and started dragging him away from the creature. He pressed one of his hands over Markl's eyes, stopping him from seeing the waterlion continue his feast.

"We're still moving," Charles said. "We'll get out of

their nest soon. Just breathe."

As if he heard that, the lion ripped his snout from inside the man and stared right at them.

"Out of my way." Micah pushed his shoulder aside as he walked past, making them fall onto their side. His lifeline dragged behind him for a second before it pulled taught. While the crew fought back the waterlions, he had retrieved his crossbow from his headquarters and now held it so comfortably that the weapon seemed an extension of his arm.

The waterlion started moving toward them, slower on land but still dangerously agile. King Micah raised his crossbow.

"The swelling is going down already! Don't argue with me anymore," Celeste said to the first mate, using her hands to touch the doorframe. She could still see out of her uninjured eye, but depth perception was tricky now. She would have to get used to it. "I miss my hammock and Augie's snoring."

Augie let out an offended gasp. "I do not snore! Don't make me trip you."

"You'd really do that to a poor blinded woman?" Celeste smiled, then winced when the movement caused the cut on her face to ache.

"Don't even try that with me. You're only half blind, I'm still better than you."

Nona chuckled, shaking her head and watching them walk away from Glenlivet's quarters and into the hold. Once they vanished from sight, she turned back to the room where her captain sat by the desk, eyes focused on the wall. She played with the green ribbon that kept her old letters together.

"We'll be arriving at Melende tomorrow…" Nona said tentatively. "Are we going to get a room together there?"

No response. Nona sighed, closed the door behind her, and started walking toward the desk. On the way, she lifted her hand and gently pushed a wooden wind chime that hung from the ceiling. The sound made Glenlivet finally snap out of her head and she looked at Nona with wide eyes.

"Pay attention to me."

The captain's surprise shifted into a satisfied grin, a small dimple appearing on the side of her mouth. The sight made Nona's chest feel warm. She brought her hand down and away from the wind chime as Glenlivet stood, leaving the letters inside a drawer. As always, Nona tried her best to ignore it. The task became easier when the woman rounded the desk and stood in front of her, holding her hips.

"Does this mean you're no longer mad at me?" she asked.

Nona groaned at the teasing tone in her voice but placed her arms over the captain's shoulders anyway. "It does not mean any of that sort. Don't think you're entirely off the hook."

Glenlivet's smile didn't falter, eyes shining. "But I'm off the hook a little bit. I see... So, you want me to make it up to you." When Nona squinted at her, pretending to think it over, Glenlivet leaned down and kissed the tip of her nose. "Was that enough?"

Nona brought her hands down to grab at Glen's collar and pulled her in, kissing her lips. The captain's hands moved from her hips to her lower back, getting their bodies so close Nona felt the air being stolen from her lungs. When she pulled away, the captain's eyes were watery and her breath desperate.

"Better," she said.

Micah was sweating, biting hard on a piece of wood as his men held him down. Charles dumped alcohol onto the length of his right arm. He inspected the wound, and the king watched the man lose color, his eyes widening.

"I can see the bone. It's broken and splintered, and most of the flesh around it is in no state to be stitched together," he said, looking away to try to gather his courage to suggest what needed to be done.

Jona Ishim, who was laying down in the corner of the room, sat up on the cot and watched the quiet room that surrounded the king, who eyed the arm with apprehension. Jona rolled his eyes. "He's saying the best course of action is amputating the limb, my king."

Charles widened his eyes at him, shaking, but Micah looked over at Jona over his shoulder and spat out the wood piece, frowning, before returning his attention to the man holding his arm.

"If you cut my dominant hand, I might struggle to do it but I will cut off your head."

While the threat was real, and everyone in the room knew it, its weight was lessened by the breathless voice that delivered it. The king looked pale and dizzy from blood loss.

"I'll do what I can," Charles said, not meeting the king's eyes, "but I can't promise it will be a neat job. Old Flick was the most experienced surgeon we had on board." He said the last part quietly, fearing the monarch's wrath but unable to stop himself from saying it.

To everyone's surprise, Micah didn't react to the remark and simply nodded. "Gather whatever you need and get to work," he said and placed the biting block back in his mouth.

"He'll have to move the broken bone," Jona said, standing and limping toward his bag. From it, he took a bottle of clear colorless liquid. "I don't have much left, Your Majesty, but enough to make this bearable."

As the king inhaled from the chemical-drenched rag Jona offered, Markl stumbled out of the room. He couldn't help but replay the events of the last couple of hours in his head, confused by how fast everything had happened.

The waterlion moved full speed toward him when the king shot at it. The creature swerved violently to the left as if to avoid the shot, but the volt lodged into its side. It caused the lion to roar in pain, catching the king's right forearm in his mouth and tearing meat as he fell. Micah managed to pull his arm out, and through his own agony, he got the crossbow ready and shot again, this time between the eyes.

The rest was a blur. The last thing Markl vaguely recalled was Charles lifting him from the floor.

"Those blasted pirates knew about the waterlions," he heard another soldier say behind him.

"We should be going back to Agara, or even Agath," Charles said, sternly. "I can try to keep the wound free of infection but we don't have the resources to—"

"No," Jona said, raising his voice. "You won't take advantage of the king being unconscious to run your mouth. We will follow his orders, and his orders are to dock in Sodra and hunt the pirates."

Markl didn't hear much else, now on the deck. He

walked across it, giving the body of the waterlion a wide berth on his way to the burn bucket. He took a breath before opening it. The stink had only worsened over the past few hours, but he faced it now without feeling sick.

The young man burned the remains alone on the deck, as the rain turned into a drizzle.

Nona woke up to light coming through the window. She rolled over in Glenlivet's bed, feeling the empty space where the captain should have been. With a sigh, she swung her legs over the bed and stood, covering herself with a sheet, padding across the room to the desk. She stole a glance toward the door.

"If you didn't want me to open the drawer," she whispered to it, "you should have been here when I woke up. So, if you don't want me to open it, you should open the door now."

No response came.

She suddenly felt silly, talking to no one in the empty room, and with an annoyed huff, she leaned down and tried to pull the drawer open. The whole desk groaned, a terrible sound as it scraped against the floor. Nona winced and looked at the door, waiting for someone to come in, but it remained closed.

Glenlivet had locked the drawer while Nona had been

asleep. Aggravated, she shook the handle, and the box clattered. The papers inside moved but remained hidden away. She fell back onto the chair, head hanging in defeat.

Right as she did, Danielle knocked and opened the door. "Nona, the captain said —Oh! Sorry, sorry!" The girl turned to look away as the first mate brought the sheet higher and wandered to the bed to collect her clothes.

"We're almost at Melende. Glenlivet sent me to tell you," Danielle said, her back still to her as Nona dressed, but she could see how red her ears were.

"She really should have told me herself; don't you think?" Nona said.

"I guess?" Danielle said, head tilting to the side. "She was busy organizing some things with Gale."

Nona grunted in acknowledgment as she finished covering herself. "You can turn around now," she said, grabbing the scabbard from its post against the wall.

Danielle turned, relieved to see Nona back in her usual garments. Before she knew it, she was speaking: "So you and the captain have a... a relationship?"

Nona looked at Danielle for a moment before averting her eyes with a sigh. "We don't call it that."

"Oh, all right. What do you call it then?" she asked. Danielle feared she was intruding in uncomfortable territory but she had spent weeks watching them dance around each other, had noticed the glances they shared and the mornings in which Nona snuck out of the captain´s quarters before the majority of the crew woke up. "Excuse me. I'm not well-versed in romantic affairs. The court in Rera isn't exactly a place for love."

Nona scoffed as she grabbed her bag from the floor. "We also don't call it that, apparently."

Seeing Danielle's confused expression made the first mate falter and redirect the conversation. "You were never in love with the king?"

The woman looked down at her shoes. "I thought I was, at the beginning. Before we got married, he seemed polite. Perfectly acceptable, according to my mother. Even kind." She peeked up at Nona for a second before looking away again. "You must think me a fool."

Nona walked toward her and placed a comforting hand on her shoulder. "No, Danielle, I don´t." Her other hand wrapped around the kraken token as she spoke. "Men like him? They´re small. So, they worm their way into people´s lives, and once they´re inside, they do everything in their power to make everyone around him feel small too."

G.

I think my father suspects. You're right as always, we should stop talking at temple. We could pretend we had a falling out so he stops sticking his nose in our business.
I find myself so tired. It's been almost two years since you arrived, you'd think he would have gotten used to you by now! I want to be able to go on walks with you to the beach, and have picnics, and show you my library as we talked about.
Next time we sneak to The Dusk Market, could we go to port as well? I'd like to ask how much it would cost to buy us passage out of here.
I intended to not speak of it until you brought it up, but I know you've been saving up to buy a ship. No use in hiding it any longer.
Would you allow me to help?

L.

Book Two

The Cursed Eel

8

Pirate Talk

Tavia slammed her cup onto the bar twice, calling the attention of the bartender, a lovely old woman with white hair and grey eyes. She waddled over to the pirate and filled her cup back up.

"Don't you have other business on land to take care of?" the woman said. "Drinking so much will only pull you back to your ship faster, won't it?"

"It's none of your business, Elena," Tavia gruffed out.

"Suit yourself."

Tavia's long blue hair fell onto the sticky bar surface as she slumped her head forward, taking another sip of rum. The captain's hands were so pale you could see blue veins through the thin, papery skin. Despite the tavern being full of people, to the point many had to stand for want of a seat, the stools next to either side of Tavia were empty.

"My business here is done anyways," she said, standing.

The room spun as she stumbled backward into someone's arms. She was about to turn and cut whoever had touched her when she heard the person's voice: "Got the supplies for Cave Island. Are you ready to leave?"

Recognizing the voice, she used the arms around her to steady herself and turned to look at her crew mate. Ashlin's short hair was messy in the back, a few strands caught in the lace choker that decorated her neck. A bag hung over her shoulder.

"More than ready," Tavia said. "I feel the pull."

Ash rolled her eyes, but smiled, "Of course you do. You stink of rum."

"Don't be mad at me. That's an order," Tavia said. "I think I can make my way back to the ship on foot, don't worry."

Ash nodded, but put an arm around her captain to hold her weight all the same, when the tavern door opened. Tavia turned her head to see who had walked in, and a wave of nausea overtook her. She doubled over and vomited a rush of green water rather than rum. The pull took over entirely—and Tavia vanished from sight. Ashlin stumbled forward, body crashing against the empty stool where Tavia had been just a second ago. A few people screamed and ran out of the door at the sight of the pirate throwing up and disappearing into thin air. Ash sighed, irritated, and looked up to find Elena watching her and shaking her head.

"I'm sorry about her."

"It's quite all right, my dear. As long as you leave now."

The pirate offered a few coins to the old woman and adjusted the bag over her shoulder. She stepped to the side to avoid bumping into Glenlivet on her way out. The captain of *The Outsider* and a few members of her crew looked at her for a moment as Ash walked past them.

Danielle looked at the door as it closed behind her. She could have sworn the woman was a mirage, the way her clothes swayed and became translucent as she moved.

The Edbris Fang was packed, forcing Glenlivet to elbow a few people to make her way to the bar. Elena gasped when the captain sat right where Tavia had been.

"Today seems the day of odd crews at my tavern," the barkeep said, propping her hands on her hips. "You lot keep costing me money."

A few men that had been drinking by the door

were walking out, staring daggers into Glenlivet's back. Danielle watched them as they stepped out, muttering among themselves.

"You know we can outdrink those assholes so you don't lose one copper," Marcya said, smiling and pushing a man off of a stool so she could sit on it.

"We will also be staying for the night if you have free rooms, Elena," Glenlivet added. "And in the morning, we'll rent horses to cross the bridge to Sodra." The barkeep smiled back at them, satisfied enough with that information.

After the crew had a few drinks, Danielle was still watching over her shoulder. The tavern was still busy, but the patrons were now much quieter, whispering among each other and stealing looks at her crew.

"Ignore them," Nona said, touching the girl's wrist for a moment. "Elena?"

The bartender drew close, leaning over the bar.

"Has Elric been around Melende lately?" Nona asked, and Glenlivet leaned forward as well, waiting for the answer.

Elena shook her head, lips in a tight line. "That little boy knows not to step foot in my neck of the woods since we had words last time. And if you ask me, maybe that is a good thing. If you keep stepping on his heels, he won't hesitate to kill you and—"

"It's a good thing I didn't ask you then," the captain

said sternly and Elena knew not to say another word about it. Glenlivet sighed. "If he kills me, then so be it. He'll die with me."

Nona turned her head to Glenlivet, frowning at her, but Elena spoke again before she could say anything. "Well, his contacts have always been on the main island, so going to Sodra is your best bet."

"We thought so," Marcya said, taking another sip of her drink.

"Glenlivet, we need to—" Nona started saying the captain was already walking away to join Julian and Blue by one of the tables, where a game of cards was starting.

Gale, who had been standing behind her with their book, tapped her shoulder. Nona turned to look at them and waited while the strategist wrote down on a piece of paper.

Don't take it to heart. She cares for you. Just struggles to communicate it.

Nona crumbled the note and threw it over the bar into a rubbish bin the old bartender kept there. "I guess..." she said, but when she turned to watch the card game table, the game was in full swing and a woman with curly blonde hair tied in a loose braid over her shoulder was apparently winning. Glenlivet smiled at her with a glint in her eye that Nona recognized. Gale followed Nona's gaze, seeing how the captain whispered something in the woman's ear and how they both stood up and went up the stairs together.

When the strategist looked back toward the first mate, she had refocused on the bottom of her glass.

Tavia fell forward in her chair, her chest hitting the edge of the desk. Water continued gushing out of her mouth, mixed with bile, rum, and pieces of algae. The burning in her throat made her eyes tear up.

She knew it would pass soon, but for a while, the room spun and her ears were clogged. She tried to take a sip from the glass that had been in her grasp a few moments ago but her hand was empty now. She groaned as she stood, her whole body aching as if under great pressure. Her nose burned, and when she reached her hand up to it, her fingers came away stained black.

The door of the room opened with a slam. "You got pulled?" Derya said, walking in without asking, her arms burdened with bedsheets. Unfazed by the state of her captain, she crossed the room to change the bed.

Derya's long, curly blonde hair draped over her shoulders. The strands looked wet, as did her dress, but her skin was dry. The dark blue veins on her neck were so prominent they looked like tree roots, crawling up from her chest to her jaw.

"It never gets easier. Thank Edbris you don't ever feel it," Tavia said, coughing one last time before walking to the open door. "Is Cecilia on board?"

"She just arrived. On foot, not pulled," the young girl said, looking sullen.

Tavia paused at her tone of voice and scratched her scalp. "I'm sorry. I shouldn't have said that about the pull, I know you really want to go on land."

"It is what it is." Derya shrugged, and Tavia stared at her, looking for any signs of dishonesty but her features were unreadable.

The shadows underneath her eyes were the deepest in the crew, and her face was cracked in random places, where water damage had broken the skin. Derya had already been dead when the remains of her soul laced themselves to the ship, so her body had taken a bigger toll than the rest of them. She was also unable to step foot outside of *The Cursed Eel*. Her dark purple lips were shut tight as she finished her task, and asked: "Anything interesting to report from the land of the living?"

She turned, spotted Tavia's vomit on the desk, and plucked a rag from her belt loop to clean it.

"No news about Mama Ruth," Tavia said, "so our plans remain unchanged."

"Are we taking the shortcut to Cave Island, then?" Derya asked, voice a bit nervous.

"Yeah. I know you don't like sinking but Ash is right. It's the fastest and easiest way there," Tavia turned to leave when she remembered. "Oh, and *The Outsider* just arrived in Melende."

"Will they give us any trouble?" Cecilia appeared, leaning against the doorway, eyeing Derya at the desk. "You don't have to clean that, darling. It's the captain's mess, she's meant to do it."

"I'm happy to clean it, I don't mind," Derya said, still wiping.

"Then how will our dear captain ever learn her lesson?" Cecilia asked, smiling with a cocked eyebrow at Tavia.

The blue-haired woman sighed and walked to the desk, taking the rag from Derya's hand. "Cecilia is right. Let me finish this." Derya shrugged and stepped back, allowing the captain to clean, and listening to the conversation. "And no, I don't think they'll be trouble. They seemed busy with their own bullshit, whatever that is these days."

"Probably the same suicidal mission they're always on," Cecilia commented, rolling her eyes. "I don't understand why Elric doesn't just... crush them."

"Perhaps he's scared of her," Derya said, frowning.

Cecilia and Tavia both stared at Derya for a second before looking at each other and bursting into laughter.

It was dawn when Glenlivet rose. The woman she had met the day before snored softly until she sat on the edge of the bed to put on her shoes. The woman stretched and rubbed her eyes before focusing on her.

"Morning," Glenlivet said, not looking at her. "I'm leaving today, Laura."

Glenlivet ignored the confused silence and stood to grab her things.

"Oh, right!" the woman said, remembering. "Sorry, I was a bit tipsy last night, I did say you could call me that."

"I hope it was worth it," Glenlivet murmured with a small smile but didn't meet her eye.

"Better than most of the men that come my way. And definitely not the weirdest request I've gotten, trust me," the woman said with a chuckle. "Will you return soon?"

"I don't know about soon but I will probably be back, yes. I guess I'll see you around."

She was almost at the door when the woman spoke up again: "So what's the deal with the name?"

Glenlivet paused, a hand on the doorknob.

"Laura, I mean," she clarified, sitting up on the bed. "Someone important to you?"

In the light that started to stream through the window, the woman didn't even look that much like her. Glen didn't say another word before she opened the door and stepped out, rushing downstairs and out of the tavern, toward the stables.

The morning progressed as it always did whenever they docked at Melende to get to Sodra on horseback. Celeste complained the horses didn't like her, which in all fairness was the truth, Augie spoiled the horses by feeding them far too many carrots, and the captain protected the group by staying at the back of the procession while the first mate led up front.

"It is technically one of the colonies," Julian remarked to Danielle, "but it doesn't give Goliath a lot of profit, so they mostly leave it to their own devices. Not to mention, all the agents they send to keep the place under control are always willing to be bought. Much better to not talk a lot about a place that gives the empire such a bad name, huh, Roma?"

The girl smiled back at him and nodded.

"You're from the Cluster?" Danielle asked.

"Yeah. Not the main island though," Roma said. "I'm from Tophia, a small village to the north. We barely got any envoys from the empire."

"Thank Mydos for that!" Mel said. "They're constantly pestering the other colonies."

"Can't really demand coin that doesn't exist," Roma

joked, slapping Mel's arm playfully, then turned to Danielle to explain. "Tophia was left destitute after the conquering and they still haven't recovered. Not entirely."

Danielle watched Roma's face. The former queen wondered just how many kids had been raised on the islands with the knowledge that a country overseas was responsible for the hunger in their bellies.

"Is that why the barkeep was so worried we were scaring off her customers?" Danielle asked, to which Roma nodded.

"Melende struck a deal with Goliath when they took over so they weren't completely destroyed, but taxes are still too high for most people."

"She said there were two odd crews. I saw that woman with the vein tattoos coming out of the tavern, is that who she meant?"

Roma exchanged a look with Celeste, who was watching them over her shoulder with her healthy eye. When she realized Danielle was looking at her, she turned her head back to the front, pretending to not be listening.

"Yeah… She's part of *The Cursed Eel*," Roma said in a whisper, "Celeste doesn't like them much."

"Why?" Danielle whispered back. "I thought she'd be happy about another crew allowing women on board."

Before Roma could answer, the captain rode ahead

to join Nona at the lead. The crew followed her with their eyes before resuming their chatter.

"*The Outsider* is the only pirate crew alive that allows women on board," Roma said with a nod.

Danielle frowned, confused. "What? But... I saw that woman leaving The Edbris Fang, she—"

"She's not alive. And those were not tattoos."

Glenlivet never knew how to start these conversations. And she had a feeling this gap of knowledge was the reason the conversation died every time without ever resolving anything. Still, it didn't stop her from trying.

"You slept well?" she asked, keeping her tone light.

"I did," Nona said smiling in a way that sent a shiver down the captain's spine and made her brace for impact. "No need to ask how you slept. I know you didn't. She looked energetic."

Glenlivet winced. "No need to be petulant."

Nona gaped at her, eyes wide. "I swear, it's like you enjoy making me angry."

"That wasn't the goal."

"I thought we were sharing a room at the inn," the first mate said, her voice so quiet Glenlivet almost didn't hear it.

"I didn't agree to that."

Nona's hands gripped the reins too tight, making the horse dance nervously in place.. She stared at her in disbelief for a second before sighing and shaking her head sadly, loosening her grip and patting the horse's neck to calm it. "I guess you're right. You didn't. You were too busy playing with those letters you're so secretive about."

"That's not—" Glenlivet started, blood boiling at that comment. She became highly aware that those letters were hanging from her belt right there, between them.

"Save it," Nona cut her off, pulling on the reins of her horse to turn around. "I'll take your spot at the back."

"Nona!" Glenlivet called out. "Come on, you know I care about you, just—"

"Then fucking act like it, captain!"

Glenlivet closed her mouth and kept riding. The gates of Sodra could be seen in the distance. Her vision blurred, her mind replaying the end of another conversation before she had even met Nona.

"I love you..."

"So act like it! Get us out of here!"

"I told you! We need to save more coin. It's too dangerous if we rush it!"

"It´s dangerous if we don´t."

She closed her eyes so tightly that white spots swam behind her eyelids. When she opened them again, the conversation faded and the voices of the crew behind her took its place.

i.

We have to leave before the end of the month. All my life I had known I would have to marry a boy from a nice family in Agath, or join the Orena Sisters at the core temple. I accepted both of these options.

Meeting you has completely shattered that compliance.

The idea of marrying someone else or joining a temple where I'd never be allowed to see you again makes me want to throw myself into the ocean. I'd gladly drown.

I think my father has sensed that change. When I was a child he often would say the decision would be made when I turned twenty but he now claims seventeen is old enough. I told him I refused to marry, and now he's making preparations with the clergy so they come fetch me.

I can steal, gods forgive, some coin that my father keeps in his office, and use it to get out of here. To The Cluster perhaps. We can save money there and buy a proper pirate ship and sail after your revenge.

Take me. I no longer fear it.

L.

9

Pirate´s Haven

"Rommely!" Glenlivet jumped off her horse, smiling wide as she walked the rest of the way toward the massive gate.

The guard was tall with a red and white beard and vibrant brown eyes. His nose and cheeks were burnt red from standing for hours under the sun. He laughed when he saw the pirate and ran to meet her halfway, receiving her with open arms.

"My favorite freebooter!" he said as she leaped into his embrace. "How long has it been? I could have sworn you were a head shorter when I last saw you!"

The pirate pulled back with an amused chuckle. "I haven´t had a growth spurt since I was sixteen, Rommely. Maybe you´re the one shrinking!"

The man ruffled her hair, messing with the scarf on her head. They walked together the rest of the way and he knocked on the wooden gate with the pommel of his sword. The clanking echoed through it, and a set of guards on the other side started opening the door.

"You brought the hard worker you stole from me?" he asked as they all waited for the door to finish moving. "The wife would be happy to see her again."

Glenlivet smiled but broke their eye contact to focus on his shoes, fidgeting with the letters on her belt. "Yeah, she's at the back. I'm sure she'll be happy to see her too."

"Uh, oh. What did you do to make Nona mad?"

Glenlivet looked up, her top lip curling at him. "Why do you assume I was the one that did something wrong?"

Rommely raised his hands in surrender.

"Because you're a mess," Gale muttered as they rode through the doors on their horse.

The captain's mouth hung open while the crew laughed.

"I swear, they only talk when they want to drag me through the mud," she said even as she joined the laughter, hugging Rommely once more.

They filed into Sodra as the afternoon sun turned duller and softer.

The group headed to the guard's home on his orders.

He insisted his wife would scold him if she found out he allowed them to stay at a bug-riddled inn. At the door Julian, Mel, and Blue separated from the rest, taking the horses to the stables around the corner.

"Start asking questions," Glenlivet ordered as they walked away.

"Will do, Captain!" Blue called out, looking over their shoulder.

Rommely's wife was a blonde woman named Claudia with a bird-like voice and movements. She received them in the kitchen, a wide tiled space that smelled of broth, charcoal, and wood.

"Bless Yrena! You're here!" she screamed, pushing Glenlivet to the side and onto a chair. "Where's my girl?"

"I'm here, I'm here!" Nona pushed her way through the crew and grabbed the woman by the cheeks, kissing her over and over while they both cried.

Glenlivet stood back up, chuckling. "I'm so glad to see you, Glenlivet! How do you do, Glenlivet? I'm happy to see you as well, Claudia! I'm doing splendid, thank you very much!" she said, sarcastically.

"Oh, hush, child!" the woman said, letting go of Nona and turning to Glenlivet. "You know damn well I'm happy to see you as well, but Nona is my starling."

"I understand that," the captain said, setting her bag on the floor.

The crew settled around the big table and Roma got busy at the counter making drinks for everyone. Celeste stood by the window, watching the street.

The main island had the most resources, but despite this, most of it was in a state of disrepair, the dirt on the streets only taken care of by occasional and inconsistent cleaners, roaches, and rats. In contrast, the district where the Empire's soldiers lived looked nothing like the rest of Sodra. The neighborhood streets were clean, and the houses, bigger than what most of them needed, were given a fresh coat of paint every couple of years.

"You all right, Celeste?" Augie asked, sipping from his glass.

Glenlivet turned to the woman, noticing her distracted gaze. "Anything on the horizon?"

"She's *seeing*," Roma said, jumping to get closer to the woman. "I haven't felt anything."

"It's just an inkling," Celeste finally answered, blinking. "I see blood in the water. Lots of it."

Claudia brought a hand to her belly. "Oh gods be gracious."

The mage turned toward the woman, frowning. "Yrena watches you closely." Her frown turned into a soft smile as her eye cleared. "Congratulations."

The woman's eyes widened, stammering out unfinished words as the crew took in Celeste's meaning and looked at each other. Finally, Nona grabbed Claudia's hands in hers. "Another one? I thought you said little Marilla was going to be your last."

Claudia laughed, shaking her head and looking at the group surrounding her table as she nervously fixed her hair. "I haven't even told Rommely or the kids yet, so quiet yourselves about it."

As if on cue, a lanky teenager wandered into the kitchen, holding a three-year-old in his arms. "She won't take the bottle, Ma. I think she just wants you," the boy said before tearing his eyes away from his baby sister and noticing the pirates in his kitchen.

A mere second later, the baby was in Claudia's arms and the pirate captain had the young man in her lap, his arms around her neck. "Glenlivet!"

"Barden, my favorite boy!" she exclaimed, mouth wide in surprise. She looked at Claudia with eyebrows raised. "What are you feeding this kid? Gods, he's grown!"

"You're late, ma'am," Barden said, looking at Glenlivet with a stern look.

"Late?"

"You promised you'd be back to visit before the year was over. Therefore, you are late."

"Ah. Turns out I am late then," the captain said, winking over at Claudia. "And I´m perhaps still late because I´m not here to visit, boy."

"Glenlivet, we just got here," Nona whispered, looking down at the table. "Can´t you allow everyone to settle in first?"

The captain looked at her for a moment, considering her, before looking at Barden again. "I´m still working. And if you´re still friends with those kids at East Port, I´d be happy to pay for some help."

Barden straightened his back, smiling, and looked at his mother for permission. Claudia nodded, though looking worried, and the young man turned to Glenlivet again. "Anything I can do, tell me."

The captain took out a few gold coins and handed them to the boy. "I need to know if *The Conviction* has been here recently. Really, any word of its whereabouts will be useful. The money is to pay whoever knows anything, but you can keep one of the coins."

"They´ll be at the docks when the sun sets. I´ll head there after supper," the boy said with a nod, putting away one of the coins. "I´ll make sure nobody sees me, as usual."

Nona sighed, looking at Glenlivet, and brought the drink back to her lips. She looked so different than when they had met a decade ago, right in this very house.

Celeste was looking out the window again, her one

eye white as snow.

The mage knew she was seeing something she hadn't been invited to see, but she couldn't pull away. The sensations were so strong that the kitchen around her shifted and she couldn't feel her hands any longer.

The crew disappeared, the table and chairs empty and silent. The street outside, hot under the sun just a few moments ago, was flooding now, and rain was hitting the window so hard she thought it might break.

Celeste pressed a hand against the glass, trying to will herself back to the present, back to the busy, lively group in the warm kitchen—lightning turned the street white and thunder split the sky.

The door slammed open with a *crack* and Celeste turned to watch a much younger Rommely enter with an unconscious Glenlivet in his arms. Just as suddenly, the mage realized which memory her gift had transported her to.

The captain and the first mate had spoken vaguely of this night, made light, and poked fun at it every once in a while, but they had never gone into much detail.

"Where did you find her, girl?" Rommely asked, setting Glenlivet onto the table.

Nona rushed into the kitchen after him. Her features were softer, in a way only innocence and inexperience could soften a face. Just like her captain on the table, she must have been eighteen that night. She was soaked head to toe, and her shoes and legs were muddy.

"Near the docks. I was helping Omell and some of the others, securing their ships and cargo," the young girl answered, opening a cupboard to fetch a pot.

"Warm water, not hot," said another voice from the door. Claudia rushed in with towels in her arms. "Barden, go to your room and stay there until I fetch you," she called out.

Before the door closed behind her, Celeste spotted a little boy, watching with wide eyes from the stairs.

"Do you know who she is? Any crew that will come looking for her?" Rommely asked, removing Glenlivet's purses and belt, as Claudia dried her off.

Nona shook her head. "She was alone. Nobody at the docks knew her," she said, stepping back to let Claudia work after giving her the pot of warm water. "Is she going to make it? We managed to make her breathe again back there, but she looks..." Her sentence trailed off, looking away from the young woman on the table.

For the first time, Celeste dared look at her captain properly.

"The storm didn't do this to her," Claudia muttered.

Glenlivet's face had a cut on the cheek, crudely

stitched with dingy thread that was coming loose. There was a nasty bruise on her left eye and clear signs of rope burn around her neck. Her left arm was twisted at an odd angle and her expression shifted in pain when Claudia moved it.

Glenlivet seemed to be trying to open her mouth. Though her eyes remained closed, they were now shut tighter.

"Laura…" Her voice was coarse, barely more than a rasp.

Nona, Rommely, and Claudia didn't seem to hear it, speaking among themselves. Celeste leaned forward, putting her ear to the captain's mouth.

"What was she thinking?" Rommely said. "She's lucky to be alive if she actually was at sea on her own. Especially on a night like this, the fool."

Celeste felt Glenlivet's lips move again. "No, please… I wasn't…" Her voice died out and Celeste suddenly found herself standing in Rommely´s parlor.

The storm had quieted outside but the rain still fell, the room basked in grey. The chimney was lit despite it not being cold. She turned, in search of clues as to why she was being shown this memory.

Glenlivet now lay on the sofa, under thick blankets. Her breathing was calm and her injuries had been tended to; her arm was in a sling, and someone had re-stitched the cut on her cheek and applied ointment to her bruises.

Nona entered the room with a small basket of clothes on her hip and sat on the armchair. She spared a look toward the stranger on the sofa to her right and sighed, shaking her head as she threaded a needle to mend a shirt from the basket.

Celeste didn´t know how long she stood there, watching them, nervous to look away in case she missed something important. Nona was still working on the clothes when Glenlivet´s eyes fluttered open and she whimpered, aching from the pain.

"Gods," Nona said, dropping a pair of trousers into the basket on the floor, and stood up. "Claudia! She´s awake!" she called out to the open doorway and rushed forward to help the woman sit up. "We were beginning to worry you would never wake up."

"Where—" Glenlivet´s voice was still rough, and whatever she wanted to say was interrupted as she doubled over the edge of the sofa and threw up.

Nona scrambled to catch her, so she didn't fall off the sofa, holding her forehead to keep her hair away from her mouth. "You´re safe. You´re in Sodra," she said, assuming the young woman was questioning where she was. "We found you on the coast."

Glenlivet had clearly not eaten recently, as only water and bile came out of her. It didn´t take long for her to recover and gently push Nona´s hands away to sit properly on the sofa. "I'm sorry. I'll clean this."

"Don't worry about it, you stay put," Nona said, looking down at the mess. "You seem to have gone through hell. You need rest."

Glenlivet slowly blinked up at her, and then down at herself. She touched her waist, as if searching for something. Her movements became frantic as she found nothing and tried to get up. Nona grabbed her healthy arm and sat her back down. "Your things are over there," she said, pointing to the side of the sofa. "We didn't touch them, but a lot of it was damaged by the water."

The pirate moved away from Nona's hand, stretching to grab her belt and the bags still attached to it. She opened one of them, struggling with shaky hands, and took out a handful of envelopes. Nona had been right, many were ruined by the water, but Glenlivet sighed in relief and clutched the letters tight as she sat back.

"I was alone when you found me," she whispered. Her eyes were closed, and Celeste wasn't sure if she meant it as a question or a statement.

"You were," Nona answered anyways. "I'm Lynona Cromwell, by the way. You can call me Nona, if you wish."

Glenlivet opened her eyes to look at the young woman for a moment. "Thank you. But I don't think I'll stick around long enough to call you anything."

Despite knowing she couldn't be seen, Celeste still tried her best to not giggle at that, covering her mouth.

"You have a name?" Nona asked, her curiosity bigger than the impulse to react to the pirate's rudeness.

"Glenlivet."

"Last name?"

"Don't have one."

"That's silly. Everyone does."

"I must be real special, then, Lynona Cromwell," Glenlivet answered, squinting at her as she said her name.

The room began to disappear, becoming blurrier and darker at the edges of Celeste's vision.

"No, wait!" the mage said, looking around in confusion. "I don't know why I was shown this memory yet!"

Between one blink and the next, she found herself back in the kitchen with the crew of *The Outsider* around her. To her surprise, she had moved during the episode and now leaned over the table, her hands open on the surface and holding onto it for dear life. Her crew watched her, eyes wide as she let go and stood straight again, blinking to ground herself.

"You're back?" Roma asked, her hand rubbing at Celeste's back. "That seemed like a strong one. I've never seen you like that before."

"It's never been that intense and clear before. You didn't feel anything?" Celeste asked, looking at her apprentice.

The young woman looked down, the corners of her mouth twitching downward, "Not even a hint..."

"Don't worry, child." Celeste caressed Roma's cheek. She realized, looking at her now, just how young her face looked. Just like the captain and first mate in the memory she had entered, she had just turned eighteen. "You're still so new to your power. Trust me, you will tune it one day."

"Any news?" Glenlivet asked, looking at her with eyebrows furrowed, a concern in her eyes that Celeste was relieved to see.

The captain had no trace of bruises or rope burns and her arm wasn't broken. She looked fuller too, not only muscle but fat making her healthy and strong.

Celeste shook her head. "Thank the gods, it was a memory, not a prediction." And yet, even as the crew moved on, she couldn't help but wish she'd had just a moment longer to discover why that memory had appeared at all.

Markl had been posted under the window of the inn. Charles stood outside the door of the king's room, and Jona was inside. All others were scattered around Sodra, keeping their eyes open for the pirates. Even the man recovering from being shot in the arm made the rounds. He figured it was another punishment for their failure in Agara.

Markl couldn't imagine those men had found anything. They would have returned to give a report if that had been the case. But the citizens of the islands were not friends of any Reran soldier. This was pirate territory. Every one of them had learned to protect them or been paid to. Even a crew like *The Outsider*, so different from the others, was inside that bubble of protection the Cluster offered. At the docks, the king's men had gotten suspicious, even hostile, looks.

Their ship waited at the southern port. The wall Markl leaned against faced east, and it was a blessing. He had had enough of looking at the ship for a while. Being near it made the image of the burn bucket return full force.

He yawned, stretching, eyes closed as he did. It was close to midnight and he hadn't slept properly in a long time. He was wondering how pirates spent so long away from proper beds when he spotted something out of the corner of his eye. A shadow in one of the alleys nearby: a tall skinny figure, taking short, careful steps. A feeling in his gut told him not to look directly.

He kept quiet, eyes trained forward, but the figure, whoever it was, walked into his line of sight and under a lamp post. For a brief second, Markl saw the freckled fifteen-year-old boy hiding around the corner of a building. His movements told Markl he was a local, familiar with every inch of the city. He wore a vest over a big white shirt, and pants that fell freely around the knees.

Another figure joined the boy behind the building. The new person was shorter, probably younger, too. They huddled together, believing themselves completely hidden by the building and its shadow. The taller boy moved to get something from his back pocket, coins, most likely. Markl waited to see what the shorter boy gave in return for it but nothing was given.

When they separated, he decided against following almost immediately. He couldn't leave his post and there was no sign, no matter how sharp his gut feeling, that this had anything to do with *The Outsider*. He looked around and up toward the window. The streets were deserted and the blinds were shut. Nobody else had seen the two figures' exchange but him. It was safe to keep quiet about the whole ordeal.

The pirates had settled in one of the guest rooms.

Celeste snored softly in one of the beds while Glenlivet sat by the window, watching her crew as she drank from a half-full cup of tea with honey. Her eyes passed over Julian and Mel, who were huddled together in a corner. On the other side of them slept Blue, mouth open and saliva running down their chin. The three of them had asked around for any information on *The Conviction*, but had come back with nothing. *Not their fault, really*, Glenlivet thought to herself. Not many would be willing to sell Elric out. She yawned, looking back toward the street. She knew she should be sleeping, too, but this place always left her feeling restless.

A soft knock from the door caught Glenlivet's attention. She hoped it would be Nona, who had stayed downstairs to help clear up the kitchen and wait for Barden. Instead, Claudia entered the room. The woman lightly stepped over the pirates´ sleeping forms and joined her by the window.

"Not at all like the weather we had the day you arrived," Claudia said, pointing outside, and sat down with a soft smile. "You´ve grown so much since. I would say you´ve become a nice, sensible woman."

Glenlivet raised an eyebrow and chuckled. "Many would disagree."

"Your first mate included," Claudia said, her eyes serious now. "Which never bodes well for a pirate crew. You should be a united front."

Glenlivet sighed. "I knew you weren´t just being nostalgic. What did Nona say for you to be busting my balls?"

Claudia rolled her eyes. "Just the truth: that you´re still being an emotionally constipated idiot."

The captain didn't answer, looking down to the street. She heard the woman sigh and felt her hand on her knee.

"Glenlivet, dear… I know you only told me because I saw the letters, but why don't you tell her? The whole story. She loves you, she would understand—"

"Barden is here," she interrupted, standing up and walking out the door.

Claudia looked out the window. Her son snuck down the street toward the house, looking over his shoulder to make sure he wasn't being followed. Relieved by his safe return, Claudia followed Glenlivet down the stairs and into the parlor, where Barden toed off his shoes.

"You didn't tell us you had the fucking King of Rera on your ass," the boy said, meeting the pirate captain at the bottom of the stairs.

"Barden, don't swear," Claudia said, stopping halfway down the stairs and looking at Glenlivet. "What is he talking about?"

"He—"

Barden interrupted her: "The King of Rera is in the city right now and asking questions about *The Outsider*. His soldiers are all over, offering coin to anyone with information."

"It's only a matter of time before someone actually takes the money and points them here." Glenlivet sighed, then looked at Claudia. "I'm sorry. I didn't think he´d catch up so fast. We will leave at once."

Nona, who had been listening from the kitchen door, started up the stairs but paused for a moment to put a comforting hand on Claudia´s shoulder. "I'll wake the crew and get out as fast as possible."

Glenlivet followed her with her eyes, but her first mate didn´t look back at her. She sighed and turned to Barden. "Do you have any other information for me?"

Barden still looked angry and nervous, looking out the windows for any approaching soldier. "Elric was at East Port less than two weeks ago. According to Samuel, he stayed on the ship most of the time until he received a message that caused him to leave in a hurry."

Glenlivet crossed her arms as she looked up at the crew making their way down the stairs behind Nona. "Any idea where they went?"

"It was expensive, but Samuel says one of his friends heard the crew talking about the hot weather in Mene and how they weren't looking forward to it."

"Mene?" Nona asked.

Glenlivet looked at her with soft eyes, not daring to speak. Her first mate's face paled as Barden nodded in confirmation.

"Samuel's friend didn't mention a specific city?" the captain asked, taking her things from Blue, who had brought them to her.

Nona's concern and anxiety only intensified when

Barden shook his head with a shrug.

"I'm sorry, dear," Claudia whispered, but the young woman just grabbed the strap of her bag harder, her knuckles whitening.

The crew of *The Outsider* left the stables an hour after midnight, leaving payment next to the sleeping guard. The sky was clear as they rode toward the bridge, the captain at the front. Their return to Melende was silent, cautious to not draw anyone's attention.

Nona rode at the back, her left hand clutched tightly around the kraken.

10

THE CROWN´S PERSUASION

Jona Ishim exited the inn and barked, "Prepare the horses. We got a lead."

With that, Jona disappeared back into the building. Markl did as ordered, frowning as he made his way to the stables. A guard had arrived a bit after three in the morning, rushing up the stairs to talk to the king. A scrappy kid dragged behind him. For a moment, Markl had wondered where the kid's parents were. He wondered what the boy's bedtime was, if he had any.

Markl stopped at the entrance of the stables, considering his mood, and forced his face to smooth away the frown. He knew he couldn't show he was upset at how fast they had gotten someone to talk. A lead to the pirates was a good thing. His face had to reflect that, or at least remain neutral to avoid punishment, even when away from the king.

They needed Queen Danielle back. He focused on that.

She was in charge of many of the country's social programs. Even though she had been under the king's watch and restrictions which limited her decisions and funds, her absence would be noticed soon. And people would suffer for it.

The queen's escape also meant tension with the neighboring nations and would make Rera look vulnerable. If The Council of Goliath thought the country vulnerable, they would send people to guarantee it wasn't so. This wasn't good for anyone, and it injured the king's ego. This was really what fueled Micah's drive to find Danielle, and Markl knew it now.

A part of him, after making conversation with Danielle during her walks in the gardens, delighted in knowing she was free and away from her husband. But a larger part was terrified of the king.

Markl was preparing the final horse with the stable boy's help, when the king appeared, his soldiers behind him. He was sweating, and pale, but his bandages had been exchanged for fresh ones and he walked with his head high, his pace unwavering. Jona, even with his injured leg, tried to help the king get on his horse but the man refused, pushing him away.

The streets were dark, but the air smelled like morning already. To Markl's surprise, they headed to the rich side of town in complete silence. He leaned toward Charles, who rode next to him. "What is this lead exactly?"

The man shushed him but whispered back: "A fucking kid from East Port told Slade where the pirates were staying. They're at a guard's house. Can you believe it?"

Markl nodded. He could believe it. He glanced at Slade, who still had the kid with him. The boy looked excited to be riding a horse, his eyes shining bright as he tried to make it go faster by kicking at the horse´s flanks, though it proved ineffective. He guessed he was about ten in the dim light they were riding under.

They stopped in front of a two-story house. It was quiet, the curtains drawn as they all dismounted to surround the main door.

The king unsheathed his sword as he approached. "Be as quiet as possible until you find the pirates."

The soldier called Slade knelt by the door, starting to work the lock with a pick he pulled out of his pocket.

"When you find them," Micah continued, "kill without hesitation. We only need Danielle alive."

"What about the siren, Your Majesty?" Charles asked.

Markl turned his head to watch his friend, whose eyes were glued to the door. There was a quiver in his voice that he didn't recognize completely. A mix of excitement and fear. The man had been raised by a woman from Greene, on stories and legends about these sea creatures. That much Markl knew, but he had never seen him in such a state before. Even his hands were shaking.

Micah paused, considering, as the door finally opened with a faint creak. The king looked at Charles before answering, giving a soft nod. "I'll let you keep a piece of the beast if you find it first."

Markl felt vomit crawl up his throat.

"They will probably be sleeping," said another soldier, a man in his thirties called Ren.

"Which is why it's vital you're as quiet as possible going in," Micah said, smiling.

"We're not giving them a chance to defend themselves?" Jona's reproach surprised Markl. His tone was severe, and his stare pierced into the king's eyes.

"You have a problem with that?" Micah held the stare, holding his injured arm.

Jona took a step back, lowering his head. "It's not honorable, Your Majesty. It's not the Crown's way."

The king turned around completely to face his soldier. His expression was unreadable, but every guard there knew questioning the king's order meant death. When Markl looked at Jona Ishim, he was shocked to find his stern expression toward the king had not wavered.

"We're in Sodra," the king said, smiling wide. "It is good manners to follow the customs of the place you're visiting."

"I brought you to the house," the kid interrupted, standing beside the two men. Markl could tell by his voice that he was trying his best to sound older. "When do I get my reward? Your man here said I'd—"

The king's sword slashed his neck.

The child fell to the ground, right onto Jona's shoes.

Jona spoke again, in a murmur this time: "He helped us." His eyes were harsh, staring at the boy's body.

Markl could tell he wanted to kneel and help, but it was too late. An impossible amount of blood gurgled from the open wound, his mouth open in a silent scream.

Micah put away his sword without cleaning it, the blade still wet with blood. "You talk about honor as if this country knows what that word means." Micah took two steps over the growing pool of blood and into the house, signaling to the soldiers to follow him.

Jona Ishim and Markl stayed outside, guarding the entrance. The silence stretched as they watched the boy grow cold. It seemed like hours had passed before Charles came out of the house, frowning.

"The king wants you inside."

"The pirates?" Markl asked, confused at Charles's defeated expression.

"Not here."

Saying goodbye to Rommely at the gate had been sour, and the crew's mood was dampened by the interaction, despite Rommely being more than understanding. They returned the horses to the stables in Melende around three in the morning and walked the rest of the way, still in solemn silence.

The docks were quiet, though a few workers were already preparing for the day's chores. The crew boarded *The Outsider* and readied to leave, while Nona woke and paid the dockmaster.

Glenlivet watched her as she approached the ship, her steps sluggish and hesitant. "Come on. You can sleep on the way there, not now." She smiled, trying to sound cheerful.

She was eager to go. The lead on Elric was fresh enough that with some luck they would catch him this time. There was some excitement there, that hunger she was so familiar with, but the circumstances stained that thrill. Still, she wanted to look strong and follow Claudia's advice. Present a united front.

When Nona met her gaze at the gangplank, all pretense dropped.

"You all right, love?" Glenlivet asked, though she knew

it wasn't, of course. Not after receiving the news that their next destination was Mene.

"Do you mean it?" Nona answered with a question. When the captain frowned, confused, she took a step back from the plank. "When you call me 'love.' Do you mean it?"

"Gods, Nona." Glenlivet looked away, to the water. She started to walk back into the ship. "We don't have time for that conversation right now."

"This is the only moment to have this conversation, actually," Nona muttered, dropping her bag on the ground.

The sound of it made Glenlivet turn, startled. "What the fuck does that mean?"

"I won't go back to Mene for someone who doesn't love me, Glenlivet," she said matter-of-factly, her jaw tight. "I simply won't."

She did call her 'love' sometimes. Her chest would jump at the word, fear gripping her for a second before she realized Nona hadn't dropped dead the second she said it. The relief was immediate, and guilt would come right after. She averted her eyes every time, to make the word seem casual, a nickname and nothing else. Perhaps doing that would stop the universe from noticing how much she meant it. Perhaps that would save her.

She knew it hurt Nona every time she changed the

subject or avoided it entirely. But she had stayed every time, loyal to the ship, the crew... and her. Glenlivet felt tears threatening to spill, gratitude so strong the docks went out of focus. She blinked the tears away. "You don't have to get off the ship in Mene. You can stay back with Marina, you know she also hates it there."

Bargaining.

"You're unbelievable," Nona said, breathless. Glenlivet knew she was crying but she refused to look. She refused to face her. "You can't even look at me!"

The captain forced herself to stop watching the water. Glenlivet stared at Nona now, her hand resting on the purse that held her letters, a comfort while she felt adrift. Nona's eyes focused on her hand for a moment, and she sighed, looking down. The clatter of the crew moving around on the ship was a distant buzz in her ears.

"Claudia said you had your reasons and that I needed to talk to you," Nona started, trying to keep her breathing even. "If you just told me why, I could try to understand, but you won't even give me a chance, Glenlivet! What am I supposed to do? Follow you into the Dread Water not knowing if you truly care about me as I care for you?"

"I'd follow you," Glenlivet whispered.

Nona looked up, startled for a second before she swallowed hard. "Except you know I love you."

"I suppose—"

"You suppose? I have told you several times, I—"

"I suppose," Glenlivet started again, her voice stern and louder, making Nona grow quiet, "it's up to you. I'm leaving now with or without you." With that, the captain started walking back onto the ship before pausing for a second to add, "I won't hold it against you, whatever your decision is."

"Glenlivet!" Nona called out but received no answer.

She stood on the dark dock for a moment, in silence, before picking up her bag. Then she grabbed the gangplank and pushed it forward, so it hit the side of *The Outsider* and sank into the water. She watched the water between her and the ship that had been her home for the past eight years. The blackness of it made her dizzy.

The morning was a chilly one for Sodra, and Rommely was glad for it as the end of his twelve-hour shift neared.

Worry pricked at his brain as he watched the soldiers atop the wall making their rounds. The crew of *The Outsider* had left Sodra in the middle of the night without being followed but the guard couldn't help replaying Glenlivet's apology in his head, her warning about the

King of Rera. Nona had remained quiet while hugging him, her eyes darkened by troubling thoughts.

Because of the pirate's message of caution, he wanted to go home, have breakfast, and be ready to face anyone who came knocking.

It was around seven when the gate opened, revealing a tall man with intricate tattoos under his eyes. Rommely didn't recognize his face, but he did recognize the sigil on his uniform. The man approached him, and his gait hinted he had been injured recently, though his expression didn't show any pain or discomfort. Something about him felt off, but Rommely couldn't pinpoint what it was about him that caused him to take a step back when he got close.

"Rommely Pohmar?" the man asked, looking him in the eyes. When Rommely nodded hesitantly, he reached into his pocket. "You're expected at home, soldier. Follow me," he added, offering him a coin with the Rera-Goliath alliance symbol engraved on it.

Mydos's bird stared back at him.

Rommely swallowed and forced his voice to remain level. "If I may ask, who exactly expects me, good sir?"

The royal guard extended his hand. "Pardon my manners, Pohmar. I am Jona Ishim, at your service." Rommely doubted that, but still shook Jona's hand. "It is my king who wishes your presence. Rera's Crown, Micah Griffith."

There was still half an hour before Rommely's shift ended, but when he looked over at his partner, he nodded, allowing him to leave.

He followed Jona Ishim through the streets of Sodra as the sun slowly rose in the sky. His house's door was wide open when they arrived and someone had broken one of the ground-floor windows into the parlor. The curtains danced in the morning air.

Jona stepped aside to let Rommely enter his own home. He did so with his eyes on the floor, terrified of what he might find.

"Rom, thank the gods." Claudia stood up from the sofa, but a hand rose from the armchair, making her stop dead in her tracks.

"I will thank you to stay put," the king said.

Claudia looked at Rommely for a second before resettling on the sofa beside her son. The teenage boy was looking at the floor, but his father still caught a glimpse of his state: a swollen eye and a busted lip. His daughter, Veliah, was bouncing on Barden's knee and playing with a small ball of yarn. She had been crying, judging by the red around her wide eyes.

Rommely swallowed his anger. "Rera's king himself requires my presence. What can I assist you with, Your Majesty?"

"Please, sit," Micah said, smiling wide. "I called you here to have the whole family together."

The guard approached the sofa and sat by his wife, in silence, touching her shoulder in comfort.

"Now," the king started, clearing his throat and standing up to pace around the room. "You were seen yesterday, Rommely, greeting the pirates I'm hunting."

Claudia grabbed Veliah from Barden's lap and held her close to her chest, a protective hand caressing the little girl's hair.

"Your informants err, Your Majesty," Rommely dared, looking into Micah's eyes. "I am familiar with this crew as I am with any other that visits Sodra frequently. I wouldn't say I greeted them."

"Oh," Micah said, raising an eyebrow. "So, you hug all pirate captains when they arrive?"

One of the king's soldiers, a man with short black hair, chuckled. "I knew the Goliath soldiers in the Cluster were corrupt, but I didn't know just how dirty they had gotten."

Barden stood up so fast his legs hit the coffee table in front of the sofa. He spat on Slade's shoes. Claudia shushed her daughter when she started crying, startled by the noise, and Rommely grabbed his son, standing between him and the royal soldier.

"Excuse him, sir. He doesn't know what he's doing," he pleaded, his eyes trained on the man's hand, which had come to rest on the pommel of his sword.

"Please," Claudia begged, holding her daughter

tighter and shutting her eyes.

"Stand down, Slade. You already gave the kid a few love taps," Micah said, an amused smile on his lips. "You insulted his papa, it's only natural he got a bit feisty."

Slade cocked his head, taking a step forward. "Yeah, only natural." His hand left the weapon, instead rising to Rommely's shirt pocket and ripping it. Slade handed the piece of fabric to the guard. "Go on. Clean it."

The king watched the scene, smiling still. By the door, Jona did not mirror his expression.

The stable boy was surprised to see Nona back so soon, but he didn´t ask questions when she paid handsomely for his best horse. The mare was a brown one with white spots called Marcilla that Glenlivet chose every time she was in the Cluster. Nona rushed the ride back to avoid traveling under the morning sun. She beat the sunrise by a sliver as the Sodra gates came into view from the winding path.

It was standard procedure to always have two guards outside to receive newcomers and two inside to open the doors, as well as the soldiers patrolling the walls themselves. Nona had lived in Sodra long enough before joining Glenlivet to know this routine didn´t change unless there was a pressing reason. Because of this, when she saw only one guard outside the entrance, she slowed down, approaching with caution.

Her anxiety, which had dulled and transformed into quiet grief since abandoning *The Outsider*, came back tenfold when she recognized the one guard as Rommely´s shift partner.

The man stopped her, but before he could ask his usual questions, Nona questioned, "Where´s Rommely?"

The man raised an eyebrow at her. "Good morning."

Nona blushed, remembering long-gone afternoons when her small hands were swatted with a branch for her lack of manners and impertinence. But she wasn´t nine anymore so her face remained unchanged. She waited for him to answer, holding the reins tighter as the scars on the back of her hands started aching.

"Had to go home early," he finally said, knocking on the gate. "Not too long ago, actually. You just missed him."

"Any idea why? He never ends his shifts early."

The man shrugged as the gate started opening. "Seems old Rommely is moving up in the world," he said with a cheeky smile. "A royal soldier summoned him. He came with a sigil coin, so—"

Nona didn´t wait for the guard to finish his explanation before sending Marcilla into a gallop through the half-open gate. There weren´t many people outside yet.

She didn't care about being seen anymore but people getting in her way would only slow her down.

After racing through the streets and alleys, she dismounted around the corner from Rommely and Claudia's home. She tied the mare to a lamppost, caressing her nose as she calmed her down. "Not a sound, precious."

She peeked around the corner, watching the house and the area around it, where guards could be posted. The door was closed, as were the windows, the curtains drawn. Her eyes were drawn to the broken glass on one of them, and Nona feared the worst as she started walking, with bent knees, close to the ground.

Nearing the door of the house, she was careful to avoid being seen through the broken window. She was focusing so hard on this that her foot slipped through something wet on the ground. She bit her lip to avoid yelping as she steadied herself. With a grimace, she wiped the hand she had used to avoid falling and started moving again.

Nona had known it wasn't water by the sticky texture, but the realization only hit her when she saw the dark red on the yellow fabric over her thigh. Her clean hand rose to her mouth, eyes closing tight as she tried to not picture her friends dead. There was no sign of an injured person outside the house. The puddle of blood stretched as if someone had been dragged away.

She pressed herself flush against the wall under the broken window and tried to breathe deeply, quieting the loud heartbeat so she could listen to any sound that would tell her what was going on inside, though she didn't recognize any of the voices.

"Should we prepare the horses to follow them, Your Majesty?"

"I don't know, Charles. Can the horses follow the schooner at open sea?" Micah responded with a mocking tone that put Nona on edge. "If they left after midnight, as they say, *The Outsider* is long gone from Melende by now."

There was a pause at which Nona overheard the king's boots hitting the floor as he paced around the room.

"Tell me, boy, where are they headed?"

"I don't know," Barden responded.

She felt a cold sweat start pooling under her shirt. Barden's lies were always stiff and monotone; they had been since he was a child.

"I recently suffered an injury at sea that almost took my arm," the king said. Nona frowned, confused and nervous at the apparent change of subject. Micah's voice raised slightly as he continued: "That is obviously causing me a lot of pain. I have found that inflicting pain onto others...helps."

"Please, no!"

"Dá!" Vehlia's voice startled Nona.

Everything in her body was begging her to stand up and rush inside. She heard Rommely's pained groans, and then Micah's voice again.

"So, I ask again: Where are the pirates heading?"

"I—"

"Barden, please!" Claudia begged.

"Mene. They're headed to Mene," he rushed out, and everyone grew quiet before the boy spoke again: "They're going to Mene to find *The Conviction*."

Nona couldn't blame him. Still, she felt her stomach drop with dread.

"He told you the truth." Claudia sounded teary, her voice shaky. "Please, let go of my husband."

"Yes, Slade. Let go of the man," Micah ordered, and his order was followed by a thud that made Nona jump. Her eyes were wide, burning under the fresh morning sunlight. She prayed to Yrena, and she responded through Rommely's whisper, that proved he was alive.

"I'm all right, I'm all right, love. Breathe."

Nona could hear the smile in Micah's voice when he asked, "Now...why are they after *The Conviction*?"

11

Mama Ruth's Home

"She could afford better lodgings with how famous she is, don't you think?" Tavia grumbled, pulling her leg out of the sucking wet sand.

Cave Island was named appropriately. The tiniest of the land masses that made up The Sodra Cluster was covered in cave formations and underground tunnels that wove together in a dark, confusing maze of limestone and dolomite.

Cecilia walked behind her captain, splashing the bottom of her skirts with every step. The uneven mushy ground at the mouth of the cave made it impossible to avoid.

"She likes to stay away from people," Cecilia said, shrugging. "Can't say I blame her."

"What I don't understand is why they can't just give us clear directions for once," Ashlin complained, walking behind Cecilia. "What? Just because we're dead we have to find out shit through cryptic riddles?"

Tavia laughed, holding up the piece of paper to read it again.

Cave Island has a mouth painted with red rain.

"Captain!" Cecilia called out, staring down a narrow crevasse between two tall rocks. There was a mound of sand that had been kicked at some point, and the entrance of another cave was clear.

"That has to be it. Good catch," Tavia said, blinking at it.

Ashlin followed their gaze, then declared, "No," she said and turned to walk away.

"Ash," Tavia called out, grabbing her arm so she wouldn't go far. "I don't see any others that fit the description. Do you?"

Ashlin knew she was right, but that didn't stop her from groaning when her captain and first mate started walking toward the grotto. Above the passageway, the stone was stained rust red in long streaks. The opening itself wasn't wide, barely big enough for an adult to crawl through it.

"It seems to get wider the deeper it goes," Cecilia commented, sticking one arm inside the cave to feel the walls of the tunnel.

This information didn't make Ashlin breathe easier, but she watched Tavia kneel next to the mound of sand and touch the stone, scratching at the red paint with her blackened nails.

"I'll take the lead," Tavia said, sitting on the floor to go legs first. She rubbed her face, wiping away sweat from under the nose ring that hung above her lip, "Ash, I know you hate tight spaces. You can stay out here and guard the entrance if you prefer."

Ashlin shook her head, still looking at her captain. Tavia had changed slightly while taking the shortcut to Cave Island. Sinking *The Cursed Eel* was risky every time. Their lives weren't in danger but there was no telling what Edbris would take as payment.

During this shortcut, Tavia's right eye and eyebrow had been covered by decaying barnacles. Smaller ones littered the left side of her jaw, creeping up toward her mouth. Ashlin had pushed for sinking, eager to get to their objective faster and avoid the trail growing cold. Tavia had agreed, of course, but she had been the most affected by the shortcut. She couldn´t help feeling guilty. She wouldn´t let her go into that cave without her to watch her back.

"I´ll go in right after you," Ashlin said, starting to sit down on the wet sand.

Cecilia glanced at Tavia, sharing a fond smile before the captain turned and faced the red-painted mouth again.

Tavia slipped inside easily, though everything in her mind screamed to not go into the dark. The crablike crawl down the tight tunnel was unceremonious and uncomfortable. Ashlin and Cecilia had a rougher time of it, their wider build making their claustrophobia much worse. Their muscles scraped against jagged points on the walls before the channel opened up slightly, allowing them a breather.

"It feels steeper from here," Tavia warned, feeling the floor with her foot.

Cecilia let out a shaky breath, nodding despite knowing it was too dark for anyone to see.

"How steep?" Ashlin asked, imagining a sharp drop.

"It's not that much of a difference, just hold on tighter to the walls," the captain said. "And don't panic."

It seemed like hours before the tunnel opened more, and took a turn. Tavia managed to kneel in the wider space. Her head grazed the roof, but she welcomed the position change after being tense the whole way down.

Cecilia sighed in the dark. "Torch?"

"Please," Ashlin answered, sounding desperate, and the fire lit the cavern with warm light.

Blood was smeared across Tavia's cheek from a small cut to the barnacles on her eye, but she didn't seem bothered by it. "Tunnel continues over there." She motioned to the passageway that luckily seemed to maintain the size as the cavern they were in. "I have a feeling we´re close so when we find her, stay alert but calm. She probably doesn´t want to be found considering—" She gestured to her surroundings.

"You´re right. Go away," said a voice ahead. It was calm, without a trace of hostility in it.

"Not happening," Cecilia said, straining to continue moving. Her body was sore, "We´ve come this far."

"We´re sorry to bother you," Tavia said, taking the torch, "but we desperately need your help. It´s an emergency."

She expected the tunnel to widen further in, maybe turn into a room where they would be able to stand. There was simply no room. It made the pirates nervous, not having the ability to defend themselves if necessary. The cavern led to a dead end.

Slumped against the wall with her bare feet stretched before her was the mage, staring back at them with wide eyes. "Hardly an emergency," she said, still in that neutral calm voice. "You´ve been dead for years. You can stay dead a while longer."

Mama Ruth looked to be around thirteen years old. She had waist-length black hair and a nasty burn scar that covered her left shoulder and most of her left arm. Her shoes were placed neatly beside her, along with a cracked handheld mirror. Her hands were busy shuffling a deck of playing cards.

"Please," Tavia said, sitting in front of her.

"I'm tired today." She shrugged. "Come back tomorrow."

"You'll be gone tomorrow," Cecilia said, frowning at the kid.

Ruth's hands stilled, and she looked at the first mate with a smile. "Smart."

Cecilia ignored the surprised tone in her voice, but Tavia took the bait: "We haven't made it this far as pirates by being stupid."

The girl's eyes traveled back to the captain. "That's debatable. Only a very stupid person would defy Edbris. Your existence disrespects the order."

"We can't even remember what we did wrong," Ashlin muttered, leaning against the stone. The wall was moist but Ash was so tired she didn't mind it.

Ruth nodded, that odd smile on her lips once more as she finished shuffling and picked a card. Her eyebrow raised as she put it back on top of the deck. "Guess your card, Captain."

When Tavia looked down at the kid's hands, she was surprised to see the playing deck had changed to an old tarot one. Cecilia looked at Ashlin briefly, an incredulous look on her face.

"We don't want our fortunes, Mama Ruth. We just want to rest."

"I am no executioner, Tavia. Now guess. Or leave."

The torch seemed to dim as the captain took a moment to think. She wasn't all that familiar with tarot. A few of her crewmates had a deck of their own but none of them were mages. She searched her brain, trying to remember any of the names to humor Ruth and gain her favor.

"The devil?"

"Are you asking me or telling me?"

"Telling you," she said with a nod.

"Wrong," the kid said curtly, taking the card and shoving it under her shirt without allowing the pirate to see it. Before Tavia could protest, she had picked another card from the deck, now looking at Cecilia, "Guess."

To Ashlin and Tavia's surprise, Cecilia answered without protest or hesitation. "The Hanged Man."

There was a pause as Mama Ruth squinted and turned the card to let them see it, "You're good at this," she said. "Thanks for playing."

"Are you going to explain what it means?"

"No."

At that, Cecilia turned around with an aggravated sigh and started her way back through the tight space. "I knew this was a fucking waste of time."

Mama Ruth didn't seem phased by this display. She grabbed another card and looked at Ashlin.

Tavia turned to look at her friend, who had been so convinced the mage would help them. Ash shook her head before answering: "Death."

"So predictable." Ruth rolled her eyes though the playful smile stayed in place while she turned the card around. "But you´re right, of course."

She placed the Death card onto the deck and started shuffling again, now ignoring the two women. Tavia stretched her back as much as she could in the cramped space. She was feeling the pull, but she wouldn't leave without some direction.

"We´re short on time, Mama Ruth. We played your game, now play ours."

The kid put the deck of cards away, "We have."

"No," Tavia grunted out, her voice higher and echoing in the cave, "You didn´t show me my card. You haven´t been playing fair."

Mama Ruth followed the movement of her hand with her eyes, "You would cut down a child for your answers?"

Tavia looked down, realizing she held her sword, the blade now exposed. She shoved it back inside its scabbard, a deep burst of shame swaying inside her stomach.

The mage watched her, her face calm. She reached under her shirt, retrieving the captain´s card and looking at it.

"You can keep it," she said, and threw it in Tavia´s direction. "As a reminder."

The captain caught it mid-air, a sting of pain striking her side as she did. A woman with blue hair and decrepit wings stared back at her. She held two cups, pouring a red liquid from one into the other. The receiving cup was overflowing, creating a bloody sea at the woman´s feet.

"Temperance…" Tavia read, frowning.

"As I said"—Mama Ruth nodded— "you can stay dead for a while longer. You´re missing a crew member. Wait."

"They're ahead of us again," Markl commented as they exited the house.

"Doesn't matter. That might actually help us this time around," the king said, pushing him to the side. Micah walked away, his soldiers filing out of the house and following him. The king put a gold Reran sigil in Charles´ hand and a purse full of coins. "Get a new ship at North Port. As different from ours as you can find."

Markl stayed by the door, confused for a moment. "What?"

Jona was the last out of the house, closing the door behind him. "If the pirates arrive at Mene's port and see no sign of our ship, they'll feel safe," he muttered, patting the young man's shoulder before walking away.

His steps were still affected by his injury but it wasn't long before he caught up with the group.

Markl looked down at the cobblestones. Charles had been ordered to get rid of the body a few hours ago but the kid's blood was still there.

That's what happened to people that felt safe around the King of Rera.

Nona watched the soldier at the door from around the corner, kneeling on the ground. His eyes focused on the puddle of blood for almost a minute before he seemed to wake up and rushed to join the others.

Her options were limited, and none were ideal. She finally stood, dusting herself off. The sounds of the waking town were finally starting and one of the windows in the neighboring buildings opened. She needed to move or she'd be spotted.

She approached the door, raising her hand to knock on it when Rommely's voice reached her through the broken window.

"We knew it was dangerous to protect them," he said, in a rough voice that made Nona realize that while he was alive, he was probably injured. "They'll understand we had no choice."

"No choice?" Barden replied, anger laced with every

word. "Nona is our family, and we just sent a pack of wolves after her."

"Go to your room. Now. And take Vehlia with you," Claudia said, her voice stern.

"I'm not a fucking child anymore. We need to talk about this!"

"Don't swear at your mother."

"Father."

"Barden!" There was a beat of silence, followed by a sigh. "You're not a child anymore. You're right about that, which is exactly why we need you to behave like an adult and take your sister to bed while your mother and I clean up here. Go."

Nona didn't stick around to hear the private conversation Rommely and Claudia would most likely have while their son was gone.

She did understand. And she wouldn't knock on their door and put them in danger again right after that scare. Claudia would patch Rommely up and they'd get on with their lives just fine without her meddling. Nona walked in the opposite direction the king had taken. It would slow her down but she couldn't risk being captured while she was alone. She needed freedom of movement to warn Glenlivet.

She didn't owe anything to her captain, she knew that. No matter how much she still thought of her as her captain, the image of Glenlivet above her, eyes shiny and imposing as she refused to answer her questions, made her want to abandon it all. Let her deal with whatever web that spider of a king was weaving.

All the same, she mounted Marcilla, petting her neck to calm her down and directing her to back up in the tight alley. The rest of the crew would go down along with Glenlivet. She sighed, also knowing that if the captain got captured by the crown, the punishment outweighed Nona's anger. As much as she wanted to shake the woman, she didn't deserve to hang.

Nona did everything in her power to avoid thinking about Mene as Marcilla trotted toward East Port. If she left the harbor today, she would arrive around the same time as the king and before *The Outsider*. Hopefully, she would be able to warn them before Micah could get to them.

The weather did not match the spirit of *The Outsider* as they finally left Cluster waters after a week and a half of sailing. The sun was clear in the sky, though descending rapidly as the day came to an end. The clouds were a fluffy white, moved by a soft breeze.

The ship was deadly quiet. Marcya, Mel, and Julian were helping Blue prepare for dinner, whispering when they needed to communicate. The surgeon's eyes were puffy and red from crying, and Julian kept giving her worried side glances as he took plates and cutlery from her.

Roma, on the mage's request, was shuffling her tarot deck. Hers was a new one, unlike Celeste's, which bore the marks of a well-loved set that had seen better days. The movement of her hands was clumsy and she bit the inside of her cheek in concentration. She kept peeking up at the woman in front of her, looking for pointers, but Celeste stared at the cards with that far-away look that had stayed on her face since her vision in Claudia's kitchen.

"Are you asking something specific?" Roma whispered as she finally spread the deck on the table. She allowed her mind to clear and open, reaching over the cards and picking three of them, thinking of the mage sitting in front of her. A headache was forming behind her eyes.

Celeste blinked slowly as the cards were chosen and turned in front of her, revealing their message. She cocked her head, then looked up at Roma who was waiting for her to speak. She felt a whirring under the patched-up eyelid, a sensation similar to a swarm of bugs crawling and moving under the thin skin.

The Hanged Man, Death, and Temperance.

"What do they mean?" Danielle asked, curiously eyeing the art on the cards. "They don't look like good news."

Roma smiled at her softly, "They look scarier than they are. I'd say they're pretty neutral, actually." She looked at Celeste again. "Right?"

"Supper is ready," Blue announced before Celeste could answer, joining the table with a black pot in their hands. "Marina, would you tell Glenlivet, please?"

The siren nodded and left the galley in silence. The entire crew gathered to get their share of the meal, sitting where they could in the cramped, dark kitchen.

When Marina returned alone, shaking her head at Blue, the group started eating in silence.

The captain hadn't left her quarters since Gale's meltdown. The strategist had been the first to notice Nona's absence around mid-morning and hadn't taken it well when Glenlivet informed them she was aware of it. It wasn't a mistake. The abandonment had been intentional. Sudden. Everyone had watched as Gale pushed Glenlivet away, screaming in her face. They had all watched in silent dread, how the captain took all the insults and blame with her hands behind her back. Eventually, the strategist ran out of air, gasping through their tears, and finally fell silent. They had disappeared into the hold, exhausted, nonverbal once more. And the captain disappeared into her room, silent as well.

"She didn't eat lunch when I brought it to her either," Blue commented. "I'm worried about her."

"Me too," Roma muttered, putting her own bowl down.

"She´ll recover," Marcya said sharply, though she started to whisper again when Mel shushed her. "And Nona will fucking come around, too. She just didn´t want to go back home."

The surgeon shook her head. "I don´t think it´s that simple."

"What´s not simple?" Marcya said, chewing a piece of potato she had fished out of the broth. "Both of them are stupid and won´t communicate about the real shit that bothers them. It is fucking simple."

A sad chuckle made its way around the group, Marcya´s colorful language lifting morale for a few minutes. The exception was Celeste, who moved her spoon inside the bowl for some time, not actually eating. Her eyes were unfocused and far away, the three cards she had pulled still on her lap.

"Something on your mind?" Roma asked, rubbing the woman´s arm to get her attention.

The mage turned to the girl, confused before smiling and shaking her head, "Oh, just…" Her sentence trailed off, unfinished.

Roma shuddered, though she wasn't sure why.

Danielle watched Gale, who sat the farthest away from everyone. The crew was trying their best to keep their voices low, to avoid overwhelming them, but they still needed space to process it all. Their leg bounced against the chair they sat on, and their eyes stared straight ahead, through the open kitchen door and across the deck, toward Glenlivet´s closed door.

The strategist stood abruptly, abandoning their meal, but grabbing Glenlivet's untouched bowl of food on their way out. They walked across the deck with it and knocked two times, as was their custom. Glenlivet didn´t answer, but Danielle watched Gale open the door anyway and step inside, pausing for a moment before closing the door behind them.

12

COLD PLUNGE

East Port was the biggest sailor spot in Sodra, combining pirate activity with official Council-approved commerce.

It was Nona's best chance of finding passage to Mene, either working or paying.

The dockmaster was nowhere to be found, but a Mangrathian sailor had been kind enough to point her to Ynos's Pride, a pub where the man usually spent his time.

"I wouldn't interrupt his drinking, though. Gralin has a temper, he does."

Nona ignored the curious look on the sailor's face as she nodded and made her way to the place anyway. She appreciated the heads-up, but it did her no good to heed the warning.

Ynos's Pride was a joke. No bar on The Sodra Cluster was touched by the god of nobility. And there was no honor within the pub's walls. The stag held its head high on the sign over the door. Nona looked at the bite someone had painted over the side of Ynos's symbol and rolled her eyes as she pushed the door open.

The inside was dark, the air fogged with pipe and cigar smoke. The bar was at the far end of the room and Nona felt the sticky floor under her shoes as she made her way there. For a sick moment, the image of her father pulling her by the kraken necklace flashed in front of her eyes.

"What would your mother say if she saw the tainted girl you've become?" His voice resonated in her mind, overshadowing the drunken screaming and singing all around her.

She smiled as she reached the long wooden bar and pushed a man off of his stool to use it. She climbed up it and onto the bartop, kicking away an empty glass, and turned to watch the crowd. It was no use. With everyone moving, scrambling over each other, and the smoke, she couldn't spot the dockmaster's uniform.

"Hey! Get down!"

She looked down at the barkeep who was screaming at her. The man held a bottle in one hand and a dirty glass in the other. She bent down, grabbed the bottle, and ignored his protests. A few eyes were already on her, but the whole pub paused and turned to watch her when she threw the bottle on the ground.

Her father would burn the town all over again if he could see her now.

"I'm looking for Gralin Lightfall! Dockmaster!"

Glenlivet lay on the floor, watching the swaying stained-glass oil lamps. The knocks on the door made her jump, but she didn't move.

The door opened anyway, and she watched an upside-down Gale walk in. The strategist paused, looking at her with a raised eyebrow before sighing and closing the door behind them.

"You should be resting," Glenlivet said, her voice soft and merely a whisper, before looking up at the lamps again. "I know this week was rough. I'm sorry."

She wondered when she would stop having to apologize for her fuck-ups.

Gale lightly kicked her arm to get her to look at them. When she did, wincing, they shoved the bowl of food toward her.

"I'm not hungry."

The strategist sighed, rolling their eyes, and sat on the floor with the captain. They put the food away and took their notebook, hands slightly shaking. They wrote quickly and placed the small book on her chest.

You're making everyone worry. Eat.

Glenlivet returned the notebook after glancing at the words, sitting up and grabbing the plate. "Only because you asked so nicely," she grumbled and was relieved to see a tiny hint of a smile on Gale's tense face.

They watched the captain eat for a moment as they fidgeted with the pen and journal. Gale opened it again, scratching their thoughts down onto the page.

I shouldn't have screamed at you in front of the others. It was disrespectful. I would understand if there was a punishment for insubordination.

"Shut the fuck up, Gale," Glenlivet scoffed when she read it, pushing the journal back toward them. "I've never done that shit and I'm not about to start. You were well within your rights to be upset."

They stayed silent as the captain finished her supper. She stood, wiping her mouth, and putting the bowl on top of the desk. She reached under the table for a bottle, and she opened it, then threw the cork out the porthole.

"You warned me this would happen," she said, merely a whisper. "I should have listened, I just—I couldn't."

Gale stood to join her, writing in their journal.

She would have understood.

Glenlivet nodded, sucking her teeth before answering. "She probably would have, yes." There was a sadness to her tone that Gale couldn't decipher. They cocked their head to the side, prompting her to explain. The captain looked back at them and sighed. "I don't think I deserve her understanding. It was easier, I guess, to just hide her."

Glenlivet touched the letters hanging from her hip, the pads of her fingers caressing the green ribbon that held them together.

Gale nodded, looking away.

"I hate when you make me admit deep shit out loud." Glenlivet forced out a chuckle, taking a sip from the bottle.

Lightfall had tried to help, as much as a drunk dockmaster could.

He was a short, wide man with short white hair and bushy eyebrows. His uneven beard had crumbs in it and Nona didn't dare guess how long they'd been there.

Gralin had led her out of Ynos's Pride and onto port, stumbling. More than once, Nona had to push him to make him walk straight. He had checked his books and pointed her in the direction of several ship captains who were to leave that afternoon toward Mene. To her annoyance, many of these ships were Council-approved. Only two pirate vessels. She started with those.

"I'm willing to work for passage. I have experience, and I—"

"I know the experience you have, lass," one of them said. "I ain't risking it. Edbris sinks ships that hire women."

"You know damn well that is a Goliath lie," she spat, snarling.

The man shrugged and walked away.

The other pirate captain was kinder, though he also recognized her. He shook his head. "I would take you. We honestly need an extra hand, but…" He sighed. "My ship has an agreement with *The Conviction*. None of us want to anger Elric. And last I heard, your captain wanted him dead."

Nona tried her best to remain neutral, but she couldn't stop the quiver of her top lip. "She's not my captain anymore. I won't bring you any trouble."

"And why are you headed to Mene exactly, Cromwell?" The way he rolled her last name out of his mouth let her know he was aware of her father's role in Old Mehri.

She couldn't bring herself to lie. "I'm headed there to warn Glenlivet of upcoming danger."

The captain nodded, sighing again. "Sorry. I hope you find your way there eventually but it won't be with me."

"I understand," she grumbled, walking away.

She didn't have better luck on the legal sailor vessels. Most of them weren't willing to have a pirate aboard, no matter how much she insisted she wasn't affiliated with any pirate ship anymore. The one crooked captain who seemed open to it was only willing for an amount of coin she most certainly didn't have on her.

A full day wasted.

To her surprise, the tavern in the main floor of the nearest inn was almost entirely empty. Soft music filtered out of the corner as a woman played an old piano. She missed a few of the notes, the musician's attention not fully on the keys. Her eyes kept drifting to the two patrons sitting nearby.

Nona paused, also taken aback by their presence.

"Cromwell!" Cecilia said.

She waved back, taking a few hesitant steps toward their table, but paused when Tavia turned to watch her.

"Gods, what happened to you?" she blurted out, an expression of disgust on her face. She shook her head, re-composing herself. "I'm so sorry, that was so rude, I just—"

"It's fine," Tavia said. "You're not the first to give me that look and you won't be the last. Please, join us," she added, motioning to one of the empty chairs.

"If that's all right with your mage, of course," Cecilia said with a sly smile and a look to the door, clearly waiting for the rest of Nona's crew to walk in.

Nona sat in the chair between them, still looking at Tavia curiously. "She's not with me..."

"Oh?" the captain said, raising an eyebrow.

"I left *The Outsider*, actually."

"Oh," Tavia repeated, frowning this time, "What about your girlfriend?"

Nona cocked her head, trying to find the words. She heard a thump from underneath the table and Tavia winced, looking at her first mate. "Ow! That hurt, bitch." She rubbed her shin, biting her lip.

"It's all right," Nona said, an amused smile making its way to her eyes. "She just... had a lot she wasn't ready to tell me." She scratched her neck, under the thread that held the kraken.

Cecilia smiled. "If you're not all right with secrets, I don't know if we're the best company, Cromwell."

"Nona. Please," she begged, tired from being called her last name all day. "I was actually wondering where you're heading next."

Tavia put her tankard on the table and wiped her mouth. "We don't have a specific place in mind yet. We've hit a dead end."

Cecilia chuckled at that, as if it was a sick joke, and then turned her head to Nona once more. "Why were you wondering that, dear?"

As Nona answered, Tavia found herself distracted,

watching Nona's chest rise up and down with every breath. She had a slight blush on her cheeks and ears and a small scar on her wrist. A small friction rash was growing under the thread of her necklace, where she had scratched. She was alive. When Nona frowned at her, Tavia realized she hadn't heard a word she had said.

"I'm sorry, what?" she stammered.

"She's interested in going to Mene, Tavia," Cecilia said, side-eyeing her. "I was just telling her we might be heading there to check out The Page Turner Dome."

"And I'm willing to pay for passage, or work, of course," Nona added, quickly, looking at the captain with pleading eyes.

Tavia took her meaning, looking away and down to the table surface. "You're barking up the wrong tree, Cromwell."

"Tavia—" Cecilia started to say, sternly, but the captain stood, taking the tankard with her.

"I'm going to get a refill," she said. "And I won't hear another word about it."

Mama Ruth's words replayed on the captain's head: "You're missing a crew member. Wait."

She wouldn't do it. The last person to join the crew had been Derya. And her addition, almost nine years ago, hadn't been planned. No other unsuspecting stranger was allowed to set foot on the ship and become one of them. She would not change that now, even if it doomed them to sail forever.

Nona laid in bed staring up at the ceiling. The mattress was lumpy and the linens didn't smell pleasant but even if it had been a bed in a royal palace, she wouldn't have been able to rest. After Tavia had refused her, she hadn't stayed around to drink with them. There was no point, and she needed to think.

The one small window in her room was too high for her to see through it, but the sky was a deep blue already, almost black. She sat up in bed, looking over at the bedside table holding a few of her rings and her necklace. She stared into the kraken's eyes and wondered why the hell she was asking for permission.

She stood and put her jewelry back on, then her shoes. She threw her bag over her shoulder and walked out of the room.

"You're leaving already?" asked the sleepy innkeeper behind the bar when he saw her come down the stairs. He rubbed his eyes and looked at his pocket watch. "You're not getting your money back!"

Nona didn't answer as she slammed shut the main door. The warm air of the night enveloped her as she walked down the steps of the entrance and down the street toward the harbor. The ships she had asked about throughout the day had already left, taking advantage of the good afternoon weather.

She looked across the line of ships moored closest to the dockmaster's cabin, then beyond them. Away from the port, far enough to avoid paying for a spot and the security Lightfall and his workers could provide, was *The Cursed Eel*.

Its dark sails were barely visible in the night, but a warm light was visible in the captain's quarters. She squinted, trying to see the faint movement on deck. The shadows of the crew didn't seem to be resting, instead hard at work.

Nona rushed to the edge of the docks, where the rowboats were tethered. She was leaning down to undo the knots on one of the ropes when she heard a pistol being cocked behind her.

"Don't."

Nona straightened up, her hands up to show they were empty, and turned to face Gralin Lightfall. He eyed her with a frown, his Council-appointed pistol still pointing at her.

She took a deep breath. "I need to get to *The Cursed Eel* before they leave."

"Ain't happening on one of my rowboats."

"I don't have time for this, Gralin!"

"And I don't have the patience. I suggest you find

another way."

Nona glanced toward the ghostly ship, biting the inside of her cheek. Someone already stood by the helm.

Gralin started speaking again: "I'm all for offering spots on my port to you pirates but you won't make me—Wait! Wait! What are you *doing*?"

Nona took a running leap and dove right into the inky black water, mentally cursing all the while. A freezing pain locked her legs and arms as she touched the rocks near the docks' wall. The water was never this cold around the Cluster, not even in the winter months. Panic gripped her throat as she failed to find the surface. She screamed underwater and started swimming forward, with as much direction as she could muster in the dark.

Her head finally broke the surface and she opened her eyes, gasping for breath. *The Cursed Eel* was moving slowly and she was halfway there. Nona started swimming again, her skin growing numb, though the cold wasn't as stinging anymore. She could vaguely hear the dockmaster hollering in her wake.

"Tavia!" she screamed, water rushing into her mouth. It froze her throat, making her dizzy. Her muscles were rigid and she felt heavy.

She had grown up in Old Mehri, by the beach. She swam great distances every day to collect sea urchins and starfish as well as seashells. She was a very skilled swimmer; even fully clothed and dragging her bag, she should have been able to clear the space between East Port and the pirate ship with ease. Something was very wrong.

"Tavia! Take me to Mene!" More water rushed in as her hands finally touched the hull of *The Cursed Eel*. She slapped at the wood, trying desperately to find something to hold on to, but the surface was smooth. "Take me home!"

Through the haze, she saw a person with greyish skin and long curly wet hair peering over the banister down toward her. Her expression was so sad, Nona found herself thinking of Glenlivet for a moment.

"You already started the process!" the person screamed, leaning even further toward the water. "Just let go! The ship will pull you!"

It seemed mad, but the confidence in their voice made her obey against all reason. Nona breathed deep and allowed herself to sink. She wanted to keep fighting, but she was so tired.

"Rest for now," a voice said, deep below her. She tried to find the source, but she had already lost consciousness when Edbris's mouth engulfed her.

13

AN INVITATION

The Outsider closed in on Skye's port, the southern city of Mene. Augie had announced it that morning, but it was clear to everyone already by the change in weather and Marina's behavior.

She was now spending most of her free time underwater, trying to avoid the dry hot air that made her skin flake and her nose bleed. But that was only part of it: the siren was also avoiding the captain. She understood Nona had decided to leave, but she was still angry, and the first mate wasn't present to have that anger directed at her. Unlike Gale's rage, the siren's was muted and simmered, not yet reaching a boil. Glenlivet was allowing her space to chew that emotion out on whatever unlucky sea creature she happened across.

The rest of the crew had resumed their routine, adjusting to Nona's absence with a taciturn demeanor. Glenlivet also had returned to her chores. She did her best to eat with everyone to avoid worrying them, but she was standoffish and quiet, unlike her usual self.

Half a day out from port, most of the crew crammed together into the captain's quarters to get a sense of their plans in the arid country.

"Jackeline is my only contact in Mene who also communicates with Elric, unfortunately," Glenlivet said, pointing at a circle on Gale's map of Skye.

"Wasn't Arlo your contact there?" Julian asked, frowning. He sat in one of the chairs in front of the desk, one of his hands around a glass of rum, his other hand resting on Mel's hip, who was perched on the arm of his chair.

Glenlivet shook her head. "She goes by Jackeline now."

Julian nodded, raising his glass in a silent toast. "Good for her. I was wondering when that egg would crack."

Mel smiled, playfully slapping him in the chest. Danielle, standing behind them, smiled at the sight.

Marcya was tapping her foot on the floor, arms crossed over her chest. "It's a long shot. They're friends, but Elric wouldn't have told her his plans."

Gale nodded, then looked at Glenlivet who was biting her lip, gaze fixed on the map. "I know...Even if he did,

Jackeline doesn't like me much. It was Nona she got along with."

The crew shared knowing looks as silence settled over the room. After an uncomfortably long silence, the captain finally looked up to find the crew staring at her. "Don't look at me like that." She had tried to smile, to give her order a joking tone, but it had come out sharp instead, pleading.

"Like what?" Roma asked.

"Like I'm gonna crumble!" Glenlivet said. "I'm fine!"

"It's all right if you're not," Blue said, reaching to touch the captain's hand over the desk.

Glenlivet pulled her hand away, as gently as she could. "Guys, really…I'm fine."

"You haven't been yourself the past few weeks," Marcya said matter-of-factly.

The captain sat down on her chair, rubbing her face. "Of course I haven't been myself, Marcya! We're so close to catching that motherfucker!" She leaned forward, though her smile didn't reach her eyes. "I've been busy planning. I'm excited!"

Danielle watched the woman who had given her a home despite how dangerous it was. She took a step forward, resting her hands on the back of Julian's chair Julian. "You've been working toward this for eight years. You wanted it to be perfect…" Glenlivet watched her, curiously. "Is it truly perfect without the person you started the journey with?"

Glenlivet stood abruptly. "Yes, but Laura is gone and there is nothing I can do about it, so how about we focus on destroying *The Conviction*?"

"Laura?"

The captain turned to Marcya, her eyes wide. "What?"

"You said Laura."

Glenlivet's mouth went dry. She searched the crew's confused faces before focusing on the map again. "Nona. I said Nona is gone, and—"

The letters were silent and yet so loud, hanging from the captain's belt. Glenlivet felt them burning against her thigh.

The fisherman's house was small, but all of Micah's guards crammed together on the second floor. The man had been smart enough to leave the premises as soon as Jona had handed him Mene´s crown-sealed letter. The document allowed them access to any house Micah saw fit for their purposes.

It was about three in the afternoon. They watched the crew of *The Outsider* through the windows as they prepared to disembark and enter the city of Skye.

As soon as the first pirates started down the gangplank, the king said, "Jona, Follow them. Don't let yourself be seen."

"Are you looking for anything specific, Your Majesty?"

The king shook his head, his eyes locked on Danielle, who walked with her arm looped around another young woman's arm. "Where they go, who they speak to, anything of interest. Report back." Jona's steps down the stairs were the only sound, followed by the door opening and then closing. In his wake, the king said, "We will board *The Outsider* as soon as they're out of sight. Search for anything we can use."

"I know what we can use already," said Charles, who stood by the other window. Markl turned his head to look at him, a nervous feeling rising in his throat. His shiny eyes were foreign to him. His friend offered the spyglass to the king with a shaky hand. "The siren stayed at the ship, Your Majesty. Alone."

The Page Turner's Dome was a red and orange building to the left of a plaza in a touristic area of Skye. While most of the shop matched the rest of the architecture in town, the building was impossible to miss. The glass bubble on the ceiling, decorated with iron leaves and flowers, distracted and attracted everyone who came into the hub of the city.

The place buzzed with activity. People from all over

Patriah gathered here for books of all kinds, and all documented research about both Patriah and Castiah was stored within these walls for those people to read. Glenlivet strode through the first floor toward the wide, ornate staircase, avoiding people and bookshelves. Gale and Celeste followed her, breathing hard as they struggled to keep up with her fast pace.

The second floor was dedicated to desks and chairs for studying. One of the students, buried under a pile of books and parchment, spared them a look as they walked past him, not much caring for how loud their shoes were on the marble floor.

A very modest door that blended into the wall color opened to a narrow set of stairs. They walked up the steps, ignoring the *Employees Only* sign.

The collection of plants under the glass dome was overwhelming. The humidity, in contrast to the arid air outside, only added to the sensation.

"Jackeline!" Glenlivet yelled, pushing a massive leaf out of her way.

A shattering glass preceded the voice of a woman ahead of them: "Fuck!"

Her head popped up from behind all the green that gathered on top of one of the many tables in the room, followed by her body as she stood up. She was tall, with broad shoulders, and slender but with defined, tanned arms. She looked to be in her late forties and had long, straight, lime-green hair, with matching eyelashes. Her grown-in roots were a rich brown color. She removed her large glasses, revealing squinty grey eyes and full but elegantly plucked eyebrows.

She stared at Glenlivet with a frown as she wiped her hands on her dirty apron. "What the hell are you doing here?"

Marina was practicing her knots in the hold, sitting crosslegged on the wooden floor, when she heard the steps above her. Her ears twitched at the sound. Unrecognizable footsteps on her home. Intruders. Danger.

The steps ceased and she forced her shoulders to relax, though her heart didn't. Marina was always on edge when left on the ship alone, even though she preferred it. She willed herself to feel the water that caressed the hull of *The Outsider*. She pressed her lips together and stopped breathing, in an attempt to sharpen her hearing. She wondered if she had been wrong, wondered if her senses had deceived her. She prayed it was just Glenlivet coming back for something she had forgotten.

Then she heard the steps again. She stood, dropped the rope, and grabbed her shortsword, watching the stairs of the hold.

"I mean exactly what I said," Jackeline said. The scorn and satisfaction in her voice and face were as clear as the glass above their heads. "No sign of your daddy around Skye since yesteryear."

"He's not my father," Glenlivet said, "and you know that."

"He might as well be. He raised you when your actual father was too busy drowning in a bottle and torturing people."

"Don't test me, Jackeline."

"You are the pirate you are because he willed it so, you ungrateful brat."

Glenlivet swallowed and tasted her own words in her mouth before letting them free. "Look, I understand. He paid you a fortune so you could set up your silly little dome. You feel indebted to him." The pirate captain grabbed a potted plant to look at it for a second before she finished. "I, however, don't owe Elric shit."

Jackeline raised her dirt-stained hand to slap the pirate over the head, her cheeks reddening with anger, but Gale drew a dagger before she could make contact. The woman stared at Gale, wide-eyed.

"You're not going to stab me, boy."

"Not a boy," Gale muttered, their dagger held against

the woman's side. "And I will if you put hands on my captain."

Jackeline nodded and lowered her hand. She let out a breath when Gale's weapon disappeared into their bag once more.

"You truly are scum," she dared say, returning Glenlivet's stare, "but you have good company, which is more than I can say for poor Elric. Where is your first mate?"

Glenlivet's eyebrows twitched at that but she stepped back, thinking about the crew of *The Conviction*. She had grown up being told by both her father and Elric to be cautious of them. She understood from a very young age that they could slit her throat without hesitation if she crossed them. This was a feeling she had grown out of with *The Outsider.*

"She left me."

Me. Not the crew. Not the pirate life. *Me*. Jackeline raised an eyebrow at that, catching her meaning.

"Good. She deserves better."

Glenlivet didn't protest that, turning to leave, but Jackeline's voice made her pause: "You kids know nothing about him and the life he has been forced to live!"

Glenlivet saw red, curling her hands into fists.

Jackeline took a step toward her. "He's nothing but a cursed man who is destined to leave this world far too young."

Glenlivet sucked her teeth, not bothering to look back at the woman. "I'm glad you know that, at least. I'll be the one to show him the exit."

"You need to calm down!" Celeste called out, trying to catch up to their captain as she made her way through the streets of Skye. "People are looking!"

"Fucking let them," Glen growled, though she knew Celeste was right, as usual.

They turned down a small street, less populated with tourists. Gale had kept track of all the turns and streets, enough to realize Glenlivet was running back to port instead of heading back to the discreet inn they had chosen.

"Glenlivet, wait!" they said, stopping their chase and taking deep breaths.

She stopped at Gale's voice, remembering her strategist had the biggest target on their back if they were recognized. She stumbled forward slightly and placed her hands on her knees for balance. She spat on the ground, trying to regain her composure, but she felt tears threatening to spill, her heart hammering inside her chest.

She had heard those words before. Jackeline had said them with a smile, knowing the jab would hurt Glenlivet. The librarian had no way of knowing just how deep they cut, the memory of a man in robes saying the same phrase in her ear as he strangled her. She forced herself to breathe, reminding herself that he wasn't behind her anymore. The preacher was dead, but his voice, and now Jackeline's, rasped in harmony inside her head.

She deserves better. She deserves better. She deserves better. She deserves better. She deserves better. She deserves better. She deserves better. She deserves better. She deserves better.

"She looks on the verge of a panic attack," Celeste muttered, glancing at Gale.

Glenlivet straightened up, fixing up the fabric covering her head. "I'm fine, I just... Go back to the inn and report to the rest of the crew. Tomorrow we should go out and scout the coast for any sign of *The Conviction*. I need to get something from home." The strategist touched her arm, but the captain didn't look at them as she spat, "That's an order, Gale."

She continued toward the docks, leaving the strategist and quartermaster standing together in the middle of the street.

The Outsider arrived," Ash said, sitting at the table.

Cecilia didn't look up from the papers on the desk, though her eyebrows raised. "You saw their ship at port?"

Ashlin shook her head, grabbing a few books from the first mate's pile. "No, I saw Glenlivet and two of her crew running past me in the plaza outside."

At this, Cecilia did look up. "You didn't stop her? We literally have her girlfriend in our hold."

"She didn't look happy," Ashlin said, opening a theology volume. "I don't have time to be stabbed today."

"Nona had a message for her, we should—" Cecilia started but Ash interrupted, holding a hand up to stop her. "A message we don't know. And seeing as Nona is still unconscious, we don't have anything to offer her but terrible news."

Cecilia nodded, deep in thought before Ashlin continued, gesturing to all the research in front of them. "And we have a lot on our plate as it is. All we can do is hope Nona wakes up in time to give whatever message she had."

The coast of The Red Land of Mene was unforgiving.

The Conviction was hidden away there, nestled between two tall and protruding points of red stone. The jagged rocks hiding under the surface of the water would have deterred most captains from dropping anchor in the area. Elric Omar wasn't like most captains, and his crew knew that well.

Elric sat at his desk, writing furiously in a worn-down notebook, full brows furrowed. His dark bangs stuck to the sweat on his forehead. He kept pushing them away, but it wasn't long before they fell back down, the hair too short to join the longer tangled mess at the nape of his neck.

Outside, he could hear his men at work, preparing the provisions they would need for the long trek through the desert. Their voices sounded irritated and gruff, but this was nothing new, and despite the protests, they would do as ordered. They all knew the consequences if they didn't.

The captain paused, looking at the words on the page. His handwriting was still clumsy, like a child's, but it was legible enough. Glenlivet had always been able to decipher his scribbles anyway, and she was the only reader that mattered.

"We're ready, Captain," called a voice from the doorway, and Elric looked up to find his first mate there. A man from Teraf called Liang Sūn. He had joined *The Conviction* right around the time the old captain had taken on his role, and was, by all accounts, a better pirate than Elric. A better man, too. Elric suspected that was the exact reason Liang hadn't been chosen. He also suspected Liang didn't like him much.

The captain stood, leaving the long coat on top of the chair, but grabbed the old captain's hat. As much as he hated the stupid thing, it would protect him against the burning sun.

Glenlivet forced herself to walk at a normal speed the rest of the way to port despite the urge to get home faster. The panic was climbing up her windpipe, ready to blow. She needed to read her letters and hear Laura in her mind to replace the preacher´s voice.

She cried every time she read them, and nightmares always followed, but they were a lifeboat in a storm when her heart beat as fast as it did now. Reading her handwriting forced it to slow.

She thought about knocking on the hold´s door so Marina would know she was there, but decided against it. The siren would know it was her just from the sound of her steps, so she headed to her quarters instead. Her hands trembled as she unlocked the drawer of her desk and yanked the wooden box so hard the envelopes flew out of the drawer, the satin green ribbon that held them together unraveling.

Glenlivet knelt to pick them up, feeling dizzy. A sharp scent made her stop.

The corner of one of the envelopes was in a puddle of oil. She frantically picked up the letter, wiping the liquid off of it. These keepsakes were already messy and water damaged, one of them stained with blood, but she didn't want them to become more difficult to read.

It was halfway through cleaning the letter that the captain's leg graced a piece of glass on the floor. The pain at the tiny cut brought her mind back, her eyes searching the origin of the oil. The stained-glass lamp that had been on top of her desk now littered the floor in tiny pieces. The receptacle of oil inside had opened and created the puddle.

The captain blinked, gathering the letters as a terrible sinking feeling settled inside her. She knew the lamp hadn't fallen on its own, and she knew with the same certainty, that if Marina had knocked it over, she would have cleaned up the mess.

She stood, left the letters on top of the desk, and ran out onto the deck.

"Marina!"

Her instincts kept scraping at the back of her brain with long, sharp nails. She almost fell on the creaky step down into the hold. Her scream had been loud. When Augie had screamed as a rat scuttled over his foot two years back, Glenlivet had heard it clear as day from her room. Marina was not nosey and didn´t interrupt unless strictly necessary, but she was paranoid. If she had heard her captain screaming, she would have rushed out to check on her.

She called out again as she searched the hold for the girl: "Marina!"

Glenlivet moved under hammocks and around the boxes they used for storage until she reached the messy cot Marina slept in most nights. Her shoes, a pair without laces that she had been using since joining the crew, were under the bed. One of her books lay on the floor, open and facedown, a few of the pages folded in a painful way. Close to it was a small piece of rope. A loose knot had been made in it, but abandoned before it could be secured properly.

But it was what sat upon the sheets that made her heart drop into her stomach: an envelope bearing the royal sigil of Mene.

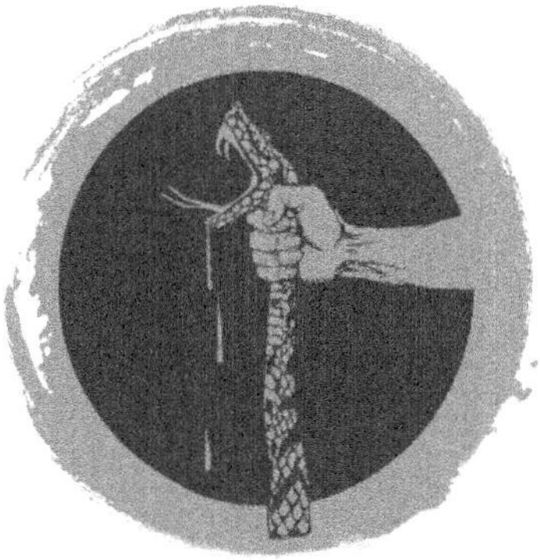

14

MASQUERADE

Derya slipped in and out of consciousness all morning, sitting on a chair by the cot Nona was in. She was vaguely aware of Tavia, coming in and out of the room, but her steps were muffled in the background. Her dreams were choppy, bright, and out of order. Images of all the sewing she still had to do that day, a greenish slush that used to be soup and waited to be scrubbed off the bottom of a pot in a kitchen she didn't recognize. Drowning while screaming into a storm too loud to allow her to be heard. Nona desperately trying to stay afloat and finally giving in to Edbris. Then those rocks again.

She was closer to them this time. She felt herself run sluggishly, the crash of the sea hitting the coastline like thunder in her ears. Derya's heart beat hard inside her chest, a pulsing behind her eyes and in her throat that she hadn't felt since the shipwreck. She didn't know, couldn't remember, why she was scared in this dream that repeated over and over again like a chanting message in a language she just couldn't translate.

For the first time, *The Cursed Eel* allowed her to grab the one letter under the stone.

Meet me at the back of the temple at sundown.

She was sure she hadn't written the letter, hadn't signed it herself. She knew it was a lie. Derya knew the terror in her body was true as she ran toward a tall building with colorful windows. Temple. Both a home and a prison. The feeling of familiarity hit her at the same time as nausea, the call from the ship wanting to wake her.

A loud sound inside the building, a scream, was the final strike that sent her flying back to consciousness, back into her dead body sitting next to their new crew member.

Nona was wide awake, staring at her.

"Queen Braya convinced Claudius that Rerans love masquerades," Micah explained, standing at the grand entrance of the ballroom. Markl stood next to him, stepping out of the way for the workers coming in or out as he watched a busy group decorate an extravagant chandelier with satiny red and yellow fabrics. The expression on his king's face was a scowl that shifted into a polite nod when people walked past.

"An attempt to amuse me, I gather," said the king.

Markl waited a few seconds, fully aware Micah expected an answer, but he didn't know what to say. He didn't know why the king was sharing these musings with him, and his instincts, animalistic and loud, kept screaming at him to keep his mouth shut and his head down. Another voice, a very human one that scared him far more, kept whispering that he should plunge a dagger into the man´s heart.

"Anything to report on the siren? Why are you here?" The king's voice startled him out of that trail of thought and he was a cowering animal again.

"She didn't sleep at all. She keeps banging her head against the bars and refusing to eat."

"So nothing. Go back to guard her, boy."

"I thought you'd want to know if anything threatened her health, sir." He swallowed hard around his next words. "She has to be healthy for cutting, right?"

Micah shook his head, turning to Markl. "I just want to know if she tries to escape or dies. Otherwise, deal with it on your own."

The soldier nodded with a slight, respectful bow and turned to leave.

"And tell Jona to strengthen security for tomorrow evening," the king added. "We can't risk the whole crew of pirates storming the mansion. Just Danielle and the pirate captain get past those doors."

If a bruised hand was the worst thing to come out of the evening, Glenlivet would count herself lucky. She swallowed the protest on her tongue as Gale continued to squeeze her hand. They made their way across the bridge, over the moat. The stench rising out of it would stay with her for weeks, she was sure. It surrounded the royal residence as protection, and as a way to get rid of waste. The captain cursed under her breath and tried to cover her nose, though the mask she wore dug painfully into her cheeks when she did.

"The smell will go away once we've crossed the gates…I hope," Danielle said, even as she suppressed a gag.

The queen's hand was closed tight around her royal sigil, the edges of the gold coin leaving ridges on her palm. Anxiety crawled its way around her intestines, stomach, and throat. The invitation from the monarchs, Claudius and Braya, was clear. Only Glenlivet was summoned to participate in the masquerade. A celebration of the arrival of the summer season, when the king and queen left their residence in Sun Capital every year. Danielle had called bullshit and had been proven right by the note from Micah that accompanied the official letter.

They had Marina, and Danielle was to use her royal sigil to be granted entry to the party, accompanying Glenlivet. Once there, she was to be exchanged for the siren.

"It's obviously a trap," Marcya had said, and the captain had agreed.

"That's why I won't be going alone."

Danielle couldn't comprehend how Gale would make

their way past the guards without their name being included in the royally signed document, and even if they did manage to sneak in, she didn't know how they would get out of Micah's claws.

The whole crew had refused to hear her out when she had offered to give in to her husband's demands to recover Marina, and now Gale walked alongside them, right toward two soldiers dressed in a red tunic, with a slim yellow trim: Mene's national colors.

"I'm sorry," the captain interrupted her trail of anxious thoughts. When Danielle looked up at her, the guilt on the pirate's face wasn't hidden by her mask.

Gale tightened their grip on Glenlivet's hand, swinging their linked arms, and shook their head. It earned them a few curious looks from other arriving guests, but Danielle smiled softly.

"I agree with Gale. You have nothing to be sorry for," she said, firmly. "Only Micah is to blame here."

The strategist nodded, lips pressed tight.

"Invitation," barked one of the guards as they finally reached the gates.

Danielle handed him the gold coin with Mydos' bird on one of the faces, the crown of Rera on the other. The guard took a quick look before returning the sigil with a slight bow.

"Queen Danielle Scott of Rera. Welcome," he said, his tone softer and more respectful now. "We've been expecting you. The king arrived about five days ago and has been incredibly helpful in preparing the mansion for the party."

She swallowed hard around the lump in her throat and forced herself to smile. "These are my companions," she said, motioning to Glenlivet and Gale.

The captain smiled, handing her letter to the guard. She carefully watched the soldier's face as he studied the letter, nodding after a bit and giving it back.

"We've also been expecting you, Captain," he said. His tone was harsher, but there was no disrespect or distaste on his face, which confused her. "I personally would like to thank you for escorting and protecting Queen Danielle on her travels."

Danielle nodded, understanding washing over her. Of course, Micah hadn't risked telling anybody where she really was and why. He had probably concocted some elaborate lie to explain her absence.

The soldier then turned his attention to Gale, who stared at their boots. Glenlivet looked back and forth between them for an uncomfortable beat while Danielle's panic spiked. The captain finally pressed against Gale's side, pushing him gently out of their stupor. They looked up, painfully meeting the soldier's eye.

"Apologies," they said, an uncomfortable smile playing on their lips. "It's been a while since I've made a public appearance and seem to have forgotten my manners."

Danielle stared at Gale. She hadn't had much of a chance to hear the strategist's voice in the months aboard *The Outsider*. But the few times she had heard it, it had been neutral, smooth, and informal. The sound coming out of her friend now was deeper, with a court-formal undertone to it that made the queen take a step back. It was familiar, in a way she did not miss. She followed Gale's hands with her eyes as they reached into their coat's deep pockets, searching for something.

Gale's royal sigil was smaller, but just as solid and real as hers. When the soldier held the gold coin up to inspect it, Danielle spotted the familiar shield of the Mangrath crown on it.

"Your Highness!" the soldier stammered, bowing and removing his helmet, revealing a full head of black straight hair. "I'm Jair Haddad. You probably don't remember me. I served your parents for many years before King Claudius hired my services. It is an honor to be in your presence again."

The soldier turned to the other guard, slapping his arm to get his attention. "Go grab the chancellor. Now."

It wasn't two minutes before the man returned, followed by a short man wearing a bird mask and a colorful coat of fake feathers.

"Chancellor," Haddad said, nodding. "We have an unexpected guest. I, however, believe the king and queen would be happy to receive him."

"*Them*," Glenlivet corrected, sharply, and Danielle didn't miss the way the captain's back had straightened, one hand reaching for the spot where she usually kept her sword. She smiled, relaxing her empty hand once more. "The king and queen will be happy to receive *them*."

Gale looked at their captain, their eyes warm and soft, while the chancellor and soldier exchanged a quick glance.

"Of course. Apologies." Jair Haddad nodded, looking away.

"And who are they, exactly?" the chancellor asked, raising an eyebrow behind the mask, which made the piece move askew on top of his face, giving him a confused and ridiculous appearance.

The strategist averted their eyes, focusing on their boots again. The bird man grabbed the sigil from the guard, while Glenlivet took a step forward.

"You're in the presence of Galear Connelly, lost prince of the Crown of Mangrath."

"Fuck!" Nona screamed as she finished throwing up green water all over Tavia´s relatively clean deck.

"I told you," Derya muttered, pity in her eyes.

The sky turned an intense orange as the sun prepared to hide away for the night. Nona had been trying to walk on land for hours now. Derya had watched her become more and more agitated as she failed again and again to leave the cursed pirate ship.

"I don´t need that shit right now, Derya!" she screamed.

"No need for that either," the girl whispered, rolling her eyes, though she didn´t take it personally. Nona was too distracted to hear, retching again. "I think you´ve overdone it. You should rest."

Nona shook her head, wiping her mouth with the back of her arm. "I slept for a month. I had plenty of rest. I don´t have time for more." She straightened up and pushed her hair out of her face. She assessed her surroundings, including Derya, who was just standing there with her arms crossed over her chest. Nona sighed. "I literally just have to reach *The Outsider*. It´s not even that far away!"

Derya looked over to the other end of the docks where the pirate ship rested. There was no movement in it, no sign of life, but Nona insisted a siren called Marina would be there. Derya didn´t argue with that. After all, *The Cursed Eel* gave plenty of signs of life and there was nobody alive on board. She wasn´t one to argue these things. And by most standards, Nona was right, it wasn´t far. But by the ship´s rules, *The Outsider* might as well be on Castiah.

"How long did it take you to be able to get off the ship, anyway? Like Tavia and the others?" Nona asked, making her way back to the gangway.

Derya didn´t answer, her jaw tense as she watched Nona take a few shaky steps onto the gangplank. She knew what would happen next because she herself had gone through it several times—so many times she had stopped trying after a while. And she still couldn't get more than a few steps away from her open prison. She didn't say that to the woman in front of her. She didn't dare tell her that Tavia and the others, as she had put it, had been traveling the seas of Patriah and Castiah since before the Empire was established and taken over the colonies.

Nona was halfway down the plank when she doubled over once more, and suddenly she was back on the main deck, next to Derya. The girl held Nona's hair as she vomited again.

"I didn't know it would be like this," she said in between gags and sobs that tore through her chest.

"I know. I'm sorry."

Glenlivet had done nothing but evaluate their plan

since it had been formed, searching for any flaws, any holes. There were glaring ones, but under the circumstances, the best they could do was hope they didn't fall down any of them. They just needed to trust that Gale's sudden reappearance, after so many years declared "missing", was enough of a distraction.

It had worked wonders so far. Word spread fast after King Claudius heard the news from his chancellor. All eyes were on the lost prince, despite the mask that covered their face. The whispers and gossip centered around them and the mysterious woman they had brought as a partner. Both a blessing and a curse. The prying looks had stopped Micah from attempting any backstabbing, but it had also stopped Glenlivet from sneaking off to find Marina.

"Dance with me," Danielle demanded abruptly as a song came to an end. She reached for the glass in Micah's hand. He offered slight resistance for a second before allowing her to take it and watched as she put it on a table behind her.

"I'm not in the mood."

"You never are, Micah," she was bold enough to say, and he whipped his head to stare daggers into her. She tried her best to show pleading with her eyes, to cover up her anger and fear. "It's my last night of freedom. Indulge your wife."

She held up her hand for him to take, a very obvious

display of an invitation. In front of the crowd, he had no choice but to take it and lead her to the dance floor. Danielle had stopped hoping for a dance without an audience long ago.

As she grabbed his shoulders, she told herself that she was playing that role again. A queen in love, and in equal power to her king. She also told herself that it was her last time doing it.

"You'll be happy to hear I solved our little issue," Micah whispered in her ear as they danced. The music was loud enough that nobody seemed to be overhearing. "If you hadn't run away like a coward, I would have been able to give you the good news back home."

Danielle stopped herself from rolling her eyes and smiled instead. "Which one of our issues have you solved, my dear?"

She felt his hand tense on her hip, his fingers digging into her flesh through her dress.

"One of the maids at the castle is pregnant with my child," he said, pulling away slightly to return her smile. "I told you it wasn't my fault."

Danielle didn´t react. She couldn´t afford to react. She felt the eyes of the room on her, the barely audible comments of nobles and servants discussing the happy couple dancing. Micah still held her, though their swaying had paused along with the music. As a new song began, Micah pushed her to keep dancing. As he twirled her, she gathered herself and looked around the room as they moved. Gale was now out of the dance floor, interacting with a duchess and her lady-in-waiting. Glenlivet had not taken another partner for a dance. She was not in the room at all. Danielle needed to use this. Buy her time.

"So you plan to replace the Queen of Rera with a castle maid. Quite below your station, I dare say."

"You dare too much," Micah growled, bringing her close to him with a scowl. "I did what was needed since you couldn't. Rera will need a ruler when I'm gone."

"I will outlive you."

She didn't recognize her own voice. Danielle flinched when he turned his head toward her. He was chuckling, his eyes bright. "And you pretend to rule on your own? Danielle! Your foolishness was always amusing, but this is your best work yet."

Danielle surprised herself with the deep desire to wring his neck and then stab his writhing body with the dagger Glenlivet had strapped to her thigh. She looked down to stop him from seeing the rage plastered on her face.

"You're wrong, anyway. As usual," he added, giving a nod to a nearby dancing couple. "I can't replace you. The Empire sees you as the queen and challenging that is too risky. My advisors recommend another course of action."

The queen looked up at him with wide eyes. "Surely you-"

"We'll compensate her as soon as she gives birth, of course. And she will leave Rera to make sure no whispers spread," he interrupted. "We will tell everyone that your little... vacation, was to ensure you didn't kill the baby again."

The pain that flashed across her face for a second made Micah smile wide. To her horror, he brought her close and hugged her, sighing against her.

"The people here..." she said, eyes frantic as she looked around, her voice slightly cracking. "I'm clearly not pregnant. They'll suspect."

Micah shrugged, pulling away with a smile. "You have managed to gain weight since I last saw you. We can tell everyone you carried small."

Danielle knew he was right and she was suddenly very aware of every inch of her body that had changed, being inspected by his eyes. They might not serve lavish banquets at *The Outsider*, but she was never afraid to eat in front of her new family, and with her new daily chores and training, she had grown stronger, too. Despite Micah's clear attempt to make her feel inadequate, she knew she looked good. Healthier, brighter. With a chill, she realized this meant that a majority of the idiots dancing around her would believe his lies, and the minority who suspected wouldn't dare to question it.

"What about the maid?"

"What about her?" Micah raised an eyebrow.

"If she doesn't want to sell you her child. What then?" Danielle asked, wondering how these months at sea managed to make her so bold. Crass, her mother would have said.

"Danielle, why do you insist on asking questions you don't want the answer to?"

15

A Desert Mission

The group selected to walk through the desert was quiet. This was the main reason they were picked, and being familiar with their captain, they were all aware of that fact.

Liang, who walked by Elric's side, matching his pace, broke the silence as the third night of their journey approached: "Two more days, according to the message."

"I know."

"We could have made a stop at Buhr for a refreshment. Akintoye is dehydrated." He whispered so the men following them wouldn't hear him, but the burning inside Elric's nose and gums returned as the ragged voice of the previous captain stabbed at the inside of his skull.

Cut him down. Cut him down for questioning you.

"We all are," he responded, hearing the weakness in his voice and despising it. He looked over his shoulder at the panting man behind them. He was the tallest of the group, muscles defined and sharpened. "Akintoye is strong, he can keep walking."

"Do I have permission to give him another sip of water, captain?"

Feed him your blood if he's so thirsty. Maybe you'll understand your place that way.

Elric didn't answer.

She stared at a long, empty corridor.

Glenlivet had slipped several floors underground, guided by the memorized map of the mansion Gale had drawn for her. She was barefoot, her heels hanging from her belt to avoid tripping and making noise. She had exchanged her gold cat mask for a basic green one and tied her hair back in a low ponytail. She had also prepared for a confrontation, getting her daggers out from under her dress skirt. She had wanted to bring Nona´s pistol but the bulky shape was too obvious under the dark dress Mel had fixed up to fit her.

But when she opened the door to the dungeons, her weapons in hand, she was met with nobody to stick them into. Gale had predicted at least two soldiers would be guarding the cell. Hopefully not more. Certainly not less.

Her heart hammered inside her chest, the sound reverberating in her skull as she ran down the hallway, looking inside every cell. Empty. All of them were empty. No guards, no Marina. She turned around at the end of the corridor, staring at the dimly lit dungeon, feeling the weight of the massive castle above her. All those rooms where Micah could have thrown Marina in. This had been one of those glaring holes in their plan and they were now deep inside it with no realistic way to climb back out.

A sound. A voice.

Merely a distant whisper, followed by a splash of water. If Glenlivet hadn't grown up in *The Conviction*, under Elric's strict insistence that she learn to orient herself by sound alone, she would have thought the echoing had come from the party upstairs. The pirate closed her eyes and stepped into one of the cells when the splash came again. She opened them, head tilted down. The dirt and dust on the filthy floor had tracks on them, signs of the ratty cot being dragged toward the wall.

Glenlivet frowned, deep in thought, and dropped her daggers on top of the hay mattress before bracing herself to move the bed. She had managed to pull it far enough that she could fit between it and the wall when she spotted it. She recoiled, disgusted, her eyes trained on the iron trap door on the floor. It was clear the lock had been broken and lay discarded and useless nearby. The stench of the moat outside returned to her mind as she stared down the pitch-black tight tunnel normally used to get rid of flooding water, piss, and feces.

She waited, hoping the sound didn't repeat itself. When it did, this time accompanied by a voice that echoed up the tunnel, she sighed, dropping her head in defeat.

"Fuck me," she grumbled, cutting the skirt of the dress the surgeon had lent her. No matter how light the fabric was, it would be near impossible to move in it where she was going. "Mel is going to kill me."

Gale rushed upstairs, Mangrath's royal sigil in hand to avoid losing it.

The strategist knew this castle like the palm of their hand, too many summers spent hiding around these halls from Claudius and Micah's constant teasing. The grandest of the guest rooms, where Micah surely stayed, was just around the corner.

A tall soldier with tattoos under his eyes leaned against the wall by the door, rubbing his left thigh just above the knee. His expression was twisted in a pained grimace. Augie's retelling of their escape from The Dusk Market popped into Gale´s mind. Jona Ishim.

They tried to be quiet as they started toward the doorway, but it seemed Celeste's account of the man's abilities hadn't been exaggerated. He didn't even look their way before straightening up and speaking.

"Go back to the ballroom and follow the king's instructions. You won't find the siren here. Micah is not stupid enough to hide her in his room."

Gale paused, startled by the use of the first name. They swallowed around the lump in their throat as they watched the hallway behind them, considering their options. The pain they had seen before on Jona Ishim's face was nowhere to be seen. The strategist nodded and walked closer to the man. "I guessed as much, but that´s not why I´m here. Micah sent me to retrieve something from his room."

They kept the lie short. Simple. Gale offered the sigil over, their hand trembling ever so slightly as they did. The soldier's fingers graced theirs for a moment, his eyes focused on the coin before he sighed and let go of it, leaning against the wall once more. Gale didn't need him to believe them, just respect their position.

Relief washed over the strategist when Jona Ishim nodded and opened the door. "Make it quick."

When they walked into the room, Gale heard the

steps of the soldier behind them and saw his shadow stretch at their feet as he stood in the doorway.

"Told you she wasn't here."

"I see that. A little bit of privacy here, Jona?" They were pushing their luck, they knew.

The man raised an eyebrow, his left eye slightly twitching, but he didn't step out or stopped his staring. "Perhaps I can assist. In looking for whatever it is the King of Rera requested, I mean."

Gale wasn't good at reading tone, especially coming from people they weren't familiar with. But the mockery behind Jona Ishim's voice was obvious enough to give them pause. They turned, looking at the man with renewed suspicion.

"Perhaps you can help by answering a question," they said, trying their best to seem unbothered by the whole interaction. Truth was, Gale was exhausted, and every word out of their mouth was getting them closer and closer to burnout. They took Jona's silence as an incentive to keep talking. "Why is Micah's supposed best soldier guarding an empty room?"

They didn't expect him to respond. The taunt was too obvious, and Gale wasn't stupid enough to underestimate the man. They still forced themselves to stare at his face, looking for any twitches in his expression, any reaction. Ishim let out a chuckle that made Gale frown. The man shook his head, and took a long look to each side of the corridor outside. After the inspection, he stepped into the room, closing the door behind him.

For a moment, Gale thought themselves dead as the king's soldier walked closer to them, eyes burning with something they couldn't decipher.

"Listen carefully, because I won't repeat myself. Pirates are no friend of my people, but neither is the Empire and its carrion eaters." The venom in his voice surprised Gale, their eyebrows shooting up.

"Your people?"

Ishim raised his hand to silence them, and when Gale closed their mouth the hand lowered, pointing toward one of Micah's bags lying unassuming by the bedside table.

"There is a hidden pocket in the seam of that bag. Inside is a copy of a pirate hunting report that your captain will find useful if you make it out of here."

Markl walked in front of Marina, to make sure the siren didn't go the wrong way by accident. Knee-deep in shit and piss, they marched forward.

"We're almost out," he said.

He sounded scared, and Marina couldn't blame him. She still wasn't convinced yet that Markl's intentions were good, though committing treason to sell a siren's tail would be a stupid decision. He would be risking his own skin for coin that wouldn´t be enough to hide him from Micah once he found out.

For the first time since being captured, Marina opened her mouth to speak, "What´s your plan?"

It startled him. Markl´s shoulders tensed as he looked over at her. She couldn´t make out his features in the dark.

"You have no reason to trust me," Markl said, "but I spoke the truth before. I´m returning you."

She shook her head. "That is the plan for me. I meant, what is *your* plan? After."

Markl kept walking, looking ahead. The silence stretched uncomfortably, and stretched again until Marina couldn´t take it and snapped, "Boy."

"It´s Markl," he said, irritated, "and I don´t know, all right? I didn´t really have a long time to plan my next move. Helping you escape was an impulse decision. I still can´t believe I´m doing it!"

"Then why do it, boy?" she asked, knowing it would irritate him further.

"I just—!" He stopped dead in his tracks, then flinched at the echo of his voice around them. He forced himself to relax his shoulders, breathing heavily. "Micah doesn´t deserve to win."

Marina stared at his back in the darkness as he started walking again with a sigh. Danielle´s opinion of the soldier had been positive, but the siren, and most of the crew, had assumed the queen's perception and standards were different from theirs—shaped by years of castle-shaped privilege. In Marina's experience, her assumptions about humans tended to be negative, but correct. Especially about royal soldiers who kissed the Empire's coin purses.

She was happy to be proved wrong occasionally.

"Remind me to not grow too attached to you, Markl. You have the smell of *corpse* about you."

The soldier laughed despite the siren's ominous warning, a bittersweet sound. "I swear that's the moat and not me."

She smiled despite herself, and after a few seconds of silence, Markl cleared his throat. "I know a man in Buhr who might take me in until this blows over."

Young. Naive.

"This won't blow over. It's treason. You'll have to go somewhere he won't dare search."

And they both knew there were only two places like that. Markl might have a shot at starting a new life out of the Empire's hand, in Castiah. But getting a ship willing to cross the Dread Water while a king hunted him would be impossible. A fool's errand. The Red Land was the realistic option. And a terrible one.

They continued walking in silence, weighed down by that knowledge when a sound made them freeze. There were steps not too far behind them, moving the water.

"You said no guards were going to relieve you until after the ball," Marina whispered, panicked.

"Nobody was supposed to!"

The sound that occurred next confused Markl so much that he grew quiet immediately. It was a clumsy imitation of a bird call. The soldier was about to ask Marina what she thought the noise was when she took off running toward it.

She found Glenlivet halfway down the tunnel.

"Captain!"

The woman hugged her tight, and it surprised Marina so much she took a few seconds to hug back. She found herself crying when she did.

"Nona is way better at birds than you," she said, sobbing and chuckling at the same time, emotions altered by her relief.

"Shut up," Glenlivet said, smiling wide as she pulled back to look at her face. "I should have known you would escape without any help."

It was at this moment that Markl made his way to them, panting from running, "Marina!"

Glenlivet pushed the siren behind her, pointing one of her daggers at the soldier. He raised his hands in surrender, but Marina pushed the captain's arm down, shaking her head.

"Actually, Captain, I did have some help."

Micah was almost dragging her now, still grabbing her forearm so hard she was sure it would leave marks.

"I knew you were trying to trick me the second that bitch showed up with Gale."

"Don't call her that," Danielle spat, and the heavy silence that followed let her know he wanted to hit her. She was glad for the people around her. Witnesses were her only shield. Micah kept walking toward the soldiers posted outside the ballroom.

He ordered something to one of them in a rushed whisper and the man, whose name Danielle didn't recall, marched down the hall toward the front gate. The other soldier, Charles, awaited orders with a familiar dread on his face that the queen recognized. She couldn't afford to feel sympathy for long though.

"Where's Ishim?" Micah asked.

"Still guarding your chambers, Your Majesty."

Danielle frowned. "Why is Jona guarding your bedroom?"

Micah didn't answer, simply tightened his grip on her arm, and motioned for Charles to follow them. To her surprise, the king didn't start leading them toward the front gate but to the back one.

"Where are we going?" she asked in an attempt to

slow them down, knowing there would be no answer. There were two guards under King Claudius's command sitting by the massive wooden door, almost dozing off. No one but Mene's king and his party used the back gate when he left the summer residence to return to the capital.

"Open this door at once," Micah ordered. "Gather every one of my soldiers who isn't guarding the front gate and tell them to find Gale Connelly. Bring the prince to me."

The two guards did as ordered, and Micah pulled Danielle so she stood in front of him. He hooked his arm around her neck, his other hand ready to retrieve his sword from his belt.

The gate opened just as Glenlivet pulled Marina up from the iron ladder and onto the bridge. They looked and smelled disgusting, a mix of mud, shit, piss, and water coating every inch of them.

The relief that filled her at seeing Danielle turned into an icy rock at the pit of her gut when she spotted Micah behind her. The soldier that followed after them was irrelevant, but Glen noted the shock in his face as he noticed Markl.

"Charles…" Markl whispered next to her.

"Should have known," Micah said, his eyes also fixed on the turncoat. "Soiled your uniform, just like you soiled your honor."

Markl took out his sword, and Charles looked away. Glenlivet counted quickly, aware the odds were not on her side. Danielle had a dagger on her, but the captain wasn't confident she would be fast enough to get it from under her gown before the king retaliated. Micah had a dagger and a shortsword hanging from his belt, easily accessible. The soldier behind them was also armed with a shortsword.

"I thought the exchange would happen in a more civilized manner, Captain," Micah said, a mocking smile playing on his lips. "But I can't say I'm disappointed."

"As far as I see it," Danielle said, bringing a soft hand to Micah's arm around her neck, "the exchange has already happened. They have the siren, and you have me."

The king didn't release her. "You forget I also have Gale Connelly. His father will be pleased to see Mangrath's heir alive and well, considering he is quite ill."

Danielle raised her eyebrows, understanding Micah's implication. If Mangrath's king was dying, Gale was the only heir, which explained the large reward for finding them. If there was no heir when it happened, Goliath would appoint a new ruler, someone easy to control, as they had done with Denea, Teraf, and Gara. Micah could sell Gale away to the highest bidder.

Glenlivet's fear was written all over her face, her hand tightening around Marina's. Grinding her teeth, the fear turned into anger as she let go of the siren and looked at Markl. "Give me your sword, and go."

"What?" Charles asked, eyes wide.

"What?" Markl said at the same time.

"That's an order: give me your sword and go. Take Marina with you."

"No!" Marina protested, startled, watching as Markl handed his sword to the pirate captain.

Glenlivet didn't look back at her. Instead, she tested the weight of his blade in her hand, then nodded. "I owe you one," she said simply.

Then she strode toward the king.

Micah smirked and pushed Danielle aside, toward Charles. The man caught her with trembling hands, his eyes not moving away from Markl.

The young man held Marina's hand, harder than he had in the tunnels, to stop her from running after Glenlivet. The siren opened her mouth to yell at her. She felt her throat constrict in that way that meant death and she slapped her free hand over her own mouth to stop the sound from coming out. If she screamed right now, they'd all be doomed. She looked back at Markl with pleading eyes.

"We have to tell your crew to prepare the ship to

escape," the man said, trying to pull her away from the scene. When the siren offered the slightest bit of resistance he pulled harder and started walking backward and away from the bridge. "Marina! We have to give them the best chance at escaping."

Just as the siren started walking after Markl, Glenlivet, and Micah met at the middle of the bridge with a clash of swords.

She knew herself at a disadvantage, and Micah knew this also, his wild smile evidence of that fact. Elric´s voice resonated in her mind, reminding her that dangerous terrain could be used against her opponent. She moved to her left, swinging her sword low, toward the king´s legs. He rushed forward and to the right in order to avoid being cut. He was agile, his years of practice and hunting aiding him. He smiled when he turned again, avoiding the edge of the bridge with ease.

"Wanted to make me fall, Glenlivet?"

The pirate didn´t answer but smiled back and rushed him, this time aiming high, at his face. Micah´s stance had faltered when avoiding the fall, so this time Glen´s attack got closer, caressing his left cheek as he tried to dodge.

"Captain!" Danielle´s voice raised in warning.

His sword slashed deep over her waist and she gasped, her eyes widening, feeling the hot gush of blood from the split skin. Her cheeks were flushed, warm sweat clouding her vision.

She blinked, shaking her head as she took fast steps backward to get some distance from Micah. The king chased her, emboldened by the sight of her blood, and she dodged his attack, circling him so Danielle could only see her back.

The queen shoved against Charles, trying to break free of his grip, but both his hands held her arms, fingers digging in. She turned as much as she could to look into his eyes to order him to free her but found him staring off into the distance. She followed his gaze toward Markl and Marina, disappearing around a corner without a backward glance.

The king prepared for the blow, and held his stance when their swords collided. Glenlivet saw her chance and she moved quickly to the left again, this time grabbing Micah's dagger from his belt.

"You—" His voice cut off as she slashed at the back of his thigh. His fist connected with her cheekbone.

"Fuck!" Glenlivet roared as the king smacked the knife away, her fingers too bloody to hold onto it.

She knew the cut had been superficial. She was being sloppy. *Unacceptable*, Elric's disappointed voice rang in her ear. In his distraction, she bolted several steps away only to throw up over the side of the bridge, the stench of the moat replaced with her own blood and sick.

"Pathetic," Micah spat out, limping toward her. He

inspected the bandages on his arm and found blood coating the material.

Glenlivet pushed her weight onto her palms, trying to get up on shaky limbs. Micah´s boots entered her periphery and she fell back down, overtaken by dizziness.

"You really thought you could just take everything from me," he said.

His words made the pirate feel like a child again, caught by the cook while stealing oranges from the hold of *The Conviction*. And just like she had done back then, she twisted her bruised body on the floor and closed her teeth on Micah's ankle. Through her blood loss stupor, she heard the King of Rera screaming.

"You feral bitch!"

The next thing she felt was the kick to the top of her head and Micah´s flesh tearing as she flew back.

Micah's leg burned, and for a second, he was paralyzed by fear, wondering if the bite of the snake would poison him slowly. He shook it off, thinking it didn't matter anyway. She was dead.

One swift move downward and he'd be rid of her, free to kill her crew at their weakest and sink her ship. Then he would hunt *The Conviction* and squash that silly rebellion brewing in Denea before it even started. All in time to go back home to an heir.

Glenlivet's eyes met his. She didn't look scared, and that only enraged him further. Raising his sword, he swung—only for his aim to alter entirely as something sharp pierced him right through the middle. He froze, suspended in time, and realized the growl wasn't wind or water but Danielle, her voice so raw it reminded him of a cornered animal.

Then the pain hit. He looked down, spying a sword punching right through his sternum, and sucked in a startled breath.

Danielle heaved the sword out of Micah, watching him fall to the bridge, and pressed the sword's point to his neck, breathing heavily as she processed what she had done, and what it meant. As blood pooled around him, he stared at her with wide terrified, angry eyes. A wave of satisfaction rushed through her.

Only a cough from Glenlivet broke their stalemate.

"Captain!" She turned to her aid.

Glenlivet was in better shape than Micah, though she undoubtedly looked worse, covered in mud, blood and worse. Her skin was alarmingly pale beneath it all. Makeup made trails down her cheeks, so she looked like a crying statue. Danielle helped her get up, putting her right arm over her shoulders, and looked her over.

"I'm going to need stitches," she grumbled, sounding more annoyed than in pain. She made an effort to open her eyes wider and smile but the effort was quickly followed by a groan of pain.

Danielle followed her line of sight to the gate and let out a breath of relief when she spotted Gale rushing toward them.

"Let's go!" she urged them, and the strategist took Glenlivet's other arm.

"Stop!"

Danielle had almost forgotten about Micah, bleeding out on the floor. Charles had taken off running to bring backup, but she wasn't sure he would be fast enough. She didn't know how to feel about the possibility of Micah dying. She didn't allow herself to wonder about the consequences for her country, which would be much grander than she could cope with right now.

"Stop walking right now! I command it!"

Half a year ago, that would have turned Danielle´s legs to stone. Today, his orders sounded far less threatening when he was choking on his own blood.

Book Three

The Conviction

16

Edbris´ Waves

The Merchant's tents were a bright yellow, impossible to miss among all the blinding red sand that Elric and his crew hadn't stopped seeing for days now. The sight should have been a relief, but knowing the man they'd encounter there, the captain wasn't sure relief was the correct emotion to feel.

"Will you explain why we're doing this once we deliver the cargo to Denea?" Liang asked, his voice rough.

Elric waited for the voice in his head to speak up, but it didn't come. There was relief again, rearing its ugly head and escaping in a shaky sigh that he followed with a nod in his first mate's direction. He wondered if he was far away enough from *The Conviction* that he wasn't able to hear him anymore. If that was the case, he might survive this ordeal yet. But this passing thought was just that: passing. Temporary. A lie to make himself feel better, to grant himself the brief respite of hope. He could still sense his old captain there, grabbing onto the top of his spine with dirty fingernails. Grinding his yellow teeth and waiting impatiently to return to the ship.

Akintoye sprinted ahead with the last of his strength, banging on the metal plate The Merchant had on the front of the biggest tent.

"Andreas!" he called out, though everyone knew the word to be meaningless. Nobody knew The Merchant's real name and he traded fake ones as much as he traded stolen and illegal goods.

It took about three minutes for Andreas to emerge. Elric didn't recognize him, but that wasn't a surprise. In the decades he had known The Merchant, he had seen him seven times and he had worn a different face on five of those occasions. This time, he appeared to be around thirty-five years old, with brown hair shaved on the sides and a short, patchy beard. He was thin, angular, save for the round, soft, and hairy belly protruding under a linen grey shirt.

"Captain!" he greeted him, though his eyes were focused on the sky and not on Elric.

He never addressed him by his name, only his title. Elric always wondered if this was by design, if he knew that was all he was.

"Your things are in there." The Merchant motioned to a smaller tent to his left. There was a rolling cart near it, and a pair of old and odd-looking oxen.

"Water," Akintoye groaned, falling to his knees.

"You'll die if you don't get it, yes" was The Merchant's response. He materialized a waterskin from behind his back. Andreas pulled the waterskin back when Akintoye reached for it. "I'm happy to provide water for a favor."

There it was. Elric approached the main tent, placing a hand on the man's shoulder. "I'll pay for Akintoye. Everyone else will pay in coin."

"Oh, good, I was hoping you would offer," The Merchant said, scratching his beard while handing Akintoye the water he so desperately needed.

Liang raised an eyebrow, watching the exchange. Then The Merchant and Elric entered the tent together; the flop of fabric behind them made the first mate flinch. He spat the bad taste out of his mouth and turned to the crew to give out orders. They needed to start loading cargo onto the cart fast so they could leave. The faster the better.

Tavia stood in front of her desk, leaning slightly on it. Her expression was harsh but Nona wasn't paying attention. Instead, she paced back and forth while biting her nails. No matter how much she chewed on them the salty water taste didn´t fade. It made her sick.

"You´re gonna hurt your fingers if you keep doing that," Derya said, her voice tentative but kind.

Nona was in no mood to regard her kindness, her softness. "What does it matter? I'm dead."

Derya tensed slightly at her tone, but shook her head and approached her anyway, pulling slowly on her arm. "Not really, and you still feel pain. So stop it."

There was something in that gesture that was painfully familiar, and Nona turned her sharp edges to Tavia. "You are absolutely sure your crew didn't find *The Outsider*?"

Tavia looked irked, but she answered, "The ship was there but we couldn't find the crew."

"What about the taverns? I gave you the list. Did your lot even search those?"

"I'm sorry, Your Majesty," Tavia said sarcastically, shoving herself away from the desk, "perhaps you've forgotten, but pirates aren't exactly welcomed in Empire territory. And even the sketchy places that welcome *our lot* don't particularly like dead pirates."

Nona snapped her mouth shut, a prick of guilt in her throat. "Mene isn't Goliath territory," she muttered. "They're just allies."

That only seemed to anger Tavia more. "You know

damn well that's the same shit! Goliath doesn't have friends. Just property."

After a moment of tense silence in which Nona refused to apologize, too scared she would crumble if she spoke, Tavia sighed, glancing toward Derya.

"Ash tried to ask around in the taverns you mentioned, but she wasn't received well. The last keeper threatened to report her."

"That's why they had to leave in a rush," Derya elaborated, eyes cast down. "I'm sorry, Nona."

Nona allowed herself to fall onto the chair in front of Tavia's desk and rubbed her temples. Sorries were all she had left.

"Here's where we separate," Marina said at a crossroads.

"What?" Markl asked, confused for a moment, and winded from running before he seemed to realize where they stood. "Oh."

"Yes." Marina nodded, pointing to her left. "That way is the fastest route to The Red Land and that way is the ocean." She pointed to her right, though there was no need; Markl wasn't looking at her, his eyes focused on the left path.

The boy considered begging to join *The Outsider,* but

found his throat dry, as if he was already trekking the desert. He couldn't ask. He thought of Charles and wondered if he would have run away with him if he had asked, but then he remembered the man's determination to get his hands on Marina and shook his head. He considered sobbing.

"Thank you," he said instead.

"Thank *you*," Marina said back. "I pray to Edbris I'll be able to return the favor one day."

Markl didn't watch her run toward port. He knew he didn't have much time. He needed to buy himself a sliver of a chance at survival.

It was dark inside the tent, which Elric was thankful for. It was the only thing inside the place that the pirate found welcoming.

It was a busy, garish place, full of items The Merchant had for sale, or had already sold and were waiting for pick-up.

"I won't keep you long, Captain," Andreas said, his voice mocking. "You must be aching to go back to *The Conviction*."

Elric ignored it, busy avoiding a figurine of a headless horse with a badger riding it. "What favor do you want for Akintoye's life?"

The Merchant scratched at his beard again, and Elric couldn't help but grimace in disgust, which only made the man smile.

"I've grown to like the fleas. They tell me much I need to know in order to survive, Captain." His smile didn't dim in the slightest as he leaned forward. "Like the fact that you'll be earning a new friend before your world burns."

Elric couldn't tell if he was joking or not, but he doubted there was truth in his choice of words. The Captain of *The Conviction* didn't earn friends. Much like Goliath, he bought his allies and awaited their betrayal with almost excited anticipation.

"The favor, Andreas. I don't have much time."

"Correct, you don't," the man replied with a conspiratorial grin. Elric didn't smile back and after an uncomfortable amount of time, The Merchant clapped, taking a step back from him. "You should be happy to be in my desert, Captain. Edbris is moving right now."

At that, Elric straightened up, his expression darkening. "You're awfully generous with your information today."

"Sit."

The captain did as told.

"The gash is going to get infected," Mel said, eyeing the dirty clothes she had cut away from Glenlivet's body before reaching for the alcohol. "Hold her down, she's going to put up a fight."

"Nona," Glenlivet called, her voice weak. "Where's Nona?"

"Easy now, sweet," Mel said, soft, empathetic eyes watching the younger woman. "She's on her way, calm down," she lied, earning a look from Marina.

The reassurance calmed the delirious captain for only a few seconds before the surgeon started sewing her like a ragdoll.

The Sodra Cluster was the closest and safest place for them. *The Outsider* left Sky's port in Mene and set sail toward the islands without anyone interfering. Marina watched Mene's port become smaller in the distance.

"It's good to have you back, kiddo." Julian placed a hand on her shoulder.

"I was only gone a few hours," the siren said, lips pursed. "Is she going to make it?"

The older man nodded, taking his pipe out of his coat pocket. "She's a tough one, that Glenlivet. She'll survive this and worse," he grumbled before elbowing Marina to get her attention. "And I know she wouldn't want you to blame yourself. She knew the risks going in."

"I'm not blaming myself," she said, though she didn't sound too convincing. "I just...I had to get out of the room. She keeps calling out for Nona."

"Glenlivet chokes on her own grip," he commented, shaking his head. "I'm only glad it's that name she's calling out and not that Laura girl. At least Nona's alive."

Nona's pacing had stopped, but she kept tapping her foot despite Derya's scolding. They had moved to the galley, and Nona now sat atop a barrel, drying dishes Derya handed to her. Tavia had put her on kitchen duty and told her to stay out of her way.

"She doesn't even sound like she wants to fix things!" Nona complained, putting a plate away.

"She only sounds that way," Derya said, rolling her eyes. "She does want to break the hold that the ship has over us. She's just been here too long to perform niceness for new crewmates."

"Trust me, I don't need her to be nice to me," Nona grumbled. "I just need her to hurry her dead ass off so I can get off this damn ship."

"Well, she's not in a rush," Derya mused, hands deep in soapy water as she scrubbed a bowl. "She's dead, after all. Most of us are."

Nona dropped a fork on the floor, and Derya watched her pick it up with a groan. She was pale, but there was a rosiness to her cheeks still, and the veins on her arms were barely visible.

"You're alive, though," Derya added. She couldn't help but think that Nona's presence might in fact be what Tavia needed to find the solution to their problems.

"Am I?" Nona asked, raising an eyebrow. "Alive, I mean."

"Technically. You were pulled to the ship because you wanted to board it, not because you died in its orbit."

"You'd think the ship would allow me to leave when I want to, then," she retorted, with a snark that made Derya smile.

"I wish, but Edbris' will doesn't work that way."

The Cursed Eel rocked violently onto its side. The tray in Derya's hands slipped and smashed against the side of the wash basin, the glass pieces disappearing into the sloshing water.

A soaked Ash slammed open the door to the galley with the force of the wind.

"Make sure our provisions are secured and sit somewhere safe, you two. We're sailing right into a storm."

***

Elric was confused. He didn´t like being confused. He

had left that tent and rejoined the men outside with all his limbs intact and the same weight in gold inside his pockets. Liang told him to count himself lucky. He didn´t have the heart to tell him that the favor wasn´t yet paid.

The three-day walk back to the coast didn´t look as daunting after all the men had their food and water, but Liang was very aware this was part of The Merchant´s charm. A false sense of security. He had heard way too many rumors of his customers dying on the way back through The Red Land, their goods returned to the tents they came from, awaiting another buyer.

"Best stay close to the coast on our way to Denea," Elric said as he watched his men pack up the last boxes onto the cart and attach said cart to the bulls.

"That´s going to make it easier for us to be spotted. I know it´s unlikely to be seen from the desert, but—" Liang frowned as he interrupted himself. "What did The Merchant say to you?"

Liang knew him too well. It irritated him. Heat crawled up the back of his neck.

"There's a storm blowing in. We should be safe if we stay close to the coastline."

"Since when do you trust The Merchant's intel? You know he always has an agenda."

The need to hit him intensified. He shoved his hands into his pockets instead and looked down at his shoes. The tips of his boots had dark dry splatters on them.

"I don't know what his agenda is," Elric said, "but it doesn't matter to me as long as we make it to Denea."

It looked like Liang wanted to say something else, but he bit his tongue. Elric stepped away from him.

The first mate didn't know The Merchant's agenda either. That wasn't of any consequence to him. The real problem, the problem that might get them all killed, was not knowing his captain's.

17

Storm Memories

"I think we should head to Denea," Marcya said, arms crossed. "It's what Glenlivet would want."

Mel scoffed. "Right now, she's in no state to make that decision. Sodra is closest and safest. She needs close and safe right now. She needs to rest."

"She'd have your throat if she heard you say that," Julian chuckled, biting on his pipe.

Mel rolled her eyes at him. "I'd like to see her try. She's not coming anywhere near my throat with her injuries."

Gale rubbed their temples, staring at the note they'd taken from Micah's room. The report which linked the captain of *The Conviction* to a faction of rebels in Denea.

"The report also says he's now associating with The Merchant," Augie said, sitting cross-legged on the floor.

"And you don't see us running to The Red Land to find the bastard."

Marina's head snapped toward him, eyes wide. Then she said, "I'm gonna scout ahead," and left the hold.

"What's up with her?" Danielle asked, an eyebrow raised.

"The Merchant has been known to sell live sirens," Blue answered in a whisper.

"Where's Roma?" Celeste asked, looking around. "She was here two minutes ago."

"Let the girl wander, she's been attached to your hip for weeks," Julian grumbled, shrugging.

"Because she's been having headaches for weeks. I'm worried about her."

Lucidity came and went. When lucid, Glenlivet was aware of the pain on her side, and of the fever was wrecking her body, making her shiver from a cold that didn't really exist. When lucid, Glenlivet was aware she lay in her bedroom at *The Outsider,* out at sea with the rain pouring down outside.

When her mind drifted, Glenlivet was in Agath, by the rocks on the beach. She moved a couple of stones aside, revealing the wad of letters they always hid in that spot, bound together with a green ribbon. She was running next, toward temple, where Laura was in danger, where Laura needed her. And a light rain was starting to fall.

Then she was back in bed, shivering and conscious of the rain pummeling the ship.

She was nauseous, but there was nothing in her stomach to throw up. The memory of waking up in Rommely's house throwing up came to her head. She missed Nona terribly.

"Nona!" she called, before remembering she wasn't there. That Nona had abandoned her. Nona had abandoned *The Outsider*. She called for her before remembering that she deserved it, and then only sobbed harder, her shaking body making the pain on her side worse.

A pair of hands held her down by the shoulders.

Roma appeared in her field of vision. Her pupils were blown, and the white of her eyes was closer to yellow.

"Roma...What's—?"

"She's lost in the storm." Roma's mouth moved, a voice she didn't recognize coming out of it.

"Nona?" she asked. Her own voice sounded weak, muffled, and distant.

"The kraken is lost in the storm and communing with the dead."

"Roma! What are you doing?" Celeste screamed from the doorway.

Roma's mouth opened again and the sea poured out,

drowning Glenlivet.

She was in temple, and two hands were around her neck. The preacher stood above her, screaming and angry. Angry that the dirty pirate had soiled his daughter. Sweet, pure Laura, who was destined for better. Sweet, pure Laura, who walked in on her father strangling Glenlivet and took a pair of scissors to his throat to save her. The blood poured onto her face. And she drowned.

Marcya, Julian, and Augie pulled Marina back onto the ship. Their clothes were already soaked from the rain, so they hardly noticed a difference when the siren's movements splashed water onto them.

"This isn't just some heavy rain," she reported. "We're headed into a storm. Water is too dark ahead to get a clear visual. Too dangerous to swim through."

Marcya turned toward the hold stairs, where Mel stood watching them, and said, "All the more reason to change course and head to Denea instead."

The surgeon shook her head, considering her options, but before she could settle on something, the door of the captain's quarters opened, swinging hard against the wood.

Mel rushed toward it. "Glenlivet! You need to be in bed!"

"No."

"Yes. Get back in there and—"

"I said *no*, Melody. And that´s final," Glenlivet said, her face ashen but determined, staring into the doctor´s eyes. "We´re going to continue on this course."

"What?" Marcya asked, incredulous. "Captain, there´s a storm in that direction and *The Conviction* is bound West. The report—"

"Gale informed me, Marcya, thank you," she interrupted, flinching and gripping her side. "I know Elric is West…I don´t need him right now. I need my first mate. And Nona is in that storm somewhere. Augie!"

"Yes." Augie stood at attention, awaiting his orders with a smile.

"Keep the course steady. Tell everyone to start securing all cargo and provisions. Storm procedure, you know the drill."

"Yes, Captain!"

"There was more water in this before! You drank it!"

"I didn't!"

"You did!"

"Get out of my face right now or I'll rip yours off, Griswold!"

Elric could hear the argument behind him, but he

tried to ignore it.

"You should stop them before they actually kill each other," Liang suggested, a playful smile on his lips as he looked over his shoulder at Griswold and Maiges.

The two men kept bickering and were now face to face, pushing each other. The group had stopped to watch them and were egging them on for a fight.

"Let them. More water for the rest of us."

Liang's smile dropped, and his head snapped back to Elric, who hadn't stopped walking. The man's voice wasn't Elric's and the first mate knew this. He also recognized the voice, though almost fourteen years had passed since he last heard it. Their previous captain—the man Elric had murdered—had spoken up through his new captain.

Liang didn't have time to process this information before Maiges tackled Griswold, the two men rolling in the hot sand and screaming.

Elric stopped walking.

Roma was unconscious on her hammock. After finding her standing over Glenlivet almost an hour ago, the apprentice's legs had given out under her and she had fallen onto Celeste's arms. Her eyes hadn't opened since, but the rapid movement behind her eyelids held

Celeste's attention and worry.

The mage sat by her, clutching her cards in shaky hands, when Augie stormed into the hold.

"Storm protocol, Celeste."

"We'll be all right," she said, raising the tarot cards so Augie could see them.

"Will *she* be all right?"

"I don't know. I've never experienced anything like this."

Augie rested a soft hand on her shoulder. "We need all the hands we can get to prepare for the storm. Get a move on, working will get your mind off of things."

Celeste stood to help Augie collect rope for everyone. The rest of the crew worked on securing loose items, but people were the priority. They all needed to be attached to the ship in storms to avoid anyone falling overboard and getting lost underwater. After hearing Glenlivet's story about Laura, they all understood just how important this rule was to the captain.

Roma was the first to be secured, the rope around her waist.

But she was already underwater.

Marina was right, the water was too murky to see through. Roma had always had trouble opening her eyes under salt water, but now she didn't feel the familiar burn. Her lungs didn't ache. She simply floated, and she had been doing so for as long as she could remember. Holding her breath.

The Cursed Eel could handle a storm.

It could handle anything. The ship would simply resurface again after it passed, but its crew would be a step deeper into oblivion, their minds deteriorating with every sinking, as if the sea took payment for their stolen time. If Tavia could avoid that fate for them, she would. She stood at the helm, doing her best to keep *The Cursed Eel* upright and on course.

She could see Ashlin and Cecilia on the deck, ordering the rest of the crew to head belowdecks.

Nona and Derya were posted by the door of the galley, far from all the secured pots, pans, and knives. They sat on the floor, backs to the walls. Nona bit the nails on her left hand, eyes tightly shut, though it did little to calm her nerves.

"I've heard of *The Cursed Eel* sinking before," she said, raising her voice to be heard over the roaring wind. "But then I see it sailing away as if nothing happened. What happens if we sink?"

When no response came, Nona opened her eyes. "Derya!"

The girl had slumped onto her side, her body moving with the swaying of the ship in the violent waves. Nona crawled over to her and got a hold of her shoulder to lay her on her back. Derya's eyes were open and wide. She wasn't looking at the woman over her, but farther away, somewhere behind her. The muscle in her jaw bunched and rolled as she ground her teeth.

Nona called her name, shaking her shoulder. She had seen people enter trances before, but never like this. Celeste's episodes tended to make her absent, but she rarely lost control of her body. Derya's breathing was ragged as a layer of sweat accumulated on her forehead, making her curls stick to it.

"It's all right, Derya, just breathe. This will pass," Nona said, cleaning her face with the edge of her skirt, hoping she was telling the truth about both this episode and the storm. She softly moved the hair away from her face and, in doing so, a flash of color caught her eye. A short green ribbon carefully braided with a lock of hair behind Derya's ear.

Her own breathing grew ragged as recognition washed over her.

The desert had a way of blinding you to the passage of time.

Markl sweated profusely, looking up at the sky to try and ascertain what time it was. The moon wasn't visible, nor were the stars. All he knew was that he could no longer see the city of Skye behind him. That should be a comfort. It meant they couldn't see him either, and that the king wasn't going to catch him any time soon. But he didn't feel much comfort as he removed his uniform jacket, exposing the shirt underneath, already soaked in sweat.

He was dizzy, and thinking clearly was a struggle. He was already thirsty to the point of feeling his lips swell up against his teeth, but he was aware that he had a long way to go before he could get more water. He was too afraid to drink even a sip.

The air felt charged and heavy. And he had a feeling he was dead, or that he would be soon. He had gotten that feeling before, when he had taken his coat of arms at Rera, to serve Micah's reign and become an ally to the Empire. He hadn't actually dropped dead back then, but he realized now that his intuition had been right. He had sold his life to the Crown and forfeited his right to die with any sort of dignity. He had ignored that sensation then, passing it off as nerves, but the sensation was back and this time he was unable to dismiss it.

The ocean was dark, but lightning illuminated its surface every few minutes.

"*The Cursed Eel* is ahead!" Marcya announced, walking into the captain's quarters.

Glenlivet sat by her desk, a bit hunched with a hand pressed to her bandages. Gale was in the middle of helping her put on a fresh shirt. Mel stood in front of her with her arms crossed over her chest.

"See? I told you," the captain said, groaning as she tucked a hand into the sleeve.

"I don't know if that means Nona is with them," Mel said. "What I do know is that you have a serious injury and should be in bed, so you don't pull your stitches and bleed all over the ship!"

"It's my ship, I get to bleed all over it if I want to," Glenlivet said, standing up. Her step faltered, and she held onto the back of her chair to stay upright.

"You can't even stand properly, Glenlivet!" Mel protested, but the captain walked around the desk and put a hand on her shoulder.

"Follow the dead," she said and limped out of her room onto the main deck.

"We have a ship on our tail," Ash said, loudly enough to make Tavia hear her over the storm.

The captain raised an eyebrow, confused, "Goliath?"

The Empire hadn´t tried going after *The Cursed Eel* in

decades. And the idea of another pirate ship following them was ludicrous. They avoided them for the whispers of decay and stench.

"Doesn´t look it. It´s a smaller vessel," Ashlin responded.

"Who the—" Tavia interrupted herself, and then smiled and motioned at the woman to take control of the wheel before jumping over the steps onto the main deck.

"Tavia! What is it?" Ash called after her, but her voice was lost to the wind.

Tavia looked like a specter under the heavy rain, the sight of her appearing and disappearing from Ashlin´s field of vision. A wave retreated and crashed over the deck, flooding it, yet Tavia barely felt it. She continued walking and opened the door to the galley, the water rushing in.

"Captain," Nona called, feeling the cold water splash against her legs. "She just collapsed, I don´t know what—"

Tavia rolled her eyes. "Yeah, she does that. I was actually looking for you."

Nona looked up at the dead pirate captain, eyes wide. "Me?"

"Yes, you. Because I think your girlfriend is chasing us."

18

Talking Corpses

"Storm has passed," Liang said, clapping his hands together.

"Good. We keep moving, then," Elric said, getting up and shoving the tarp away from his body. The sand that had covered it in the last half hour fell off of it. "You pick that up, Griswold."

Griswold groaned as he stood, throwing the tarp on the ground instead of folding it to put it away like he had been ordered.

"You got any complaints?" Elric said before the man could open his mouth. "Because I'd be happy to handle it like I did Maiges."

Griswold stopped, eyes wide, despite one of them being swollen shut from Maiges punching it on their fight.

"No complaints, Captain," he said hurriedly.

The crew silently exchanged worried looks. After the crew gathered to watch Griswold and Maiges's fight, Elric had stopped walking, hot rage wrecking through his body to the point of nausea. He had ordered them to stop. Griswold had followed the order, Maiges hadn't. Griswold got to continue the journey, Maiges didn't.

It was already dark when the sandstorm caught up to them. The wind was too loud outside the tarps for any of them to get any sleep. They were all exhausted. Liang considered speaking up, telling Elric the men needed at least a couple of hours to rest but one look at his captain advised him to keep his mouth shut.

Elric grabbed his things from the floor and started walking again, not bothering to look back at his crew. His own feet burned inside his boots.

Markl couldn't breathe. He had sandpaper under his eyelids and inside his nostrils.

Even though he had tried his best to keep his mouth shut, he could feel the grains of sand between his teeth.

He tried coughing them out, but more sand got in whenever he tried. He thrashed his body as much as he could, but there was pressure over his chest and head, though his legs were free. He felt a twitching in them, then managed to kick, but he couldn´t get his body to break free.

He was dying. Buried by red sand.

"He´s alive?"

A voice. He was hallucinating a voice.

"Shit. Pull him by the legs," said another hallucinated voice.

Markl then hallucinated a hand around his left ankle, and another around his right one. Then the pressure was relieved from his chest and he was born again, wailing, though his voice was hoarse, broken. And he was unconscious again, the pain too much to bear.

He didn't know how much time had passed before he was conscious enough to hear voices again. More this time.

"We should kill him."

"He's already half dead. We really could just leave him here and he'll die within a few hours."

"He's a Reran soldier. These rats don't die properly until you finish them off."

He wanted to explain he wasn't a soldier anymore, that he was running away from that life. He couldn't speak.

"Pick him up. We're down a man, he might be useful."

That voice was stronger. It drowned out all the others, and drowned him, pushing him back into unconsciousness.

***

"Tavia!" Screaming alone caused Glenlivet to double over in pain.

Mel grabbed her shoulder to hold her weight up, a worried look on her face.

The two pirate ships floated side by side. *The Cursed Eel* was bigger than *The Outsider*, but so dilapidated that the difference was barely noticeable. The storm still raged around them.

Tavia Bisset stood on the deck of her ship, staring down at the other pirate crew. Glenlivet looked up at her and, through her pain fog, understood why everyone feared her so much. Her long blue hair moved with the violent wind. One of her eyes was almost entirely covered by barnacles, and her veins were dark and protruding, crowding on her neck and jaw.

"What can I do for you, young Glenlivet?"

Nona sat on the deck, her heart in her throat. Hearing Glenlivet's voice again had given her whiplash. She realized now she had forgotten how she sounded. She had forgotten her captain's voice in just a few weeks aboard *The Cursed Eel*.

"One of my crew had a vision that has led me to believe you've stolen my first mate," Glen groaned out.

Her hand shot to her side, her face scrunching in agony.

Tavia frowned, then shot a look toward Nona, who chewed frantically on her fingernails and had managed to rip the skin under one of her cuticles, which now bled. Nona didn´t remember Glenlivet´s voice clearly, but she was sure she didn´t sound like this. There was pain laced with every word. She looked up at Tavia with worried, confused eyes.

The Captain of *The Cursed Eel* dipped her chin and looked back toward Glenlivet. "You´re injured?"

"That doesn´t matter. Do you have Nona or not?"

"Why do you care?" Tavia challenged, her frown deepening.

Glenlivet´s eyes widened, her mouth agape. "Why do I— Why do I *care*?" she asked, incredulous. "She´s my first mate, Tavia. I need her!"

Tavia scoffed, shaking her head and stepping away from the banister.

"No! Tavia!" she called after her, a hand on the wooden rail. "Captain, please!"

That gave Tavia pause. All eyes went to Glenlivet. Even the storm seemed to grow quieter. Nona stopped chewing on her nails, waiting.

"I do need her," Glenlivet begged, trying her best to breathe deeply through the pain. "Not because she´s my first mate. I need her because she´s Nona."

Gale placed a hand on Glenlivet´s shoulder, a comforting pressure that took her mind off of her injuries.

"She´s my best friend," she continued, staring at the back of Tavia´s head.

Nona closed her eyes, pressing her fingers against her temples.

"I need her because I love her."

Nona scrambled to stand, holding onto the banister. "That's the first time you've ever said it," she whispered, knowing full well Glenlivet wouldn't be able to hear her over the storm.

"Nona!" she screamed. "I'm sorry! I know it's not enough after everything I've put you through but I am! I really am!"

"You weren't ready!" Nona replied, shaking her head. "I understand now, and—" She stopped herself, considering if she should share this information now, if it was the right time, but it was pressing against the forefront of her mind, begging to escape: "...and I know who sent you those letters you can´t let go of!"

"What?" Glenlivet interrupted, most of Nona's words getting lost to the loud wind, "Wait, I'm coming aboard!"

"You can't!" Nona sobbed, shaking her head.

Glenlivet stopped moving, looking up to find Nona holding onto the banister for dear life, her hand bleeding.

The Captain of *The Cursed Eel* eyed the blood with a somber expression and placed her blue hand over

Nona's. The girl turned her head to Tavia, unable to find the words.

Markl woke to the sound of a door slamming shut. It took him a few minutes to open his eyes, too afraid of moving his eyelids and feeling sand underneath them.

When he finally dared to look, and he adjusted to the dim light of the room he found himself in, he realized someone had washed his face and forced water down his gullet. Whoever had done it wasn't in the room now. He was alone, in a bedroom lit by a couple of old candles on pewter chambersticks.

It was a wide space, but it barely had any furniture or decorations. A cot in the corner, with fresh bedding that wasn't neatly folded. A bar counter with shelves behind it. A rug with indents in it from where a desk had been placed for years in the middle of the room. But now the desk had been moved against the side wall, along with its chair.

He checked his body for any discomfort and only found a few scratches, perhaps where the strong wind and sand had cut through the skin. His clothes had taken the brunt of it, especially his thin linen shirt. His uniform jacket was nowhere to be seen.

He stood tentatively from his spot on the floor, swallowing hard, and took a few steps toward the desk. He stumbled on the rug and had to catch his weight on the chair. He sank his weight onto it, breathing hard, and slumped his head onto the desk.

The surface was covered in pieces of paper, books, and pens. His mother's voice was clear in his brain, a memory from his early teens: "You can tell a lot about a person by how tidy their workplace is. Your father's mind is clear, and so is his office."

Markl raised his head, searching for any clues about whose room this was. His mother was never one he turned to for advice, not since he was a kid, but now she was loud and present.

"Whoever works at this desk doesn't have a clear mind, that's for sure," he muttered to himself.

"I take offense to that." A voice interrupted his snooping, and he turned, startled, to find a figure in the doorway. "You would think an officer of the Empire would have better manners when it comes to the man who saved his life."

The man closed the door behind him and took a few steps toward Markl.

"So, what's your name, kid?" he asked, raising an eyebrow. When the younger man failed to provide an answer, the older one chuckled. "Look at me talking about manners, demanding a name when I haven't given mine…"

He extended his hand toward Markl, who was so shocked he shook it without thinking.

"I'm Elric Omar. Captain of *The Conviction*. That's where you are."

***

The fog of the memory Derya floated in was thick, but her hands were clear when she looked down. She held a pair of scissors. They were clean. For sewing. And then she was plunging them into the preacher's neck. Over and over again.

She should feel guilty. She wanted to feel guilty. But she didn´t. Somewhere in her brain, she was aware there was a reason for this. She knew there was a reason for the blood on her hands. A reason she felt at peace with, but that she couldn´t grasp. She only felt free after his body stopped fighting and fell to the side.

There was someone under the preacher, but the fog was too thick. She couldn´t see their face, or remember their name. But they were alive, and the relief made Derya cry. Heaving sobs made her lose her breath.

The memory shifted to them running, crossing a long bridge. She vaguely recognized it. She knew they didn´t have enough money for a decent ship. The man at the docks looked suspicious of them, but didn´t say anything about it. He just took their coin and gave them his shittiest sailboat with a quick warning about incoming bad weather. But they couldn´t heed the warning, not when they were leaving a corpse behind.

She wasn't sure if she was awake the next time she opened her eyes. She was on a ship. There was a storm. And she was alone. If this was *The Cursed Eel*, Nona would be there. She was still deep in that foggy memory. The episodes never lasted this long. Dread settled in her stomach, and she felt the need to hug herself. She wrapped her arms around her ribs, and when she looked down, she realized her skin wasn´t bloated or grey. She hadn't drowned.

Yet.

A wave hit the broken-down little ship. Hard. And she was flying. She heard someone scream before she hit the dark water. She broke her arm when she hit the surface hard, and she was sinking next, unable to swim because of the pain and the cold, unable to see except when lightning flashed over the ocean.

Derya swallowed salt water.

Roma swallowed salt water.

Still floating in the unending darkness. Still confused as to where she was. She looked up, or rather, she looked toward what she thought was *up*, and tried swimming there. She didn´t feel like she was drowning, but she hoped breaking the surface of the water would give her direction.

Instead, something else broke the surface; not coming from the direction she was swimming in but to her left, far away. She only noticed its presence in the dark because it shone like a beacon. A bright, sickly green that drew the eye. And inside the glow, a person.

After the first body broke the water came more of what Roma recognized now to be corpses. The glow of them allowed her to see better in the overwhelming darkness, and her eyes drifted upwards, to where a massive shadow was starting to materialize. She tried to swim away, realizing the shadow was the bottom of a sinking ship. She needed to avoid being sucked in, needed to avoid being touched by it by all means possible. But her limbs refused to obey.

There came a rumble from deep within the darkness. For the first time since waking in this dark, underwater dream, Roma thought to look down, following the sound. Her mouth opened in a silent scream, bubbles coming out and obstructing her vision. She slapped the bubbles away with slow hands. When the bubbles dissipated, she wished they were still there.

The sight of the giant eel moving beneath her made her body freeze up. The green glow of the bodies slowly sinking toward the body of the monster made its scales shine. Roma had the startling realization that one of these scales was bigger than her. She couldn't see its face, she didn't want to see its face; if its scales were bigger than her entire body, she didn't want to see its mouth. Its teeth.

She tried swimming away, to no avail.

"Tavia Bisset calls upon the gods to understand life." The voice boomed just as the monster's head became visible in the murk. "Tavia Bisset *demands* an audience with me to escape death. Tavia Bisset will instead become it. Become death."

She hadn't recognized her at first, because her skin was a regular color and her hair was longer. Her cheeks were fuller and her eyes, which were now open, weren't dull and vacant as the few times she had seen them in person. Roma now recognized the first body that fell to the water as the captain of *The Cursed Eel*.

Edbris opened its mouth, revealing teeth and a long, pale tongue, and Roma found herself swimming as fast as she could, this time toward the monster. She tried to scream, to get Tavia's attention, but the pirate captain didn't even blink as the giant mouth closed around her.

Then it was dark again, the green glow disappearing alongside Tavia, just as fast as it had appeared. The overwhelming and unending darkness felt like she had been the one swallowed whole. She continued to swim forward despite it. She needed to get to Tavia.

"No need to rush… This already happened. Centuries ago, in fact," said Edbris.

She turned around, trying to locate where the voice came from, but she was blind, still floating. Lost.

"I want to wake up," she said, and to her surprise, her voice traveled, unbothered by the water. "I want to wake up!"

"I thought you would be happy to experience a vision for the first time. It's what you've been wanting for years… and yet it took me almost a month to grant you one. You´ve got a stubborn mind."

Roma stopped moving, her ears perking up at that. She remembered Celeste's cryptic advice to open her mind, to let her walls down. She had tried, but all the hours practicing had only resulted in headaches and dizzy spells whenever she stood up too quickly.

"Sorry," she said numbly. "I´d like to wake up now, please."

She had a sense her politeness amused the giant eel, but only silence met her for several long seconds before the green glow appeared again in the form of two eyes a few feet away from her. If she stretched her arms as far apart as possible, she wouldn´t have been able to touch them at the same time.

The eyes stared at her. Through her. *Into* her.

The voice continued: "Tavia will continue to be death until she remembers what made her become it in the first place."

"Why are you telling me this? I'm not—"

"Tavia must remember what caused her to rot. That is what pulls people to *The Cursed Eel*."

"Stop, stop! This isn't—I'm not with Tavia, why are you—"

Edbris interrupted again: "Give back to the sea the ashes of what made them rot. I will eat them like I did their memories."

Roma felt teeth around her, perforating the skin of her left shoulder and the top of her scalp. The water around her filled with blood. Though she couldn't see it, she tasted it when she opened her mouth to scream.

Roma's scream made Celeste turn around and run.

Glenlivet paused mid-climb up the rope ladder that would allow her to be closer to *The Cursed Eel* without boarding it, and watched as Celeste disappeared down the steps into the hold of *The Outsider*.

She struggled to hold onto the ladder, and she was sure she was pulling her stitches, but her mind was clear. The fever remained, but the hallucinations were gone and so was the intense shivering.

"Augie! Go with her and help!" she ordered from her spot before continuing the climb, until she was at the same level as the main deck of *The Cursed Eel*.

Nona looked pale but alive, a stark contrast to the corpse of Tavia standing next to her. She looked beautiful. But she had been crying, her eyes swollen and red.

"I know why you couldn´t love me," Nona said, leaning over the banister.

If they both reached out, they´d be able to touch each other´s hands. Glenlivet itched to do just that, but what Nona said stopped her. "I did love you. I love you still," she said. The declaration had once stuck to her throat like cement but it flowed now, unstoppable. Glen didn´t think she´d ever grow tired of saying it. "I just couldn´t tell you before and I´m sorry. I´ll explain why once we—"

"I know why!" Nona said, interrupting her. "I understand! You couldn´t say it because you were grieving."

Glenlivet´s hand shook around the rope ladder, the roughhewn threads digging into her palm. She was suddenly captaining a different ship, smaller even than *The Outsider,* in a different storm. She held the helm, trying her best to keep the ship from sinking. Her eyes searched for her, frantic. One second ago, she was on the main deck, the next second she wasn´t. Glenlivet couldn´t stop screaming. Her throat was raw, and she was sure something would tear. She was now quiet, staring at Nona, and terrified that, if she blinked, she would disappear just like…

"I know because of the letters," Nona continued. "I

know about Derya. She has the same green ribbon."

Glenlivet frowned. "Derya?"

"Yes! Derya!" Nona rushed to explain, confused by Glenlivet's expression. "She's the one you were with when your ship sank and you washed up on the rocks at Sodra. She's the one who sent you those letters."

"Nona, I don't know who—"

Nona was about to explain when she felt a soft hand on her shoulder. Glenlivet's eyes widened as they drifted to the person behind Nona.

"Laura..."

19

THE DROWNING KRAKEN

Elric Omar was a peculiar man. Markl watched him as he poured them a glass of something that looked like piss. When he handed it to him, the younger man took a tentative sniff. It smelled like piss, too.

"It´s what we have. Blame the Empire´s trade laws."

"You respect the trade laws?" Markl raised an eyebrow at him.

The captain chuckled, leaning on his desk and sipping on his drink. He grimaced slightly as the liquid went down. "Of course not. But they are a pain in the ass to break. It's not worth my time."

Markl considered his response, wondering if it would get him murdered. Despite his uniform, the man had already spared him, but he didn´t know how much he could push.

"Booze isn´t worth it, but military-grade weaponry is?"

Elric stopped swooshing the contents of his glass around and looked at him. His eyes were unrecognizable, a red glint to its pupils that made Markl feel small.

"You got a chance to read the papers on my desk after all…" His voice was different too, with a drawl that wasn´t there before.

"No," Markl was quick to clarify, placing a hand on the desk and then quickly retrieving it. "I was a soldier of the Crown of Rera. Assigned to protect the king on his travels."

The red glint in Elric´s eyes slowly faded as he sat back in his chair, returning his focus to his drink. "And Micah Griffith has taken an interest in little old me?"

"Goliath has. The king intercepted a report about your… activities from a tax collector ship after it was attacked by *The Outsider*."

That got Elric´s attention again. His frown was pronounced between his dark eyebrows.

"*The Outsider*?" An odd expression washed over his features: a mix of satisfaction and terror, which Markl never thought could co-exist before. "Little Glenlivet's ship?"

Glenlivet lived by the coast in Agath. Or rather, it would be more appropriate to say she lived on the coast since she had been dumped there unceremoniously by Elric's men.

She was allowed to sleep on a cot in the temple's basement, but all her belongings—the few she had managed to grab before being abandoned—she kept hidden under rocks and among palm tree roots. At fourteen, she was embarrassed to tell the preacher's daughter where she lived. She was older than Glenlivet by a year and educated in a fancy school, the name of which the abandoned pirate struggled to even read. Her eyes were the sweetest brown and so shiny Glenlivet felt blinded whenever they made eye contact in the temple. The girl had a bad habit of smiling whenever they did, even though Glenlivet looked dirty and tired all the time from cleaning. Glenlivet had the bad habit of smiling back.

And her name was Laura. Laura Melendez.

Derya looked the same. For a long yet fleeting dark moment between lightning strikes, Glenlivet saw Laura how she remembered her in dreams. Countless memories of seeing her at night, by the shore of Agath, far enough from temple that the gods couldn´t hear them laugh together, had trained Glen to recognize her features by moonlight. The high cheekbones, large, round eyes, and dark eyebrows. They were all there.

She registered the sight of dead, bloated skin and wet matted hair afterward.

"Is that my name?" Derya asked, taking a step forward. Glenlivet nodded so softly she worried Laura missed it, but the girl nodded back and said, "You were my person... When I first woke up I knew I had someone. I waited for you."

"I watched you die," the pirate captain said, just as thunder broke the sky in the distance and the sea moved.

"You´re Nona´s person now," she said. There was no bitter jealousy to her voice, only a hollowness that Glenlivet was too alive to comprehend.

Derya, or rather Laura, watched the edges of the storm all around them. It seemed closer now, the hurricane continuing its path. Not long from now, it would be on them again, threatening their ships.

Nona, in the meantime, watched Laura with mournful eyes, her hands tightly pressed against her sides. She wanted to offer comfort in some way, but knew there was no relief she could grant, no solution.

Elric had finished his glass a while ago as Markl explained all the events that had led him to become buried by red sand. The captain was particularly interested in all his interactions with the crew of *The Outsider*.

"Glenlivet has a fucking siren," Elric said, smirking. There was disbelief but also a hint of amusement and, to Markl's surprise, pride. "A loose siren. No gag or anything?"

Markl shook his head no, mirroring Elric's smile. "She's completely free. Very quiet, not easily trusting."

"Can hardly blame her, right?" the captain commented.

"But she's loyal once you earn her trust," the young man clarified. "And she's kind. Maybe not nice by court standards, but she's good."

Elric watched Markl for a few seconds, his chin propped in his hand. "So she's *that* kind of captain…"

Markl tilted his head to the side, confused. "Glenlivet?"

"Yeah. She's the type of captain who attracts loyal and kind people." Markl couldn't decipher the expression on his face as he suddenly stood up, his eyes watching the men outside his quarters through the porthole on his door. "Good. That's good. I always had a feeling."

That got Markl's attention. "We only interacted briefly when we were escaping. Do you know her well?"

"Something like that," he replied, noncommittal.

"Is *something like that* the reason she's hunting you?"

When Elric turned to look at him, the red glint was back. Markl straightened his back. He had the feeling that he was about to be attacked despite the captain's relaxed posture.

"She's hunting him because he murdered me in cold blood and then abandoned her in Agath with nothing but a silly scarf."

Next thing he knew the glint was gone and Elric stumbled forward, tripping over the leg of the desk and falling on his face. The empty glass in his hand shattered on impact.

"Captain!"

The man chuckled, the sound muffled with his mouth smushed against the floor. "Which one?"

"Elric..."

His palms got cut on the tiny shards of glass as he sat upright, but he didn´t seem to notice or care. "That´s me."

Markl stayed silent, watching him, frowning. Elric Omar was talked about all over the Empire in hushed whispers, stories of slaughter and wit beyond measure. The tales of his name made most vessels steer clear of any areas he was even rumored to be close to.

This couldn´t be the pirate those stories were about. Elric looked small, younger now that the red hue was gone. Despite the resignation on his face, the most prominent emotion radiating from him was sadness.

"I can feel you judging me, little soldier," the man said, rubbing his face with one hand. A shard of glass got stuck in his stubble and he swatted it away. "Not drunk after just one drink, I´m not seven. Those… flashes just take a toll on me."

"Flashes," Markl said, slowly.

"Flashes, trances, episodes, call it whatever you want."

"I don´t know what to call it because I don´t know what you´re referring to exactly," the younger man clarified. "That wasn´t you, right? Your voice was different, and your eyes were… weird." It was the best word he could find to describe it. "Are you a witch? I know they get visions."

Elric shook his head. "Not a mage. Just the result of one; it´s a long and complicated story."

"We´re going to Denea, right?" when the pirate nodded to confirm with a tired look on his face, Markl relaxed on the chair, "So we have about a week and a half for you to tell me this story."

Celeste almost slipped going down the steps into the hold. She heard Augie running after her but she didn't look back. She was familiar with that type of scream. It was a scream out of a trance. She had heard others in her profession scream like that. She had woken herself up screaming that way a handful of times.

She had left Roma on the hammock, but she wasn't there when Celeste ran into the crew's quarters. She panicked for a second before looking down. Her student lay on the floor in the fetal position, her eyes wide open, her pupils nowhere to be seen.

"How is she? She sounded in pain," Augie called out from behind her as she rushed forward to help her up.

"She's on the floor, help me with her!"

Augie knelt by Roma along with Celeste and pushed her up while the woman pulled. Roma's eyes didn't change but her shoulders and jaw tensed up. Her hands were locked in fists. An odd murmuring rumbled from her mouth.

"Are we sure this is your field and not Mel's? It could be a seizure," Augie said, not able to make out the words.

"It's my field. I recognize the signs, I feel it... But pray to Yrena anyways," she added quickly, holding Roma's face in her hands.

"I don't pray to any god," Augie said curtly, caressing Roma's back in hopes of relaxing her.

The Outsider rocked violently and Augie fell onto his side, and Celeste tumbled over his legs. Roma, however, stayed upright and screamed again.

"What was that?" Augie grumbled, trying to get up as the ship steadied.

"You three all right?" Marcya asked, rushing into the room.

Celeste nodded as she got to her feet. "That wave hit us hard. Is everyone safe up there?" the mage asked, getting up.

"Everyone is safe, yes. It didn't hit us as hard because it broke on *The Cursed Eel*."

"Celeste?"

"Is everyone there all right?" Celeste asked.

"Tavia is trying her best, but their ship is taking in water."

"Celeste."

"They're sinking? What about Nona?" Celeste took a step toward Marcya, eyes wide and panicked.

"Celeste!" Roma finally snapped, making everyone look at her. The effort of screaming made her dizzy, but she stood with Augie's help. "I know…-I know how to get Nona back," Roma said, her head lulling forward as she pressed her weight against the young man.

Celeste stared at her, then back to Marcya, who watched them with a terrified expression before nodding and motioning for them to follow her. "We need you up there, then. Now!"

Celeste started walking, dragging Roma with her, up the wet steps out of the hold. The rain pummeled the deck, and the wind tested the tension of the rope ladder. Glenlivet was still on it, holding on as tight as she could.

"Captain!" Marcya called, but her voice was drowned by the sound of another wave crashing against *The Cursed Eel*.

"I don't want to forget! I don't want to forget Glenlivet, please!" Nona screamed, holding onto Laura.

She hugged her back, tight. She had been through sinkings before but if Tavia didn't get *The Cursed Eel* under control, it would be Nona's first. And that was the most devastating one. Laura held the back of her head to keep her close as the ship started capsizing.

"Nona!" Glenlivet screamed, watching them, just as one of the ropes holding her ladder snapped, flinging her body into the main mast. When she hit the deck, her side ached as blood stained her shirt. She heard her crew screaming.

Mel held Julian's hand tighter, her other hand covering her mouth. "My gods!"

The old pirate turned her around, stopping her from

looking. "She'll be all right. We'll patch her up and she'll be all right. She always is," he lied confidently, with the years of deceiving experience he had under his belt.

Mel nodded, and with her years of experience reading people, she knew he was lying and chose to believe him anyway.

Marcya and Celeste shoved them aside, holding a very pale Roma upright. She clutched onto the banister, watching *The Cursed Eel.* The rain had woken her up, but she still felt faintly numb. There was too much light flashing and a lot of loud sounds at the same time. A part of her wished to be back in that unending darkness. She closed her eyes for a moment to center herself, and when she opened them, she was back. However, she could still feel *The Outsider* and hear her crewmates around her.

"Give back to the sea the ashes of what made them rot."

Her voice echoed over the storm, making Celeste and Marcya flinch in surprise. But they didn´t let go of her, holding her as she shivered, her eyes unfocused and lightless. Her mentor watched her with a mixture of fear, worry, and pride.

"She´s got impeccable timing," Marcya commented, smiling.

Tavia heard the voice from her place at the helm, sweat coating her forehead from the effort to keep the ship from sinking. She repeated the words in her head,

"What made us rot..."

She couldn't remember. She couldn't remember what led her to become the captain of *The Cursed Eel*. She had always been dead, she had always been rotting. There was no reason behind it, no origin, it had always felt that way. But she remembered Derya's arrival. And she remembered Nona's. "Cecilia, hold her steady!"

Her first mate grabbed the helm and watched her captain run down the steps toward the two girls hugging on the main deck. Water reached her calves and slowed her down.

"You heard her, Connelly! Derya! Go grab matches!"

Nona pulled away from Laura, who only took two seconds to process before running to the galley.

"I heard her, but I don't-"

"We need to burn what brought you here. Quickly. Cecilia is buying us some time but the ship is sinking and you need to break the bond before it does." Tavia grabbed Nona's shoulders. "Think! What brought you here? What made you rot?"

"I wanted to warn Glenlivet about Micah, I don't have anything to burn, I don't—"

"That's what you said to me. That's what you explained calmly and rationally. What did you scream while you drowned?"

"Take me to Mene," she murmured as the memory

came back to her. "Take me home."

Her hand instinctively flew to her chest. Home was *The Outsider*, with Glenlivet by her side. But home had first been Mene. Mene was where she had been born and raised. Mene was where her mother died, passing down a kraken necklace to her. A kraken necklace, resting now over her chest. It seemed to move now at even intervals, like a fluttering heartbeat.

"Nona!" Tavia shook her to get her attention, just as Laura returned.

The water was now at their knees. Nona looked between Laura and Tavia before ripping open the first button on her shirt and pulling out the necklace. The captain grabbed the matches from Laura's hands.

On *The Outsider*, Marcya rushed forward, as did Julian to throw the gangplank between the two ships. They were now at the same height, but it would soon become unequal again as *The Cursed Eel* continued to slowly sink. Ashlin and Laura rushed to hold it steady from the other side.

"Nona!" Julian called out. "We're ready for you!"

Tavia tried her best to cover them both with her coat to avoid the matches getting wet, then handed the small box to Nona.

"Are you sure about this?" Nona questioned, frowning as she finally processed what was being asked of her.

"No," the captain answered quickly, securing the coat

better over them now that her hands were free. "But you have to try anyway. Before we sink."

Nona nodded, swallowing hard, and pressed the necklace's charm into her palm before taking it off properly. She lit a match, the small orange flame flickering in front of her. She felt like a coward when she held the flame to the thin rope rather than the kraken itself. Her eyes widened when the flame caught on the material and turned bright green. She flinched, expecting it to burn her skin, but the sensation didn't come.

Her hands felt warm, though they weren't in pain. The fire devoured the rope, slowly nearing the black metal of the kraken. A part of her doubted it would burn, but when the green flames touched the metal, the kraken started melting in her hand.

Dark smoke filled the space under Tavia's coat. When Nona looked up, she could no longer see the captain's face. She coughed, holding the burning necklace lower.

"Tavia, I don't feel—" Her sentence was interrupted by another coughing fit. She tried to take a deep breath in, but smoke filled her lungs. It felt like drowning all over again.

She felt the woman's hands on her shoulders and rain hitting her head which meant the coat had been removed, yet her vision hadn't cleared. The screen of smoke was still there and she blinked a few times, trying to clear her eyes. Nona still felt the warmth of the necklace on her left palm, and through the fog, she could see the outline of her hand. Her necklace was gone, but a dark stain remained on her skin.

"Nona," Tavia said, "you have to cross over *now*."

When Nona blinked again, the fog was gone. She found herself with water up to her belly button and her legs growing cold.

"You have to leave. Now!" Tavia urged her again. She looked in pain. Nona looked her up and down in search of a wound and found that the captain's right palm had a nasty burn, bubbling and blistering.

"Tavia…" She tried to catch her attention but the captain used her good hand to push her toward the gangplank that united the two ships.

Nona grabbed onto Laura's shoulder for support and climbed on top. The wind and rain slashed at her face. She needed to cross as fast as possible or she could fall to her true death, but the memory of the green ribbon gave her pause. She turned to Laura, who held the plank, and smiled weakly at her. Nona plunged her hand in the mass of the woman's wet curls. Finding the strand she was looking for, she brought it forward and pressed it against Laura's shoulder, then handed her the matches.

"Your bond is that ribbon," she said, looking into her eyes.

Laura nodded, and broke eye contact, pensive, before hiding the matches in her pocket. Her hand reached up to touch the ribbon. "I'll keep that in mind, Nona. Thank you."

Nona Connelly recognized the sadness in her voice, and knew she wasn't ready to let go. "I'm sorry, Laura. You deserved to be happy with the woman you loved."

The young woman opened her eyes again, finding Glenlivet with her eyes.

"It sounds like I was happy...I'm just mad I don't remember it." When she looked back at Nona, her eyes were watering. "You go. You deserve to be happy with the woman you love, too."

Nona pressed her lips to Laura's cold cheek and bolted across the plank.

The Conviction sailed the closest it could to the coastline of Mene, as instructed. It was hardest to do at night, so the crew members with the best eyes were put on the night shift.

Akintoye still felt sick from the walk in the desert, and his sight had never been good. He settled on his hammock for the night and started working on the shoes he had worn to The Red Land. The pair was almost destroyed but he still cleaned them and had started polishing them when Griswold entered the room. Astrahd, a Terafian who had only been with the crew for about a year and a half, walked in after him.

"Still off night shift because of the black eye," Griswold grumbled. "Liang won't get off my back for the fight."

"Liang?" Astrahd questioned, laying down on his bunk. "Not the captain?"

"Elric is busy," the man replied, raising his eyebrows as he took off his boots.

Akintoye paused his polishing while Astrahd shrugged off his jacket.

"Still in his room with the prisoner?" he asked. The mocking tone in his voice disgusted Akintoye.

"Some prisoner," Griswold complained, putting away his dirty boots. "Elric promised we would throw him overboard as soon as we got information from him. It's been two days already."

"Stop questioning the captain," Akintoye finally interceded. "You're already on thin ice here, Griswold."

The man grunted, ignoring Akintoye's pointed look, and allowed himself to fall on his dirty mattress. "What are they doing all day together anyway?"

Astrahd snickered from his bunk. "I have an idea or two about what the captain might be doing to the little soldier."

Griswold laughed at the jab, though he at least had the sense to look around nervously as he did.

"Or perhaps it´s the soldier doing all the work," Astrahd continued with a smirk, glancing to Akintoye for a reaction. When Akintoye just stared at him, continuing to polish his shoes, he rolled his eyes and sat up. "Oh, come on. They're locked in the captain's quarters all day. What else could they be doing?"

"Talking from experience, Astrahd?" Liang's voice interrupted, making the men flinch and turn to the door. "What the captain decides to do with his prisoners is none of your business."

"Apologies, *captain*," Astrahd said sarcastically with a sly smile before laying down again, putting an arm over his eyes.

Akintoye watched Liang pause at the doorway, considering what to do. Elric would have cut a few fingers for the disrespect. The moment the first mate made the choice to ignore Astrahd's comment, Akintoye experienced a flavor of dread he was unfamiliar with; the wish that Elric was there instead of his right-hand man. Hearing Astrahd's satisfied chuckle in the dark only solidified the feeling.

Liang closed the door behind him with less force than he wanted to. He didn't like Astrahd. His ego was bigger than his skill, and the circumstances in which he had joined the ship spoke volumes of his character, but they were already down a few crew members and *The Conviction* was a big ship. They needed the hands.

He walked across the main deck, ignoring the light

rain that hadn't stopped falling since they returned to the sea. The door to the captain's quarters wasn't locked but everyone knew not to bother Elric when he requested to be left alone. Everyone but Liang apparently, who knocked on the door and allowed himself in without waiting for a response.

The prisoner, Markl, sat on the captain's chair behind the desk, writing furiously on a black book with a focused look in his eyes.

"What's… going on here?"

Elric stood from his bed in the corner, stretching. He had a sour look on his face, but it wasn't directed at him, as far as Liang could tell. That was something to be thankful for, he thought. Except the expression on the captain's face didn't seem to be directed at the Reran soldier either, which created uncertainty. Uncertainty was never good.

"Markl here will accompany us the whole way to Denea."

Liang's eyes widened, looking between his captain and the young man at the desk. "You're bringing a soldier of the Crown of Rera to the job?"

Elric simply shrugged before turning his back to both Liang and Markl to pour himself another drink.

His first mate took a step toward him. "Elric."

"Yes, Liang?" he responded, exasperated.

"Do you really think is a good idea to have him as a

witness?" At Liang's question, the captain turned to look at him but didn't respond, so Liang kept going. "He's the enemy. The Deneans might not realize if you take away his uniform, but the Duskians will know the second they get a whiff of him."

Elric seemed to think about it, but the first mate didn't spend long looking at him for answers. The scratching of the pen on paper and the flipping of the pages made Liang's blood boil, and he turned to look at Markl.

"And what are you even doing?"

The soldier looked up, startled. He had an ink stain on his chin. "What?"

"What are you doing, boy?"

Markl looked at Elric, who shook his head, prompting him to look down and continue writing. The first mate returned his attention to the captain.

"Elric."

"He's doing as he was ordered. And so will you, Liang. Out. Now."

Being alive again was exhausting. Though Nona knew she hadn't actually died before being pulled onto *The Cursed Eel*, the ship's magnetism had paused her lungs and heart like broken clocks. Feeling these organs start-up inside her body again took some adjustment once she realized. And that adjustment took so much energy that she spent most of the following days sleeping.

Glenlivet also spent a lot of time sleeping, on Mel's orders. After her stunt on the rope ladder, she was only allowed to sit up for meals, much to her dismay. She didn't dare push the rules, though: the surgeon's wrath was something fierce, and Glenlivet was aware she needed to heal as much as possible for when they finally caught up to *The Conviction*.

For all the talk about Glenlivet being a child with barely any experience, the ship ran perfectly while its captain and first mate were unconscious. Every other crew member knew their role, and well.

Augie continued selecting the best path toward Denea along with Julian, who had experience with how *The Conviction* moved. Marina regularly monitored the course ahead, to be safe, while Celeste read her cards. All her readings were inconclusive and vague: murmurs of conflict brewing, which they already knew. She kept having repetitive visions of Glenlivet's quarters while meditating. She guessed this had to do with the captain's wounds, and her only outlet was pestering Mel about it. It all seemed to be healing properly, so the mage was puzzled.

Roma kept insisting she wanted to help but, much like Mel, the mage was stern in her recommendation of rest. The trance that helped them get Nona back was quite taxing, and the young seer struggled to sleep without nightmares. The migraines that had preceded the trance were gone, and she was so relieved it almost made up for being stuck on galley duty. Blue's company was also a comfort.

The storm had eased once *The Cursed Eel* sunk, the bad weather leaving with it, but a light rain persisted even three days later.

"You reckon it will stop soon?" Danielle asked, eyes trained on the sky.

Marcya sat next to her, sharpening one of her knives. She smiled and looked up at the sky too. "Should ask the mages for that kind of information, 'cause I don't have it, Princess."

"Queen. Thank you," Danielle said back with pretend offense that was overshadowed by a chuckle.

"Oh, I'm sorry, Your Majesty!" Marcya responded, fake bowing with a hand to her chest. "Feel free to throw me overboard."

"Nah, we need you to fight Elric's goons," she said, waving her hand before focusing on the sky again. "We have enough weapons, right?"

"I only wish we had more than two pistols," she said. "We're outnumbered. Firepower would be our best shot at winning that fight."

Gale sat by Glenlivet's bed, taking advantage of the

hours she was awake to discuss strategy. They needed to foresee all possible scenarios with the information they had about the crew. The details were murky due to conflicting reports about how many people worked under Elric, so they needed to be smart about how they boarded the brigantine.

"You keep repeating yourself, Gale," Glenlivet said, her head lulling to the side as she closed her eyes, giving the notebook back to her strategist.

Gale's lips tightened as they took the notebook back and started writing again: *We always knew this was a suicide mission, Captain. We need to consider every angle to give ourselves the best possible chance.*

She nodded after reading, sighing. "Is there any way I can go in the ship undetected? Kill Elric on my own?"

Gale shook their head and wrote a note under the last one: *If you want to die, sure*. They allowed her to read it, but before she could answer, they started writing again: *Do you want to die?*

Glenlivet chuckled. "No. That has never been in any of my plans…Especially now." She looked to the other corner of her room next to her desk, where the crew had set up a cot. Nona lay there, snoring softly, with an arm slumped over her face, the other one over her belly. Glenlivet smiled softly before speaking again. "She's back on the ship, but I need time to actually win her back. Make up for everything. I sort of need to be alive to do that."

The strategist followed Glen's line of vision, then rolled their eyes with a fond smile, quickly writing: *You're a sap.*

20

SILENT DOCKS

"Why not tell her?" Markl asked the captain. Elric looked drained and ashen, his hands limp by his sides on the bed. "If you're certain she will catch up to us in Denea now, why not tell her everything yourself? In person, I mean. Why the book?"

Elric looked up, though his eyes were unfocused, lost. Markl searched for that hint of red but didn't find it. The captain lifted his hand to his temple and tapped it twice. "You know I'm not the only one aboard this ship. I can't count on the other captain to not take over when she's trying to kill me."

Markl nodded, biting the inside of his cheek. "You're worried he might take over completely."

"´Might´ is not the word," he grumbled. "I know he will

take over. He does whenever he or *The Conviction* feel threatened."

Markl nodded, thinking back to every time he had seen that telling red glint in his eyes. Elric's information matched everything he had seen since boarding the ship four days ago.

"What makes you think she'll believe you?"

Elric sighed again, sitting up straight and rubbing his eyes. "She will have to believe it because once she kills me—"

Markl stopped writing again, looking up with wide eyes. "Kills you? I thought—"

Elric continued speaking as if Markl hadn't interrupted: "—once she kills me, she will feel it. She still has a right to *The Conviction*, and it will try to take her."

"That's when I come in."

"Exactly," he answered, nodding, but his head fell forward in exhaustion, his breath ragged. His fists tightened around the sheets. "That's the reason why I kept you around, and you have to write fast because it's taking everything in me not to kill you right now."

Denea was a fisher community, built by modest people who kept their heads down when Goliath lay claim over the island's resources. The Empire claimed taxes, fish, nets, and other goods once a year.

"Last I checked," Danielle explained calmly, "Denea is not big or profitable enough for Goliath to place more than fifty soldiers there."

"And I don't reckon these soldiers are their most competent, either," Blue commented with a mouth full of food.

Danielle nodded, then looked at Glenlivet again. The captain had been allowed to finally join the crew on the main deck for dinner, the day before arriving at Denea. She looked like herself again and didn't flinch every time she moved anymore. Despite this improvement, Mel kept checking the wound at Celeste's insistence.

The captain stole a glance at Gale, who wrote frantically in their notebook but didn't share those notes with the rest of the crew.

"That explains why Elric chose that location to do whatever it is he's doing," Glenlivet said, cutting up her food.

"What *is* he doing, exactly?" Marcya asked, frowning. She pushed her plate away, leaning back in her chair and crossing her arms. "Did the report say?"

Gale shook his head and opened their jacket, searching in the inside pocket for the piece of paper.

Marcya grabbed it and read it. "It´s not an official report. There's no seal," she observed, turning the paper over a few times.

Gale wrote quickly. *It's a copy Micah had in his things.*

Marcya read the note out loud and nodded before making an odd face that made Nona cock her head to the side. "What is it?" Nona asked.

"Denea's population is poor for the most part," Marcya said, "yet Elric is smuggling things there? It's just weird. Who there could afford him?"

"Gale thought about that," Nona said. "He could be getting paid by someone that isn't from there. Denea could just be a venue."

Glenlivet chewed on her food, looking at the floor. "Doesn't matter what he's doing or why. All that matters is him going to Denea soon to drop off whatever he's smuggling."

"He might see us coming," Nona said, placing a soft hand on Glenlivet's arm. The captain didn't push it away. "We need to be prepared for him to already be there."

"Or that he might already be gone," Augie interjected. "There is a chance he already did the drop-off."

Glenlivet smiled softly, though Nona saw the familiar twitch in her top lip that told her the notion affected her. "In that case, we take an interest in that smuggling job, find out who paid him...And we go back to hunting him."

"He'll be there," Roma said, her eyes staring off into the horizon.

Celeste turned her head toward her apprentice. "You just know that?" she asked, frowning, watching the young girl's face.

"What?" Roma blinked repeatedly before turning to return Celeste's gaze. "Oh, yes. I just...knew."

Celeste looked from Roma to Glenlivet and back to Roma, worry in her features.

"What about you, Celeste? Any more of those dreams?" Glenlivet asked, smiling nervously.

Celeste didn't know how to answer. She had had more of those dreams. There was one pretty much every time she fell asleep, but each time she woke up with more questions and fewer answers.

In them, she found herself standing in the middle of the captain's quarters, always alone. In all the dreams, *The Outsider* was always rocking, with big waves, but she could hear no storm outside. The movement caused all the hanging lamps in the room to sway. The light coming from the flames in them always made Celeste cover her eyes, but it became a comforting sight right before she was startled awake.

So despite the dreams' recurrence, which was a sure sign that there was an important message in them, she had no answers, no clues, no useful information to give. Celeste shrugged. "They're still happening. No clue why."

Glenlivet bit the side of her tongue in deep thought,

considering. "It's all right. I'm sure whatever it means we will find out soon."

"What?"

"You heard me, Liang. Now go tell the crew."

"That makes no sense, Elric! We can't do that!"

Elric turned to Liang, and the first mate saw Markl take a step back from them. When his eyes returned to the captain, the captain's nose was almost touching his.

Liang tried his best to not step away from those red eyes and the alcohol on his breath. If he gave in like an injured animal, Elric would see an opening and kick him while he was down. He stared back at him, longer than anyone would find comfortable, and then Elric was clapping his shoulder, almost affectionately, as he broke eye contact and took a step back with an almost relieved sigh.

"Ah, Liang, be a good man and follow your captain's orders."

Liang watched Elric slump into a chair. He found himself wishing he could ask him why he looked so sick. He held himself back. There was a time years ago, when Elric was the first mate to the previous captain, that he would have asked. They had never been friends but they had been crew mates, close enough to wonder out loud why the other looked close to dying. Things were different now. Instead, he shook his head.

"The men will have questions."

"They're not paid to have questions," Elric answered, and though his tone was cheerful, his voice was rough, strained.

"They're paid to look after *The Conviction*. Your orders contradict that. Their questions are valid."

Elric rolled his eyes. "Just tell them that if they have questions, they can ask me directly."

They would never. Liang knew that. And so did the captain.

"That makes no sense," Marcya said.

Augie shook his head. "It has to be a trap."

"Doesn't look like one," Marina insisted, repeating herself. "It seems like they arrived recently. Most of the crew is on land. At a tavern. That's why it took me so long to come back, I followed them to confirm."

Glenlivet had been quiet since Marina had returned, her mind running wild with possibilities while the crew gathered around her and discussed the siren's report.

A couple of hours before arriving, Marina had swum ahead to scout the port. She had found *The Conviction* docked, quiet, and suspiciously unguarded. Most of the crew had left the brigantine and had gone inland, toward a tavern far away from the coast.

"I didn't see Elric or his first mate at the tavern," Marina continued. "He must be very confident, thinking he can guard a whole brigantine with just two men."

Nona frowned. "He is a confident man but he's not stupid. There has to be a reason why he sent all his protection away when he's in the middle of a job." Then she paused and glanced at Marina. "Did you manage to count how many of his crew were at the tavern?"

"Hard to say. They were being very rowdy."

"Estimate," Marcya insisted.

"Around thirty-five of them were drinking and gambling," Marina said, squinting as she tried to remember more clearly. "A few more had gone up to the rooms, but I didn't get to count them."

Glenlivet raised her head. "Did you see Akintoye at the tavern? He would have had a scar down his arm." Marina shook her head, and Glenlivet bit the inside of her cheek. "If he's at the ship, it makes sense why Elric is so confident in his safety."

"We're not boarding them, right?" Marcya said. "There has to be another way."

Glenlivet smiled. "It wouldn't be the first time we walk into an obvious trap and come out the other side with everything we wanted."

Mel slapped her upside the head. "You came out of that trap with a stab wound, you fool!" she snapped, as the captain rubbed the spot the surgeon had hit.

Marina looked over the outline of Denea against the tinted orange sky of the evening. "We're only a couple of hours off, so we better decide our course of action fast."

The Conviction didn't hide. With its crew's reputation and the size of the ship itself, it was almost impossible. And among all the tiny fishing sails, it stood out, even at night.

The Outsider also stood out as it approached the harbor, but no alarm bells were rung. Glenlivet watched the ship she grew up in, imposing and beautiful, as she got closer to it.

A group composed of Blue, Mel, Roma, Augie, Danielle, and, after much insistence from Glenlivet, Nona, disembarked *The Outsider*. The docks were deserted save for a few rats that scurried away. A sign over the dockmaster's booth indicated the work day started at four in the morning. The exception to that rule would have been the night custodian, who was supposed to be awake and sitting behind the desk at the booth, but nobody was there.

"The ink's wet," Blue said, fingertips touching the open book on top of the desk. "The custodian left not long ago."

Nona sighed, looking around for any movement. "And even at midnight, there should be some foot traffic."

"This sounds more and more like a trap," Danielle murmured.

"We better move," Roma replied, pointing to the high street.

Roma, Danielle, and Blue ran up the street in a hurry, toward The Duskian Largemouth, the tavern where Marina had seen Elric's crew. Nona, Mel, and Augie guarded the silent docks, watching the two ships side by side, waiting for a signal that their captain might need their help.

Much like the docks, *The Conviction* was quiet. Standing on the main deck after so long felt foreign, perhaps because Glenlivet was taller now. She was seeing the old brigantine with fresh eyes.

"Elric has allowed her to fall into disrepair," she commented, glancing at the old paint and the scratches on the floor.

Her comment wasn't loud enough for the others to

hear. Marcya sprinted toward the galley door, opening it, and looking around. Next, she opened the pantry, just in case. Both spaces were empty.

"They planned on having dinner here," Julian whispered, looking at a pot of stew on the counter. "So why go to the tavern all of a sudden?"

"Let's go. We have to search the rest of the ship." Marcya closed the door behind her after everyone left the kitchen.

Glenlivet turned her head to look at the other side of the ship. The captain's quarters of *The Conviction* were impossible to miss, both because of the swinging open door, and because she was so familiar with it. Past the threshold, Elric's room was shrouded in darkness. A mouth waiting to swallow her. When Marcya, Julian, Gale, and Augie prepared to open the door down into the hold, Glenlivet still stood on the main deck, watching the open mouth. Once her father's room. Now Elric's.

"You four clear the hold," she ordered before taking a step toward the doorway.

"Captain," Julian called out in a hushed, alarmed whisper.

She stopped, sighing. "I'll be fine."

"Glenlivet?" Marcya raised her head to look at her, but the captain was already walking away.

Julian held her back. "You heard your orders. We need

to clear the hold."

Marcya snatched her arm from Julian with a roll of her eyes, but listened to him, with one final worried look to her captain's back.

The door to the hold was loud, and Gale physically cringed at the sound.

"You can't shake. No matter how scared," he instructed, holding the stick and observing the nine-year-old in front of him as she attempted to do the same.

"I'm not scared of you. This shit is just heavy," Glenlivet snapped in annoyance, allowing the end of her stick to fall to the floor.

Elric lunged forward, hitting between the kid's ribs.

"I wasn't ready," she yelped, taking a step back and rubbing the sore spot. It was sure to turn purple and blue, but she would survive.

"Bruises make the lesson stick" was the captain's only instruction to Elric when it came to his daughter's training. He wasn't involved otherwise, except for the occasional instance in which he would silently observe.

"That's not fair," she insisted, trying to bring her defense up again.

"Fair doesn't win you fights," Elric said, smiling. Out of the corner of his eye, he spotted Akintoye peeling an orange as he sat down on a barrel to watch them. "Your enemies won't allow you to be ready. Neither should you."

Glenlivet watched the open door, knowing Elric was ready for her. It was foolish to attack when it was the most obvious, when it was a clear trap. But it was also her only chance at an actual fight with him. She crossed the threshold, her sword high and her senses alert.

Markl wasn't struggling anymore, though the ropes around his wrists were uncomfortably tight and the rag in his mouth was making his jaw ache. He could only thank Elric's consideration for tying his hands over his lap and not at his back.

The room was in darkness, except for the faint moonlight coming through the window. Elric stood, hidden in the shadow behind the open door. His eyes shone bright red, waiting as Glenlivet approached the doorway with slow, measured steps. Markl thrashed around when she started closing in, screaming as loud as he could with the rag in his mouth. Glenlivet's attention was on him only a second, recognition and confusion washing over her face, before her eyes drifted to the door again.

He watched the thoughts travel frantically across her

face. Markl swallowed hard, eyeing the two pirates, and knowing one of them would be dead within the hour.

The kick to the door threw Elric against the wall, a groan knocked out of him. He kicked it back, holding onto the wall, and the door closed with a slam.

Glenlivet was running toward the small bar in the corner of the room. She looked older, obviously, but her face was the same. She still held the softness of childhood about her. He could see that defiant nine-year-old who used to curse at him during training, though her eyes were strikingly like her father's. A thought occurred to him, that the red tint of *The Conviction* would suit her gaze. But he would die slowly and painfully to avoid it.

His legs moved on their own, reacting to the threat she posed, and started rushing toward her. Glenlivet turned sharply, throwing something at his head. He raised his arms just in time to avoid a half-empty bottle shattering against his head, his arms taking the brunt of the scratches when the bottle shattered. A part of him couldn't help but smile, a swelling of pride in his chest. The feeling was soon overpowered by that voice, raw and panicked. *She's here to destroy everything we've worked for.*

When he opened his eyes again, Glenlivet was five feet away, her eyes wide and frantic. When she swung, he moved, and her blade pierced through his right shoulder rather than his chest. The splatter of blood, as Glenlivet brought her sword higher and deepened the wound, stained her white shirt and neck.

Just as he taught her, she pulled her sword out of his shoulder and stepped back and to the side, away from his sword. She had affected his dominant hand; he could already feel his fingers growing numb around the sword hilt. He switched the sword to his left hand, and with the weapon now closer to his opponent, he stepped up to her.

His technique wasn't as clean with his left hand, and Glenlivet blocked his strike with ease.

"You've lost your edge, old man," she grunted, pushing him back.

Elric kicked her knee, making her stance buckle. Her sword didn't stop moving toward him, and he found the reverse grip on his sword wasn't enough to stop her advance. He was relieved. This would be quick, he'd be injured and disarmed, and Markl would be able to warn Glenlivet of the danger she was in.

His right hand shot out and stopped the edge of her sword from reaching his chest again. His palm bled against the metal as she tried to pull it off of his grip.

"*I gave you yours*," Elric responded, his throat burning.

Glenlivet's eyes searched his face, confused by his voice. It had been years since she had last heard Elric, but his was the voice that raised her, that taught her to fight and survive. And it didn't sound like this. Elric pushed his sword toward her, aiming for her neck. Her line of thought was interrupted, and she instinctively dropped to the floor to dodge the attack. The friction of the floor against her back burned her on the way down but she ignored the discomfort and kicked her legs up as hard as she could, into Elric´s groin.

The man cursed loudly as released Glenlivet´s sword, staggering back, doubled over in pain.

She had to move. She had to attack him again to get the upper hand, but standing back up quickly was a struggle with the stitches and bruising on her side. She grunted, grabbing onto a bar stool for balance, not taking her eyes off Elric.

"*You came to this fight injured?*" he asked, eyeing the way she held onto her side as she stood, "*Is this the sort of training he gave you? Fucking pathetic.*"

Both pirates' heads snapped toward the door, as the sound of a heavy impact echoed somewhere in the ship.

The hold of the brigantine felt cold despite the hot, humid weather outside.

Marcya led the group down the steps, her mind focused sharply on any sounds or signs of a crew member walking about.

At the bottom of the stairs, the group found themselves staring down a dimly lit hallway. Unlike *The Outsider*'s, the hold of *The Conviction* was spacious, divided into rooms with actual walls instead of just curtains.

"Split up?" Celeste said, watching the other side of the hallway, behind the stairs. Her voice came out nervous, shaky.

Marcya walked to the right, with Gale following behind, covering her back. That direction had the most doors, all closed. Celeste and Julian locked arms and headed to the other side.

The mage opened doors as fast and as quietly as possible. She was under no delusion that the crew was unaware of their presence. They had to be hiding somewhere, waiting to strike.

"They couldn't have all gone to the inn," she muttered after the third empty room they searched. "It makes no sense to leave such a large ship unguarded."

Julian checked behind a large box inside the room, frowning. "It's not unguarded. Elric stayed back."

"Still," she insisted. "Just one man for a brigantine seems…"

"Elric is not just a man," Julian interrupted, walking out of the room. His voice cracked slightly at the end of his sentence, his eyes focusing on the figure in the hallway. He extended an arm, stopping Celeste from exiting the room after him.

"Julian...I thought you died in Goliath Bay," Astrahd taunted, with a smile that showed off his dirty teeth.

"I thought you did, too." Julian's voice was tense now.

"You're in that bitch's crew now, then."

"I could say the same to you."

Astrahd laughed with a hand over his belly. A cough interrupted the outburst. Phlegm rose in his throat, and he held it in his mouth for a moment before letting it dribble onto the floor. His eyes remained on Julian as he did. The older man grimaced at the sight.

He saw Astrahd reach for his saber but no attack came. Instead, he was pulled back, a cloud of white smoke appearing in front of him. Celeste's powder blinded Astrahd, who yelled out a curse. The pull came just in time as the saber appeared through the cloud, missing its target.

The mage kicked the sword up and heard it fall to the floor with a clang. Julian patted Celeste's hand, his breathing quick as he smiled thankfully in her direction.

As soon as Julian pulled out his sword, she said, "Don't die," and pushed him back toward Astrahd.

His blade struck metal, the smoke dissipating and revealing his past crewmate had pulled out a long, curved dagger.

On the other side of the hallway, Marcya and Gale were facing a wall of a man.

"Akintoye…" Gale murmured. It was impossible to not recognize him from Glenlivet's description. They had really hoped this man in particular was at the inn with the others.

The captain's words resonated in Marcya's head, the conversation from a few days ago still a fresh memory.

"Akintoye is the strongest Elric has. You'll have to be fast against him," she had said. Then, after a pause, she added, "He was polite. Never bothered me much. Perhaps he could be reasoned with, spare his life…"

"Did he defend you when Elric abandoned you in Agath?" Danielle had asked. When their captain shook her head, the crew exchanged glances. There would be no sparing.

Now, the man stared them down, watching them with a lack of expression that made Marcya tick. Gale looked between them. The two weapon masters could not look more different.

"Astrahd said you'd be attacking tonight. I didn't want to believe him," he said, unsheathing an odd-looking blade. It had a serrated edge, but the point was sharp and forked.

Marcya frowned, staring at it. Gale took a step back, assessing just how much space they had to fight side by side in the cramped hallway.

"I didn't want to believe little Glenlivet would be so craven as to attack at night, with most of the crew far from home."

"It's not her fault you lot are stupid," Marcya spat back, racing toward him, crouching low on the ground.

She stepped sharply to the left, dodging his sword but meeting Akintoye's right hand instead. The impact was deafening, as Akintoye's palm covered almost her entire face, and when she felt his fingers dig into her scalp she blindly stabbed at the arm holding her. To her horror, his grip only tightened in response to the pain. She switched targets, aiming now for the man's abdomen, right in front of her yet so far.

Gale moved fast, unsheathing both their longsword and dagger. The strategist remembered Glenlivet's warnings about him. They saw his right hand, occupied holding Marcya down. They saw Akintoye's eyes move to follow their movements and the way he raised his blade in preparation for their attack. Gale raised their sword to meet the serrated blade, holding it high above him. The edge of his longsword was trapped there, but so was Akintoye's arm unless he was ready to drop his only visible weapon, or let go of Marcya.

It wasn't elegant. The slashes were messy and uncoordinated due to the position but they drew blood and a scream, causing enough damage to get Akintoye to let go of Marcya, pushing her away as far as possible to grant himself some time.

Gale stepped back, recognizing the danger of being

so close to him when one of his hands was free. Akintoye looked down, frowning, at his right arm and chest. Marcya had gotten her short knife inside his forearm about four times and had slashed at the skin at least five. He opened and closed his hand, testing out the movement with a pained expression.

Marcya wasn´t on the floor for long, getting up and throwing herself at him again, this time forgoing the dodging misdirection. Before she could make contact, he slashed his sword against her thigh. She screamed, her throat burning from the strain, even as she scrabbled up his body. Akintoye thrashed around, trying to get Marcya off, and threw his weight against the wall, crushing all air out of her lungs. She brought the knife down again, the piercing point stabbing him behind the ear, plunging deep into his skull. At the same time, Gale plunged their dagger into his lower back, twisting upward.

21

FIRE AT SEA

Elric moved first to attack, but his sword hit the wood of the bar as Glenlivet jumped over it and rolled onto the other side.

The motion shot pain to her injury, and the sensation only heightened when Elric pushed the counter, hitting her ribs and throwing her back into the wall. The bottles on display behind her rattled with the impact, dangerously vibrating toward the edge of the shelves.

"Fucking!" Glenlivet cried out, "asshole!"

She struck Elric between the eyes with the pommel of her sword. He stumbled backward, his eyes going cloudy. Glenlivet used that second to move the bar away and push her sword forward. Elric was still holding his head, and her weapon reached his left clavicle.

"If you had a fucking heart," she bit out, "you would be kind enough to stop moving and let me stab it."

Elric's sad smile was hidden by the hand that held his throbbing head. Blood poured from the wound and onto Glenlivet's sword. There was no part of his body that didn't hurt.

It was a precarious balance he had to strike. He needed to die by her hand, but not so fast that Glenlivet didn't have time to save herself. His body wasn't cooperating. The shouting parasite that was *The Conviction* still roared and writhed, forcing him to fight back, to defend himself. He watched the back of his hand slap Glenlivet's sword away the second she pulled it out of his body and felt his legs propel him forward to attack her.

Glenlivet blocked in time and pushed back, swords clanging together with a nasty sound that made Elric grind his teeth, his ears ringing.

When he was younger, the sounds of battle were something Elric had enjoyed. He sought them out like a moth did a flame. It was those sounds that landed him on *The Conviction* when he was just fifteen, proving himself in front of its captain to join the crew. It was only fitting that these same sounds finalized the course of his insanity.

He closed his eyes, straining against Glenlivet. The sounds grew sharper, his headache reaching its peak.

"Let me die slow." he surprised himself by being capable of getting the words out, though when he opened his eyes again, Glenlivet didn´t seem to have heard him. Probably for the best.

Glenlivet won the upper hand with brute force and caused him to fall backward, his extremities shaking.

Elric was vaguely aware of his back hitting the floor.

She stood above him, the tip of her sword pressed firmly over his chest, above the beating organ he could hear so clearly pounding in his ears.

"Is this how you felt…" she began, but Elric could barely make out the words. She needed to hurry before his body kicked in again and fought back. "…when you threw my father overboard? When you abandoned me?"

Markl groaned against the rag, trying to call out to Glenlivet.

Elric had almost forgotten about his presence in the room. He weakly moved his head to the side, feeling the wooden floor beneath his temple. He tried to control his breathing. A part of him still screamed, begging for a fight. The voice was only quieted by the sword slowly sinking into his chest.

"Look at me!"

For all the boasting, when he finally gathered enough strength to do as ordered, Glenlivet didn´t look proud, or satisfied. She was panting, blood staining her shirt and hands. Her dark makeup painted streaks down her face, tears flowing freely.

"What do you want me to see, Glen?"

It almost made him smile to call her that again.

Blood filled his mouth.

The first mate was supposed to go with the crew to the inn, have a few drinks on Elric´s tab, and watch over the group, but he had decided against it at the last minute. It meant disobeying an order, but he reckoned what Elric didn´t know wouldn't hurt him. He had stayed in his private chamber, going over the ship´s records, searching for anything he had missed that would explain the captain´s behavior. Seeing the kind of contraband they were supposed to hand over tomorrow, it was natural to feel nervous. Even scared, if that wouldn´t be so out of character for Elric.

But this wasn´t anxiety.

He had racked his brain for an explanation for the bad feeling he had, his instincts flaring to the surface. Everything about Elric the past few days indicated to Liang that the end was near and that the captain knew it, like a cat that hides under the bed after days of not eating. To die alone. And to rot the same if nobody disposed of him properly.

Once he had recognized the feeling, it was a matter of finding out why it was happening. Asking Elric outright was no use. Liang´s only course of action was to try to find proof of the cause in their records. It was his job to dispose of the cat.

Nothing in the correspondence with the Deneans indicated anything was amiss. The one letter from the Agarian group, or Duskians as they called themselves, was short, lacking any formalities or niceties but also lacked any signs of betrayal or danger. He grew more and more frustrated, replaying conversations he had witnessed between Elric and the rebels in his head. Nothing had raised any alarms then, and nothing raised them now.

Liang heard the commotion above him. At first, he only grumbled, imagining Akintoye had finally lost his patience and was giving Astrahd the beating he deserved.

When another big slam moved the lamp above his head, he finally sighed, exasperated, and got up to check on them. He knew Elric wouldn´t.

The sight of Akintoye laying on the ground caused him to freeze. His hands grasped the ladder so hard his knuckles started going numb. The puddle of blood under the man had almost reached the trap door where Liang stood.

He took a step down the ladder, making sure his head

wasn't visible as he paid attention to the sounds coming from the floor. He could hear hushed voices from one of the rooms past the stairs.

Astrahd had been an easy fight. Julian knew the younger man's style, having seen him countless times at his previous ship. He was the type to brag about his skills and demonstrate them for everyone willing to give him the time of day, generally always against opponents smaller and less experienced than he.

It was no more than two minutes after Astrahd had taken out another sword that Julian had overpowered and outsmarted him. The new sword had also ended up on the floor, out of his reach. To his credit, or stupidity, Astrahd didn't turn and run but instead raised his fists to protect his face.

Julian had put his sword to the side and kicked high, getting Astrahd's own fist to impact his nose, making it bleed. The man groaned, raising his head to stop the bleeding, and Julian took the opportunity to kick him, this time squarely on the chin, causing the man to lose his balance. The hit to the head upon falling had rendered him unconscious.

Celeste and Julian dragged Astrahd into one of the rooms, quickly tied him up, and recovered his discarded swords. The mage was searching the unconscious man's pockets when Gale walked into the room, carrying Marcya.

"I'm fine," she insisted when Celeste started fussing over her thigh.

"No, you are not. Look at it!" Julian said, his pitch so high it caused Gale to cover their ears.

"Oh," Marcya said, looking at her thigh for the first time. "That's my bone."

"It is!"

Julian put pressure on the wound like Mel had taught him, covering it with the cleanest piece of cloth he had at hand, and begged the gods no infection would come from it. "We have to get her to Mel."

"Mel's on dock watch duty," Celeste said, turning to the door. "I'll get her."

"We haven't searched the lower gun deck yet!" Marcya called out, trying to stand, but Gale pushed her back down, shaking their head.

"Your thigh's still bleeding bad," Julian commented, ignoring Marcya's scowl. "You won't be searching anything."

Celeste dashed out of the room and headed toward the stairs. She was reaching for the door of the hold when something heavy and sharp slammed into her back. Pain bloomed seconds later, the impact of her hands and knees on the steps as she fell muted by comparison. She felt hot liquid run down her back, and a gasp escaped her as her mind struggled to process what happened.

Before she could make sense of it, someone said, "Who sent you?"

The voice behind her was new to her. She was vaguely aware of the Terafian accent lacing the words. She stayed down, mind racing through the shock. Liang Sūn, first mate of The Conviction, was the only crewmember from Teraf, according to Glenlivet's accounts.

The sound of the steps behind her grew closer, and when she heard his boot land on the first step of the stairs, she gritted her teeth and kicked back at him. She missed by a few inches, pain from whatever was lodged into her shoulder blade making the world wobble around her. She cursed out loud, both from frustration and agony, but her blood raced, fueling her with energy, her pounding heart drowning everything else.

Liang's hand landed on the weapon in her back, all his weight descending onto it, and she screamed, only for it to be cut short when he slammed her head against the step beneath her.

"How did Elric know you were coming?" he asked with rage in his voice, gripping her by the hair and yanking her head to the side so he could look at her face.

She twisted her neck painfully to reach him, and bit into his palm, teeth tearing flesh. With a roar of pain, his weight seemed to collapse on her, digging the blade somehow deeper. Beneath the pain, beneath the tearing flesh and weeping blood, there was a tiny sliver of worry that he might have struck something irreparable.

The pressure vanished, and she gasped for breath, terrified to move as stars sparkled in her vision. She heard a fight happening behind her, then a runt, and finally the sickening gurgle of a throat being cut.

Celeste´s vision narrowed and went dark.

"I don't know what the fuck you're playing at," Glenlivet said, out of breath, as she approached Markl with her sword raised.

Markl braced for a killing blow—only to feel the rope around his wrists suddenly fall away. While she cut the one around his ankles, he undid the knot on the gag and spat it out.

"What the fuck are you doing here?" Glenlivet demanded. "Marina said you were headed to The Red Land."

"Long story," he said, rising to his feet. "No time. We have to leave." His legs were sore from sitting for so long but he shook it off, grabbing Glenlivet's arm to pull her toward the door.

The pirate yanked her arm away. "Calm down, the

snake is dead."

"Not yet."

"What?"

Elric's chest was still moving with each breath, though slowly and unevenly. His eyes were unfocused but open. Glenlivet made a noise of distaste with her tongue, looking away. "Whatever. He will be in a few minutes. *The Conviction* is mine."

Markl shook his head, a panicked look on his face. "Trust me, you don't want it. And I'll explain everything later, but you can't be on this ship when Elric dies. We need to destroy it. Sink it, burn it, doesn't matter how, but *The Conviction* needs to die alongside him."

Glenlivet scoffed. "Is that what the arrogant bastard told you? I won't—"

"Glenlivet!" he shouted. The sharp, sudden noise made them both flinch. "Back in Mene, you said you owed me one. I'm calling it now."

A heavy but short silence followed. Glenlivet stared at Markl, as if trying to read his mind, growled, and broke free of his hold. She whirled and strode to the door, unceremoniously stepping over the agonizing Elric.

"You know," she spat over her shoulder, "I only said that shit because I thought you were going to die in the desert."

"But I'm alive." Markl swallowed hard, following her. "Marina said you were good on your word. Was she lying?"

With an unamused huff of a laugh, the pirate captain looked around in the dark, her eyes focusing on the main mast of *The Outsider* and following it up to the crow's nest. She knew Marina was sitting there, waiting. "No, she wasn't."

"Burn it down?" Mel asked, incredulous, holding the axe steady in Celeste´s back while Julian held the mage down.

"It´s the fastest method," Markl said.

"Why are we listening to him?" Mel asked, raising an eyebrow.

"I owe him," Glenlivet grumbled before her eyes drifted to the street past the dockmaster´s booth.

The group she had sent to watch over the crew at the inn was returning.

"Most of them went to bed," Blue reported the moment Glenlivet met them halfway, "and the others are asleep at the bar. We thought you´d need us here."

Roma tried to rush past the captain when she saw Celeste, but Glen held her back. "Mel is taking care of her. You can´t do anything for her, but I need you—" She paused, looking at the others. "All of you to search The Conviction for oil reserves."

"That´s useless," Markl said. "Elric ordered the crew to throw all flammable liquids overboard before we even got to Denea."

"We can move our oil barrels to—"

"No time," Markl interrupted Augie, shaking his head. He looked more and more panicked the longer they stood at the docks.

Glenlivet looked about to snap at him when Celeste mumbled something.

"Everyone shut up!" Mel said. "What did you say, love?"

"The lamps," Celeste coughed out, the words clearer this time. Blood dribbled onto her chin. "Oil lamps."

Gale´s eyes widened as the words set in, and the crew of *The Outsider* disappeared into the dark for their ship. Markl caught Glenlivet's arm before she could follow them.

"You should stay here," Markl said. "The second Elric dies, you will want to defend that ship with your life. You´ll be a danger to your friends if you´re near them."

"What?"

"Trust me."

"You ask that too much," Glenlivet said, frowning. "You better have a damn good explanation."

Markl nodded gravely and reached into his coat´s inside pocket, extracting a black book. "I do. And I´m sorry."

Glenlivet yanked the book out of the soldier´s hand.

Julian, Marcya, Mel, Celeste, and Markl watched from the docks as the rest of the crew threw the collection of oil lamps from *The Outsider* onto *The Conviction*. The colorful stained glass shattered, oil spilling over the deck. Under Markl´s instructions, a few were aimed at the captain´s quarters. One of the lamps crashed through the porthole.

"I´ll light the match," Julian said, leaving Marcya´s side and rushing to the brigantine.

Glenlivet hardly registered anything as she read the pages filled with Elric´s recognizable handwriting.

"Why am I reading Elric´s crazed ramblings about joining *The Conviction*?" she asked, rolling her eyes on route to looking at Markl. "He was fifteen. He was an asshole. I know the story."

The young man shook his head. "He wanted you to have the full context for everything, so he started from the beginning. But everything is there. It will take a while to read, but my handwriting might be easier to understand."

"I can read his handwriting." Glenlivet felt petty the second she snapped at him, but bit back the apology to start turning pages.

The first page in Markl´s penmanship read: *The old captain´s behavior became erratic on the days before I threw him overboard. I didn´t fully understand it then, but*

I do now. The Conviction has a way of knowing when it's time.

The confusion on Glenlivet's face was obvious, so Markl said, "I told you context was necessary."

"Fuck that. Explain yourself, Markl!"

"I really think you should—" he started protesting, then realized Glenlivet's attention had been stolen by the sight of flames growing inside the captain's quarters of *The Conviction*. "Captain?"

"*No,*" she said in a voice not her own, dropping the book to the dock.

The fire spread faster than Julian could have ever predicted when he threw the lit match into the captain's quarters. He stood there for a moment, staring at Elric's body on the floor. This was the man who had ordered his ship and crew sunk to make a quick escape, the man he hated and had sworn to see dead. And yet, as he watched blue, unnatural flames engulf his body, pity crawled up his throat. The dead captain of *The Conviction* looked young now, smaller, and smaller still as he was consumed by fire.

The vision was entrancing. The urge to step into the space and lay down next to the burning body was so powerful Julian reached for the doorknob. It scorched his hand, but he left it there even as his palm melted against the metal.

It was Glenlivet's ragged scream that broke the trance. Julian had heard people being skinned alive, had heard the sounds a human made in their last moments. The screams crawling out of Glenlivet's throat were nothing like anything he had ever heard before. He pulled his hand away from the door with a yelp, blinking as he realized what he had been doing. Cursing himself for a fool, he ran just as the fire reached the doorway, licking flames dogging his every step.

Nona led the crew out of *The Outsider* when Julian planted his boots on solid ground.

"Glenlivet!" the first mate cried out racing toward the dock.

Julian was a faster runner and arrived before her. The only reason he didn't throw himself on Markl was Mel, who stood in his way with her bloody hands outstretched to stop both of them.

"Julian! No!"

Glenlivet was on the floor, thrashing and screaming at the top of her lungs. Markl was on top of her, holding her down. Her weapons had been tossed aside, and the captain was trying her best to use her nails as knives against the young man's arms.

"He's helping her," Mel said, though she looked as confused as Julian and Nona. "She went insane when the ship started burning."

Glenlivet's teeth snapped together, a useless attempt to bite Markl, who struggled above her. Her forehead was wet from sweat and exhaustion, and her eyes were bulging and irritated. Around the screams were rib-cracking sobs, a mixture of rage and grief as she tried to free herself.

"At this rate, Elric's crew will hear her all the way from the inn," Marcya grunted. Her thigh was wrapped better now and Mel had managed to stop the bleeding with a crude line of stitches with the promise of cleaning it up afterward.

"Glenlivet," Nona whispered, voice broken at the sight of the captain.

The first mate knelt at her side and placed a soft hand on her cheek. Glen turned to her like a caged animal but Nona didn't flinch.

"My home." The captain's voice was more her own now, though a horrible rasp after all the screaming. "They're burning my home."

Nona stole a glance over her shoulder toward *The Conviction*. The mighty brigantine still looked grand and enormous next to *The Outsider*, but its captain's room was sinking into itself, devoured by flames. She shook her head, a worry line forming on her brow.

"No, love," she said, then moved her body to bring Glenlivet's head onto her lap. "You're home now. It's all right. It'll be over soon."

The dockmaster returned with the morning. He was a tall and lanky man, with pronounced crow's feet.

"Are you the new holders of the cargo?" he asked, looking unimpressed.

Nona stared at the man, confused, but Markl finally moved away from Glenlivet and nodded. "Yes. They are."

The dockmaster took out a pack of chewing tobacco and opened it, eyeing Glenlivet for only a moment. "The Duskians are set to arrive in two hours. Our people will meet you here, so be ready."

And with that, the man walked off toward his empty booth. He did not spare even one look to the burning brigantine.

Nona watched him go, then turned her head sharply to look at Markl, snatched up his collar, and hauled him closer. "What the fuck is he talking about?" she demanded. When Markl hesitated, she gave him a fierce shake. "Start talking fast before I do something stupid."

He nodded, then slowly pried Nona's fingers off his clothes. "Elric was here to do a job. But he knew Glenlivet was coming for him, and that it was likely he would die before he could hand off the contraband."

"So? He would have been dead. Why would he care if the job got done or not?" Augie asked, frowning.

"It mattered because of who the job was for," Markl explained. "Elric got a lot of weapons for The Duskians and Deneans. They're planning an insurrection against Goliath's stronghold on the island."

"Firearms?" Marcya asked, mouth hanging open in surprise, her eyes shining. "Are you kidding? It's almost impossible to get your hands on them."

"The Merchant provided them."

Roma, who had been holding an unconscious Celeste's hand, looked up at that. "Shit."

Glenlivet coughed and winced in pain, her irritated and inflamed throat aching. Blue rushed forward with a cup of water, helping the captain drink.

"So, Elric left the hand-over to us," Glenlivet murmured with her face scrunched.

"You shouldn't talk right now, captain," Mel advised.

Markl grabbed the black book from the dock, and gave it to Glenlivet. "Nona already read it. You should, too."

Your mother's name was Ava. We found her in Rera, working as a server. Originally from Agara, she moved to Rera in search of fortune and a chance to make something of herself. The Empire has never been one to grant opportunities. It still isn't. When she boarded The Conviction, she thought that's what it was—an opportunity.

Goliath had already banned women from their Navy and had launched a very powerful campaign of rumors across Patriah that implied this decision was taken because women were bad luck at sea. A part of me wants to believe the captain knew this was bullshit, but he didn't fight the notion or reprimand those around him who believed it. Most of the crew was uneducated, stupid, irrelevant, or all the above. I became very aware of how they felt about Ava's presence by hearing them speak to each other and grew worried about her safety on the ship.

The captain appointed me to watch over her when I told him of my concerns. "You're the only one who cares, so you're the man for the job," he said.

"Akintoye cares," I responded, but I wasn't entirely convinced he cared enough. Not like I did.

That was part of the problem. I cared.

Ava was snarky and hated my guts at first. Which only made me like her more, of course. I think you would have loved her, Glenlivet, I really do.

She was with us for almost a year when she revealed to me one of the clauses of joining The Conviction. She was pregnant.

She had learned quite a bit during her time at sea, with me shielding her from most of the crew's mistreatment, but she grew anxious about her fate once the baby was born.

The more I insisted I would keep both her and the child safe, the less faith she seemed to have in me. She didn't have any in the captain to begin with. If there is something you should hate me for, it's the fact that I never kept her safe from him. No matter how much I stopped the crew from berating or hurting her, I never took a second to question who presented the biggest threat.

He cut her throat a few days after giving birth to you when he discovered she attempted to poison his supper.

I helped him throw her body overboard because the idea of leaving her to the crew made me want to throw up. Akintoye hugged me later when I cried.

When you did, I held you.

Ava was thrown into the water near Cave Island.

～⚬～

It was an unspoken thing between the captain and me. We were the only two who knew you were born a girl. Seeing how the crew had treated Ava was enough to make us address you as a boy from the beginning.

You were a messy and active kid.

Rambunctious, Markl says. I dont even know how to spell the word. You probably do. Unlike me, you caught on quick to your letters and numbers. You were attempting to write when you were just three, though clumsily, and read your first sentence at four. This didnt impress your father, but both Akintoye and I bragged about you at every port.

I always thought those who enjoyed their books werent cut out for a life of piracy, but you proved me wrong early on. This pleased your father but he kept his distance. Knowing what I know now, I suspect he needed to. You were next in line to be captain. You were a threat, no matter how necessary.

This was the same reason I was made first mate instead of Liang. He was stronger, more experienced, and smarter. He didnt consider me, a nineteen-year-old brat with barely a muscle in his body, a real threat. As you know, this would cost him later.

It became more and more difficult to hide that you were a girl, as you know. Around the time you were thirteen, the captain started to isolate himself, and whenever he spoke to the crew, he insisted The Conviction was in danger.

He was paranoid, scared out of his mind. One morning, a couple of hours away from Agath, he revealed his plan to me: he needed a new heir. A boy this time. Someone his crew would respect without a costume.

"What of Glenlivet?" I asked.

I did not like his answer.

You witnessed the result of that argument.

I do not regret throwing him overboard, especially because the memory of your mother was fresh in my mind as I did. But I do regret how I treated you right after.

I ordered Akintoye to put you in the captain's quarters to control the riled-up crew. The last thing I needed was any of them looking at you too closely when emotions were high. I told them to continue course to Agath, but a gnawing sensation of doom was taking over me the closer we got. By the time we reached the coastline, I was sicker than I'd ever felt in my life. I knew the old captain was dead and that The Conviction had begrudgingly taken hold of my mind, with the blood heir too young yet to captain it.

I knew, too, that once you were old enough you would kill me, and that The Conviction would get its rightful owner. So, I tried my best to postpone that fate for both of us. I revealed your gender to the crew and allowed the idiots to believe this was my reason for murdering the old captain. I abandoned you on the rocks, hoping you would make it out of the life.

You didn't. And I'm proud to hear of the reputation you've created for yourself, the people you chose to accompany you, and the code you live your life by.

As we approach Denea, I know the end is coming, and The Conviction scratches at my brain like nails on a chalkboard. I am of two minds: relieved I will be free at last, yet every move I make is to avoid it and to defend the ship. It controls my every breath. I know I dont want this for you. It's a macabre puppet-show with no applause when the curtains close.

The storage building behind the dockmaster's booth held nothing but Elric's cargo.

Glenlivet was still exhausted, but she leaned on Nona as she opened one of the boxes to confirm what Markl had told her. The box was full of firearms, marked as Goliath's property, though the identifying numbers on them had been scratched.

"An insurrection," Danielle muttered, almost to herself, standing next to the captain and watching over her shoulder. "Do you really think the Deneans will be able to get rid of Goliath?"

"With all these?" Glenlivet said, closing the box. "Yeah. They could."

"If an island like Denea manages that, it will spark more revolutions down South," Augie said, a timbre in his voice that betrayed his excitement. "Especially if the Duskians are helping them. It could impact all of Patriah."

"That's the point," Glenlivet said, smiling sadly. "That's exactly what Elric wanted. Impact." She looked toward Markl by the door. "Right?"

Markl nodded, arms crossed, before looking out onto the street. "The Deneans are here."

Glenlivet pushed away from the box. Nona held her up, an arm around her waist.

"Are you sure about this?" the first mate asked, taking a deep breath.

All her adult life had been dedicated to murdering Elric Omar, and now he was gone, a different man than she remembered. Not the heartless monster who betrayed her, not the loving man who raised her. Her inheritance was firearms and the chance of a revolution.

She had never been a friend to the Empire, but she also never saw herself as the one to fight it. Every fight meant danger, pain, and death. She thought of her family, standing behind her. All of them had become acquainted with those things before they stepped foot in *The Outsider*, because of Goliath and its power over Patriah.

The captain sighed and looked around at her crew. All of them waited for the answer, determined to follow her.

"Yes. I´m sure."

Gods of Patriah

Edbris:

Also known as the great serpent, or great eel, depending on location. They oversee bodies of water and punish those who are disrespectful to the life in them.

Yrena:

Represented as a mother bear, protector of her cubs. They're the deity of familial bonds. These bonds are not restricted to blood.

Ynos:

Deity of nobility and status. Ynos is said to be inside every person with honor. Often drawn as a stag with their head held high. Sometimes the stag is represented with a bite taken out of its ribcage.

Takdos:

They are depicted as different bugs depending on the region but is mostly seen as an ant. They are the deity of soil and prosperous land.

Mydos:

Known as a golden bird. Deity of coin and riches.

Acknowledgments

This book was a collaborative effort.

Glenlivet was born out of a costume party while I was at university, but she didn't become a proper character until the COVID-19 pandemic. That was when I decided to cosplay as her on TikTok, and invited my mutuals and followers to create pirate characters of their own. This is how the crew was born.

I made some of my closest friends through this tag (#glenlivetscrew), and together we created character relationships and dynamics, storylines, and inside jokes. Once we had a crew going, I gave Glen goals and desires, along with a backstory, which my friends were enthusiastic about. The narrative grew bigger and bigger, and I couldn't hold back any longer. TikTok was quite a messy medium to communicate a linear plot, so I needed to write it down. I loved telling the story through videos, but books have always been my preferred storytelling method.

All my friends who agreed to have their characters in the book and worked with me for almost three years, I thank them for being so patient with me.

I encourage everyone who enjoyed this book to find their videos and be a part of the community. It's the best way to get a lot more content and meet all of the crew individually. Their stories expand and change over there, like different timelines to explore.

Special thanks and love to Jordan Hancock, the creator of Danielle, Julian, and Micah. She's an incredible writer, and such a kind and helpful beta reader. I hope to keep working with her.

To Andrea Carreras, who watched me become the writer I am throughout university, and read every version of this book. I hope to keep adding to your TBR for many years to come. Forever your egg.

To my entire family, who always supported my artistic side and made sure I had every opportunity to pursue it. From the comics I made by hand in La Habana, to the poetry and short stories I wrote in the subway in Madrid and the essays I went crazy editing in Bangor.

To my partner of twelve years, Carlos, who kept me sane and made sure I remembered to drink water, eat, and go to the bathroom while I was deep in hyperfocus when writing. The common sense to my chaos.

Cover art and lettering by the talented and hardworking Logan Howard, @wraithofthavalon. Their enthusiasm for the book and my very messy mock-up of a cover only fueled my determination to publish the book.

Turns out writing isn't the lonely affair is advertised to be.

The Outsider Crew:
　-*Nona*: Leah Corckran
　-*Danielle, Julian, and Micah*: Jordan Hancock
　-*Gale*: Lando Bridgeman, @spacedoutandtired on all forms of social media
　-*Blue*: Nyah Henderson
　-*Augie*: Maddox 'Madz' Bourdeau
　-*Marcya*: Talea
　-*Celeste*: Paige Royal, @pixxi.biz on Instagram
　-*Roma*: @magpie_moon on TikTok
　-*Mel*: Kaite Thompson, @kaitecosplay on TikTok
　-*Marina*: Cass Dune

The Cursed Eel Crew:
　-*Tavia*: Moon Metreyeon, @skeksisgossip on Instagram
　-*Cecilia*: Ace
　-*Ashlin*: Hedge Xochipilli Metreyeon, @hungryhungrybaker on Instagram

QUAN

CROWN
CAPITAL

THE
DOOR

QUIMAR

LEHIAM

CARPENT
FOREST

IRIAH

DREAD WATER

THE EMPTY ISLES

Printed in Great Britain
by Amazon